Seeds of Hope

HARVEST OF HOPE SERIES

Seeds of Hope by Barbara Cameron

Published by Gilead Publishing, Grand Rapids, Michigan
www.gileadpublishing.com

gp GILEAD PUBLISHING

ISBN: 978-1-68370-055-5 (paper)
ISBN: 978-1-68370-056-2 (eBook)

Scripture quotations are from the King James Version of the Bible.

This is a work of fiction. Names, characters, places, and incidents are products of the author's imagination or are used fictitiously. Any similarity to actual people, organizations, and/or events is purely coincidental.

Edited by Susan Brower
Cover directed by Larry Taylor
Cover designed by John Wolinka
Interior designed by Amy Shock

Printed in the United States of America

Seeds of Hope

HARVEST OF HOPE SERIES

Barbara Cameron

GILEAD
PUBLISHING

Grand Rapids, Michigan

Dedication

For Evelyn White
who taught me English all four years of high school
and encouraged me to write.
Thank you, dear lady!

A Note to Readers

Life really does come full circle sometimes.

Years ago, Sue Brower, my new editor here at Gilead Publishing, read my first Amish novel when she worked at another publisher. While she wasn't in the market for another Amish author at the time, she wrote a lovely note saying it was a good book and it would sell. Her encouragement meant a lot. While I had sold other novels and nonfiction books, this novel and two Amish novellas I sold around that time were my first ventures into Christian fiction, which I now love to write.

I approached Sue with *Harvest of Hope*, my new Amish series, and we finally get to work together on it. I'm so excited to be a part of Gilead in its venture into Christian publishing!

So much time and work go into a book, and it all starts with an editor who believes in an author and her story. From there, a lot of other people become involved, from those who financially back the company to line editors and proofreaders to marketing and distribution. The author's name is on the cover, but there would be no book without these people I may never meet. I want to thank them for their hard work and attention to my "baby."

I'd also like to thank Monica Peters, friend, fellow author, and the person who is the first to read my manuscript and check for errors. She lives near an Amish community in Pennsylvania and helps me with research, and is not only my first reader but such a wonderful encourager. I love her "You got this!" emails!

I was reading Facebook one night and found myself laughing at Renee Pierce's tale of where her knitting needles disappeared to ... I asked her if I could use it in this book and she agreed. Thanks, Renee. Your family sounds like it is so much fun.

I never fail to be amazed at God's plan for me and for other people.

So often He has truly shown us that when one door closes, He has better things in store for us!

Thank You, God!

One

Miriam Troyer guided the horse-drawn buggy into the lane that led to John Byler's home. She was lost in the beauty of the scene that unfolded before her. Wind ruffled the tall grasses about to be cut into hay. Livestock grazed in a pasture. The farmhouse itself was a rambling white wooden home that had been added on to by generations of Bylers as the family grew. The old house was the embodiment of Amish peace and tranquility.

John Byler sat on his front porch, his gray head bent as he wrote in a notebook.

How John loved writing letters, Miriam thought fondly. She hated to interrupt him, but when he glanced up and smiled at her, she could tell he didn't regard her dropping by as an unwelcome interruption.

And it wasn't just because he knew she brought baked goods. He had become a good friend, someone who listened and encouraged and offered wise counsel. They were a generation apart, but age had never made a difference in their friendship.

She waved and called for him to stay where he was, but he was already up and making his way to her. He was limping more than usual today. It had rained earlier and she knew his arthritis always acted up worse then. It had become more and more of a problem the last year or so. Still, he was determined to keep going each day and take care of his farm. "If you stop doing, you'll stop being," he'd say when she worried about him.

"It's *gut* to see you, Miriam."

"You, too, John."

He reached for the handle of the basket in her hands.

"I'm not some frail *maedel*," she told him. "I can carry this. I put it in the buggy."

They had their usual tug-of-war, which he won like always.

He grinned and laugh lines crinkled around his eyes, the color of faded denim. "We should help each other, shouldn't we?"

"*Ya*," said with a sigh and a smile. His gentle charm and courtesy reminded her of her *grossdaadi* who had passed years ago.

Both qualities had seemed to be lacking in the men she'd dated.

He set the basket on a small wooden table on the porch and waved a hand at one of the rocking chairs flanking it. "Do you have time to visit a bit?"

Now it was her turn to grin. "And when, I ask you, don't I have time to visit with you? So, how was your day?"

"*Gut*." He gestured at the pad of paper and pen on the table. "Just sitting here writing my *grosssohn*."

She didn't need to ask which one. John had only one. Only one *sohn* as well. Most Amish families had many *kinner* and thanked God for them. John had never complained that he hadn't had a larger family with his *fraa*, long dead now. But he reveled in the times his *grosssohn* visited.

Mark had visited many summers after he turned fourteen. Apparently he'd wanted to know his *grossdaadi*, and his *dat* had decided to let him. He and John had become close.

Miriam had been twelve and just noticing boys. And over the years, she'd developed a fanciful crush on Mark—one that no one but God knew about.

Mark was so different from anyone she knew. She'd been intrigued the first time he'd visited. Years before he became a high-powered attorney, he seemed to carry himself with a confidence the boys she knew lacked. He was outspoken, too, and had often had spirited discussions with John about the Amish faith and God.

He stood out with his dark good looks, too. His black hair shone like the wing of a raven when he stood hatless out in the fields with his *grossdaadi*. His eyes were a vivid blue, stronger in color and more direct than the older man. She hadn't seen him for a year, but the memory of his face was as vivid as if he was standing right here in front of her.

"Miriam?"

She realized she'd been daydreaming and felt warmth flood her face. "Hmm? Oh, sorry, I was just thinking of an errand *mudder* wanted me to run on the way home."

"You don't have to leave already, do you?"

"*Nee*. So, you were saying you're writing to Mark."

He sighed and leaned back in his chair. "*Ya*. I've asked him if he's coming home to help with harvest."

"He usually does."

John rested his hands on his knees. "The last time he wrote me, he sounded busy with his work at the law firm. But I'm needing his help more than usual." He rubbed at his knee with his big, gnarled hand. "I don't know how much longer I can take care of things. The doctor's tried some of the new medicines on my arthritis, but I'm not getting much relief."

John seldom talked about his age and his increasing problems with his arthritis, but Miriam and her *mudder* and other women in the community had noticed and tried to help out by bringing him food. The men in the community helped with chores, too.

"I just wish . . ." he trailed off.

"You just wish?" she prompted as he gazed off into the distance.

"I wish there was someone to hand it over to."

"Hand it over?" She wasn't following him.

"My *sohn* didn't want the farm. And I doubt Mark wants it."

She felt her heart leap at the thought and cautioned herself not to show her reaction. "Mark has his work in Philadelphia."

John nodded and looked sad. "I know."

He sat staring out at the fields he'd worked for more years than she'd lived. "There have been Bylers working on this farm for generations. All the way back to the time the Amish first came to Pennsylvania."

"So you've said."

"I don't want it to stop with me." He spoke with such passion she could only stare at him.

"I don't want it to stop with me," he said again, softer now, and he lapsed into silence.

"So you're writing to Mark about harvest?" she prompted again.

John seemed to gather himself and stared at her. "*Ya*," he said. "*Ya*. I was just finishing it." He reached for the pad of paper on the table, ripped the top page off, folded it, and tucked it into an envelope. After dashing the address across it—from memory—he looked at her. "All I need is a stamp."

Miriam held out her hand. "I have one in my purse. I can mail that for you. I'm driving into town."

He handed it to her. "*Danki, Miriam.*" He smiled at her. "Mark is a smart young man. A caring one. He'll come and we'll talk."

She bit her lip, worried that John would be disappointed. Mark had a busy, successful career in the *Englisch* world. The last few years he'd visited, he'd driven a fancy, expensive *Englisch* car and worn fancy, expensive clothes. And although he appeared to love his *grossdaadi*, he was the last man she'd expect to be interested in a farm.

John, always the gentleman, walked Miriam back to her buggy, even though she could tell the effort of walking was hard on him.

"Don't forget the basket," she reminded him as she climbed into the buggy. "There's baked chicken and potato salad and a big baked potato and a jar of the chow chow we made today. And a sweet treat that'll be a surprise."

"You make me a happy man," he said. "I know you worry I don't eat right."

She knew his arthritis made it harder for him to take care of the farm, and what Amish man really liked to cook? But she wasn't going to say either of those things. "I love visiting with you and talking. You know that."

He smiled. "You make me happy when you visit."

She sincerely hoped Mark would make him happy and visit soon, too.

SSS

"Mark!"

Mark Byler turned as his assistant rushed up to him. "This just came in the morning mail. I saw it was from your grandfather and knew you'd want to take it with you."

Mark took the letter and slid it into his briefcase as he stepped into the elevator. Judge Patterson insisted on attorneys being on time, so he wasn't about to risk stopping to read the letter right now.

He made the short trip to the courthouse, found a parking space, and headed inside. The district attorney was right behind him and both were relieved to see that they'd arrived in plenty of time.

His client was brought in a few minutes later. Mark watched as the man's leg chain was secured to a leg of the table where they sat. He could literally hear his client's nervousness as the chain rattled faintly.

"Chill," he whispered. "Everything's going to be fine."

"I hope you're right."

"I'm always right." Mark figured it wasn't arrogance if it were true.

Mark focused on Dan's closing statement, noting on a yellow legal pad an adjustment to a point he'd make in his own closing statement. When Dan finally finished, Mark was ready.

He walked slowly to the jury box, taking his time, making eye contact with each of the men and women sitting in it, measuring his words.

His favorite law professor had always said that cases were won by careful, steady work, relentless study, investigation, and the slow, careful laying out the defense in steps the often-tired and overwhelmed jurors could understand.

"And so, ladies and gentlemen of the jury, that's why you should acquit my client," he said. He made a final eye contact with each of them, nodded, then walked back to his seat at the defendant's table.

"Man, that was good," Maurice whispered in his ear as he sat beside him.

Maybe so, but Mark couldn't help noticing the poor man still shook as he sat beside him. He'd sat there shaking throughout most of the trial. The guy was built like a linebacker, yet he trembled like the frailest client Mark had ever defended. He was accused of being in a gang and gunning down a rival. Mark hadn't believed it from the time he met the gentle giant.

He hoped the jury would believe in Maurice's innocence as well.

Two hours later the case went to the jury.

"This is gonna be a quick one," Dan said as they rode down in the courthouse elevator. He wore a hangdog expression like he always did while the jury was out. He shot a sharp look at Mark. "Want to bet on the verdict?"

Mark shook his head.

"I'm going to the coffee shop. No point in leaving," Dan said.

And since Dan was almost always right about how long the jury took to deliberate, Mark replied, "I'll join you."

"Your treat?"

"Sure." Mark had a good feeling about this one, but wasn't one to gloat.

Two women who were assistants to Judge Patterson got on the elevator. One smiled flirtatiously at him. He tried not to notice. It wasn't a good thing to get too friendly with the staff from the judge's office. Someone could yell conflict of interest.

Besides, he was happy with Tiffany Mitchell, his fiancée. Well, happy wasn't exactly the right word—more like content. Tiffany was a little high maintenance, but she was beautiful, smart, and would make a great wife for an up-and-coming lawyer. Tiffany was a little wound up from all the wedding planning, but she hadn't become a bridezilla, and he'd felt a little distance between them lately.

They got out at the ground floor and headed for the coffee shop.

Dan checked his watch. "I figure we have time to split a BLT, if you're hungry."

"Sure." They ordered the sandwich and two coffees and found a table.

They'd just finished the BLT and Mark was thinking about getting out his grandfather's letter when they got the phone calls to return to the courtroom.

Dan stood and tossed his paper napkin onto his plate. "Here we go."

The courtroom was buzzing with excitement. Reporters lined the first row of seats. Behind them were members of the families and behind them, the regular contingent of senior citizens who attended trials as a form of entertainment.

Officers brought Maurice to his seat and secured his restraints. The chains shook even more than they had that morning. "A short time out's good, right? I heard the shorter the deliberation, the better the verdict."

"I'm afraid that's not always true."

Maurice gave him a desperate look. "Lie to me, man. Tell me a jury coming back so quick means they found me innocent. Otherwise, I'm gonna pass out right here."

The bailiff called for all to rise as the judge walked in. He gave his traditional stern look at the assemblage and recited his admonition for the courtroom to remain calm when the verdict was announced.

"Have you reached a verdict?" the judge asked the jury.

"Yes, your Honor," the foreman said.

The bailiff took the square of paper from him and carried it to the judge. Mark stood with his client and waited for the judge to read the paper.

"Is this your decision?"

"Yes, your Honor."

"On the charge of first degree murder," the judge read aloud, "not guilty."

"No! You killed my son!" a man shouted.

Mark turned and saw two officers wrestling the father of the victim to the ground. He screamed threats as they dragged him from the courtroom.

Maurice stood still for a moment, then threw his arms around Mark and hugged him so tightly Mark was afraid he was going to end up with cracked ribs.

Grinning, he extricated himself and the officer in charge of security went to work releasing Maurice from his leg chains.

"There's some paperwork and then you're free," Mark told Maurice, slapping him on his shoulder.

"Can't thank you enough, man."

"No problem. Now I don't want to see you again, right?"

"You won't. Like I said, I gave up that life years ago."

Mark grabbed his briefcase, accepted the grudging congratulations from Dan, and headed out of the courthouse. He paused briefly in his car to text the verdict to Lani, his paralegal and assistant.

A brass bell clanged the minute he walked into the law offices. It was the celebratory greeting for an attorney when he or she won a case.

Mark thought it was kind of silly, but it was a tradition and law firms loved tradition. Especially staid, well-established firms like this one.

His boss came out of his office to clap him on the back and other attorneys joined him.

Mark finally extricated himself and went to see if his assistant had any messages for him. He took them into his office, scanned quickly, and then settled back in his chair. He was tired—a good kind of tired. Satisfied tired. There them had been a lot of long days and long nights preparing for this and other cases.

"You look exhausted," Lani said.

"Gee, thanks."

"Think about taking some personal time soon. You've earned it."

He gave her a cool stare. She just laughed. Ten years older than he, she'd been with the firm for a long time and wasn't intimidated by any of the attorneys. He was lucky she chose to work with him. She knew what he wanted and produced it.

"Let's just say the rest of us could use the break," she said as she collected the stack of work. "I'll get these out right away."

Mark glanced at the clock on the wall and decided to quit for the day. For once he didn't have anything to take home and review, due mostly to Lani's usual good work of keeping his calendar clear for a day or so after a case expected to wrap. He'd been careful not to plan anything with Tiffany so he could go home, find something to eat, have a glass of wine if he wanted, and relax.

His condo was blessedly quiet and spotless. The cleaning service had been there that day. When he looked in his Sub-Zero refrigerator, he found a couple takeout containers that looked like they were growing science experiments. The inside of the freezer was an arctic wasteland. He sighed. It looked like he was ordering in one more night. Tomorrow he'd make himself shop for groceries. But tonight it wasn't going to happen.

He rooted through the takeout menus in a kitchen drawer and ordered his favorite baked spaghetti and Greek salad, then changed into sweats while he waited for delivery.

Later, he sat eating his solitary dinner on the coffee table in the elegantly decorated living room—done with the help of an expensive interior decorator—and watched ESPN.

Such was the life of a successful big city attorney, he thought wryly.

Reaching into his briefcase, he pulled out the letter from his grandfather and ripped it open. "Dear Mark," he read. "I need to see you to talk about an important matter. Can you come to the farm?"

That was it. Two sentences. Well, one sentence and one question. His grandfather was a man of few words, but this was very terse even for him.

He frowned. Was his grandfather ill? He pulled out his cell phone and dialed, then frowned again when the call went to voicemail. The call was being recorded out in the phone shanty, but who knew when his grandfather would check the answering machine. Phone calls weren't a high priority in his grandfather's world, unlike Mark's own smartphone-driven life.

A couple hours later, Mark lay awake in bed, unable to sleep. He'd been in his line of work too long. His imagination ran wild with worry about the reason his grandfather wanted to see him.

He needed to go visit him right away.

Two

For the next three days, Miriam found herself experiencing a tingle of excitement every time she thought Mark receiving John's letter.

Mark hadn't come home for the last harvest, but maybe he'd come now since John had written him.

She was no teenage Amish *maedel*, but she'd never gotten over the crush she'd had on Mark. It probably had to do with him being *Englisch* and therefore different from the men she'd known since they were *kinner* together at *schul*. While it was nice to know someone so well that there were no surprises, somehow she couldn't help thinking it must be nice to discover your mate when you were both adults.

Her *dat* was in the barn feeding the stock. He came out to help her unhitch the buggy when she arrived home after dropping supper off at John's farm.

"How is John?"

"He's well. He hasn't heard from his *grosssohn* yet. I told you he wants him to come help with the harvest."

"John knows he can depend on all of us in the community to help him."

"I know." She sighed. "John is worried about the future of the farm. He talked about how there's no one to take over the farm from him. His *sohn* left the community, and Mark has his job in Philadelphia. John doesn't want the farm to go out of the family after so many generations."

Daniel nodded. "I understand."

Miriam led Bessie to her stall and fetched her water and feed. "I hope Mark will at least come for harvest and talk to him. He's been so busy, he hasn't made it here in some time."

"Well, if it's God's will, it'll work out."

She nodded. "I'm going in to help *Mamm* unless there's something you need me to do."

"*Nee*, go help her."

The kitchen was a hive of activity. Miriam had three *schweschders* and five *bruders*, and if they weren't working in the fields this time of year, they were in the kitchen where the work was almost as hot and almost as hard. Jar upon jar of corn and green beans and fruit jams and jellies lined the counters.

Her *mudder* looked up from stirring a huge pot on the stove. She fanned her face with her hand. "How was John?"

"*Gut*. He thanked both of us for the food. Especially the baked chicken. You know he loves baked chicken." Miriam went to the sink and washed her hands. "What do you need me to do?"

"Supper's almost ready," Sarah said, unflappable despite the flurry of activity in the room.

Miriam's *schweschders* were everywhere, setting the table, pouring glasses of water, carrying jars downstairs to store them for the winter months. Her *bruders* were still helping their *dat* with chores in the barn.

Her youngest sister, Katie, sat in her high chair banging the tray with a wooden spoon. "How are you doing, sweet *boppli?*" Miriam asked, leaning over to kiss her on the cheek.

Katie grinned, exposing a mouthful of cracker crumbs.

Like many Amish households, there was a big gap between the ages of the oldest and youngest *kinner* in the house. Miriam was the oldest and she loved taking care of her siblings as they came along.

She stepped out onto the back porch and rang the bell several times, alerting those working in the fields. They began streaming toward the house looking tired and sweaty.

Supper was a noisy affair as Miriam's big, boisterous family gathered at the wooden kitchen table. Well, until the blessing was said and all the bowls and platters were passed around the table. Then silence descended as everyone ate.

Her *mudder* often said the kitchen was the heart of the home, and mealtime was *schur* the family's favorite time.

Miriam's thoughts wandered to Mark as she ate. What he was doing right now? Was he sharing a meal with the woman he'd become engaged to? Her name was something fancy. Tiffany, she remembered. She took a bite of chicken and wondered if Mark was enjoying a fancy supper with Tiffany.

As appetites became satisfied, there was more talk. Her *bruders* discussed the weather—all-important at this time of the year as the crops were being harvested—and her *schweschders* gossiped about who might be getting married after the harvest.

Katie babbled and clutched a green bean in one chubby hand.

After the plates were cleared, Sarah presided over the scooping of warm peach cobbler into bowls. She handed them to Miriam who topped each with a scoop of vanilla ice cream.

Her brother Jacob smiled and sighed when Miriam handed him his dish. "What a nice ending on a long, hot day."

Katie used her hands to put some of the ice cream in her mouth and smear the rest of it on her face. She grinned, delighted with herself.

"She *schur* loves ice cream," Miriam said, leaning over to wipe her face with her paper napkin. "You have a birthday in a few months, big girl."

Miriam finished her own dessert, then lifted Katie from her high chair. "I'll give her a bath."

She carried her upstairs, ran a bath, and after pulling off her ice-cream-smeared clothes, dunked her in it. Katie laughed and splashed as Miriam used a washcloth to scrub her face and hair. "Messy *boppli*."

Katie chuckled and patted the water with pudgy hands, splashing Miriam in the face. When she screeched in surprise, Katie laughed even harder.

Miriam wrapped her in a towel and hugged her. It was nice to have a *boppli* to cuddle since she didn't have one of her own yet. She was just twenty-four—which wasn't considered an old *maedel* by any means—but there were moments when she couldn't help thinking how many friends she'd gone to *schul* with who had married and started families already.

Would she ever have her own family, her own *boppli*?

Dressing Katie in a diaper and a cotton T-shirt—all that was needed on a warm summer night—she took her downstairs. It was too early for Katie to go to bed and she was too wound up to go to sleep just yet.

Emma and Mary were finishing up the dishes. Their *mudder* sat at the table sipping a glass of iced tea and looking tired.

Miriam joined her and held Katie in her lap. "I was telling *Daed* that John hasn't heard from his *grosssohn* yet. I'm worried that Mark might not be able to come visit him."

"Family's important," she said quietly. "I'm *schur* Mark will at least come to help with harvest. I hate to see John disappointed. He's such a nice man."

"Well, it's God's will what happens." She smiled. "Someone's trying very hard not to fall asleep."

Miriam glanced down, surprised to see Katie's eyelids were drooping. "I'll go put her in her crib and see if everyone's taking their baths."

"*Danki.*"

She carried Katie upstairs, laid her in her crib, and tucked her favorite stuffed animal under her arm. Katie snuggled it in her sleep, smiled her angel smile, and drifted off.

Moments like this were so sweet. It was easy to forget what a handful Katie always was.

Miriam walked out of the room and closed the door quietly behind her. As she headed down the hall to the bathroom, she heard shrieks and splashing. Her six-year-old *zwillingbopplin* sisters sounded like they were in the bath tub, but the racket they were making worried her.

When she walked into the room, her mouth dropped open. The girls had evidently found the bottle of bubble bath that Miriam used occasionally. They must have dumped the entire bottle into the tub and were enthusiastically tossing handfuls of suds at each other. Water had slopped over the sides of the tub.

"What have you done?" she cried. But she had to bite the inside of her cheek to keep from laughing.

Hadn't she done such a thing once as a *kind*?

"Finish washing off and when you get out, you're mopping up the water in here," she said sternly. "*Mamm* and I aren't doing it. And be quick about it before it leaks downstairs and *Daed* gets mad."

They stopped and stared at her, their eyes huge. "We're sorry!" they chimed at the same time. "We were just having fun. We'll clean it up right away."

"Be *schur* that you do. Then it's bedtime for the two of you."

She went out and closed the door. And as she headed down the hall to check on her *bruders*, she couldn't help thinking it was just another night in the crazy Troyer *haus*.

SSS

Mark didn't have court the next day and that was just fine with him.

Lani breezed in and took a seat in front of his desk. "What's wrong, boss?"

He looked up. "What makes you think something's wrong? And don't call me boss."

"Okay, boss. I've known you for years. You're on edge."

"It's my grandfather. I left a voicemail, but he hates anything to do with phones and rarely goes to the phone shanty."

"You think he might be ill? You can call the local police and ask for a wellness check. I did that once when my grandmother didn't answer her phone for two days."

He glanced at his cell phone, then shook his head. "I'm going to drive there to see for myself."

Lani frowned. "You *are* worried."

"Yeah. Listen, about my schedule."

"I'll work on the Epps interrogatories, schedule depositions for the Reynolds case for next week, and file your motion for the Carrington trial. Anything else?"

"No, smart aleck. I'll be back in a couple of days. You have my number if you need me."

"I won't. Take a week."

Mark tried to look stern, but chuckled as she got up and left the room. It took a few minutes to toss a few files in his briefcase and stop to let his boss's assistant know he was going out of town.

An hour later, an overnight case packed and tucked in the trunk, he was heading out of Philadelphia toward Paradise.

He'd been cooped up inside too much lately. It felt good to be out taking a drive on such a beautiful day. He put the top down, slid his sunglasses on, and turned the music up loud.

It would have been more enjoyable if he wasn't concerned about his grandfather. He couldn't help worrying about the man until he saw him in person.

He drove past fields with crops of corn, wheat, every kind of vegetable being harvested. Huge machines worked the fields of *Englisch* farmers. As he approached the Amish farms he saw horses pulling equipment. He remembered the summers when he'd helped harvest and would wonder why the Amish had to do things the backward way. His grandfather had been patient in explaining the Amish faith and their way of doing things, and Mark learned to accept, even appreciate, this different way of life.

He still liked *his* world very much. Especially this car that purred like a big jungle cat and tempted him to cut it loose and see what it could do.

His better judgment kicked in before he could and soon he took the turn to his grandfather's farm.

He pulled into the drive and shut off the engine. Getting out, he scanned the fields surrounding his grandfather's farmhouse. There were men out there, but he couldn't see if one of them was his grandfather. He took the front porch stairs two at a time and knocked on the front door. When he got no answer and found it unlocked, he stuck his head inside and called out, but there was only silence.

He stepped inside, went from room to room, and felt relieved when he didn't find his grandfather lying on the floor. Of course, he hadn't really believed he'd find such a situation, or he'd have done as Lani suggested and made a call to the local authorities to ask for a wellness check. But still, he was concerned.

He heard the front door open. "John? It's Miriam."

A young Amish woman carrying an enormous basket hurried into the room. She stopped and stared at him. "Mark!" she cried. "You came!"

"Yes. Where's my grandfather?"

"Oh, he's probably out in the fields." She set the basket on the table.

He stared. Miriam Troyer had always been pretty, with her creamy skin and corn silk blonde hair beneath her *kapp*. But if it were possible, she'd gotten even prettier since the last time he'd seen her. "Good to see you."

"You, too."

The back door opened and his grandfather walked in. "You came!"

Mark frowned at him and put his hands on his hips. "Granddad, I called and left you several voicemails on your answering machine."

"Did you?" John filled a glass of water from the tap and drank thirstily. "Haven't had time to check my messages. Busy time of the year. But you're here now."

"I was worried."

John swiped his hand over his mouth. "No need to worry. God's always in charge."

Exasperated, Mark crossed the room and gathered his grandfather in a hug. "You can't tell a person not to worry."

It seemed his grandfather had lost weight since he'd last hugged him. He felt ... frail. And it seemed the older man's movements were slower, awkward, as if he were in pain. His arthritis must be getting worse.

"So why did you ask me to come?" Mark asked as John sat down at the table, took off his wide-brimmed straw hat, and wiped his face with a bandanna.

"We can talk later, after we've eaten," John said. "Since you're not dressed to help in the fields, why don't you set up the tables for the food?"

It wasn't what he wanted, but what else could he do? "Sure."

John turned to Miriam. "It was so kind of you to bring the food today."

"The other women will be here soon to feed everyone helping you with the harvesting today." She lifted her basket. "I'll take this outside and start setting up."

Mark took the basket from her and wondered how a little slip of a thing like her had carried it in from her buggy. It weighed a ton.

They walked outside. He set the basket down and glanced around. "So where are the tables?"

"In the barn. I'll show you."

The tables consisted of sawhorses with planks of plywood set atop them. Miriam took cloths from the basket and spread them on the tables. Her *mudder* came out with several women and they set benches and some old chairs around them for seating.

Several women came around the side of the house carrying baskets and tote bags. Mark and Miriam hurried to help them. Bowls of potato salad, corn on the cob, and sliced baked chicken were set out on the tables.

"Miriam, look who's here!" her friend, Fannie Mae, cried when she saw Mark. "Haven't seen you in some time. Have we, Lovina?"

"*Nee. Gut* to see you!"

A boy about ten years old approached, pulling a little wagon with a cooler in it. "Is that your fancy car out front?" he asked Mark. "Does it go a hundred miles an hour?"

Mark laughed. "Well, it might, but the police wouldn't be too happy with me."

The women made quick work of setting out food and filling glasses with ice and tea from the cooler.

"Johnnie, go ring the bell to call the men."

The boy ran to the back porch and tugged on the bell.

Men streamed in from the fields, greeting Mark as if he hadn't been gone any time at all. After they washed their hands at the pump, they sat around the table. A blessing was said for the meal, then everyone began filling their plates.

The scene was familiar and yet felt a little surreal. Yesterday Mark had sat in the boardroom wearing an expensive suit and eating a catered lunch with his fellow attorneys. Today he sat among simply dressed farmers and their wives eating food that had been harvested just days before. He felt comfortable in both.

He glanced at his grandfather at the head of the table. The old man was watching him with an inscrutable expression.

Three

Miriam had never felt more self-conscious.

Here she sat at a table just a few feet from Mark—someone she hadn't expected to show up today. He looked cool and immaculate in his *Englisch* polo shirt and khaki slacks, a pair of expensive sunglasses shading his eyes.

No one wore their best on a work day, especially a hot summer harvest day. Although they'd tried to set up the tables under a shade tree, the temperature was in the nineties and there wasn't much of a breeze today.

"Aren't you hungry?" Fannie Mae asked her.

She forced herself to take a bite. "I don't eat as much when it's this warm."

"Heard it's one of our hottest summers ever."

"Summer is always hot and humid in Lancaster County," Naomi piped up. "I think spring was only one week long."

The men were silent as they wolfed down their food. They'd been working since sunup in the fields and would toil more hours until they were done. Each worked his own farm, then helped others in the community as needed.

While they'd worked, the women had prepared food for this meal and supper and would continue to can the vegetables and fruit that had been harvested earlier. And Miriam and her friends felt their kitchens were every bit as hot as the sun-broiled fields their men labored in.

No one complained. At least not out loud. Summer and fall were the busiest seasons, yet offered the most proof of God's abundance. And who wouldn't be grateful for that?

Soon enough the bitter winds and snow of winter would be here, and the arduous schedule would ease. Farmers would spend their time making repairs on equipment, and their *fraas* would sew and patch clothing and quilt to their heart's content. All would be grateful for the hard work of raising food and preserving it come winter.

As appetites eased there was more conversation, mostly about the possibility of rain and what crops should be planted next year.

"So how long will you be visiting, Mark?" Amos, owner of the farm next door, asked.

"Just a day or two," he said, passing a bowl of potato salad to the diner next to him.

Miriam glanced at John to see his reaction, but his face didn't reveal what he was thinking.

What she'd give to be a fly on the wall when the two men talked later. She was dying to know if John had talked to Mark about the farm.

Then she chided herself. It wasn't her business. It really wasn't. But her heart ached for John because she knew how much he wanted to pass the farm down to family. But Mark was not interested in farming. Was John thinking about selling it? It made sense that he would seek advice from Mark since he would inherit the farm at John's passing. He loved Mark so. That had been so obvious through the years. He'd doted on him when he came for visits in the summer and talked about him often. The Amish loved family and he'd only been blessed with one *sohn* who hadn't wanted to stay here.

Mark was his last hope. His only hope.

Big helpings of strawberry shortcake were served for dessert. More cold water and iced tea was drunk. Then the men headed back to the fields and the women packed up their baskets and said good-bye before hurrying home to finish their chores.

"I'll go change," Mark said as he stood. "I have some work clothes in the guest room."

"It's not a guest room," John said. "It's your room. Always has been."

"Of course." Mark paused beside his grandfather's chair, laid a hand on his shoulder. "Shouldn't you go inside and rest for a while? I bet you've been out here since the sun came up."

John started to protest, then he nodded. "I think I will go inside for a bit. We'll talk later."

Miriam frowned as she watched John make his way into the house. He seemed to move slower, more painfully.

"How long has he been like this? Limping because of the arthritis?"

She jerked as she realized Mark had come to stand beside her. "It's hard to say. He tries to hide how much he hurts. I'd say since last winter."

"I see. He never told me."

She looked at him, then away. "Well, it gets worse as people get older, from what I've seen." She packed the now-empty plastic containers she'd brought into her basket.

"I never think of him getting older. I worried when he wrote me about coming for harvest and then he didn't answer my phone calls. So I came." He shoved his hands into his pockets and looked out at the fields. "I'm going to go change my clothes and see what I can do to help in the fields. I might as well do something."

Miriam nodded. "That would be *gut*. We all help each other here."

Mark picked up the basket and carried it inside the house, then went upstairs. Miriam busied herself washing glasses and straightening the kitchen. When he came downstairs, he was dressed in well-worn pants and a chambray shirt that brought out the blue of his eyes. A baseball cap covered his dense black hair. He nodded at her, slipped on his sunglasses, and left the house.

Miriam glanced around the kitchen and then, as comfortable as family, found herself examining the contents of the refrigerator. It didn't look like there was anything prepared for supper. And she doubted that either of the men would feel like cooking after working in the fields. So she set about gathering ingredients and peeling vegetables, and in no time she was sliding a casserole into the oven. Soon the kitchen was filled with delicious aromas.

"Something smells *gut*."

She turned and smiled at John. "Hope you don't mind I made myself at home in your kitchen."

He grinned. "Any day you want to take it over, be my guest."

"I figured you and Mark might be too tired to cook supper after working in the fields. Everything's done and ready to eat when you are."

A rumble of thunder sounded overhead.

The back door opened and Mark stepped inside, shaking off rain like a dog. "It's really coming down out there."

Miriam looked out the window. She hadn't thought to watch the weather. Now she'd have to walk home in the rain.

"I didn't see a buggy outside," Mark said as he came to stand at the window beside her.

"I walked over. It's not far."

"It is when there's lightning. I'll give you a ride home."

"*Nee*, you really—"

"I insist."

"Me, too," John said. "Miriam stayed and cooked us supper," he told Mark.

"Then I'm definitely giving you a ride home. Unless you'd like to stay and eat with us first?"

Miriam felt color creeping up into her cheeks. "Uh, *nee*, I should be getting home to help *Mamm*."

"Then I'm ready when you are. I'll be out in the car."

Miriam checked to make sure she'd turned off the oven, glanced around the kitchen, and found it spotless. "I'll be seeing you tomorrow then, John. Call if you need anything."

"*Danki* for the help."

She picked up the basket and hurried to the front door. When she'd started over to help today, she'd had no idea she'd get to see Mark. And certainly she'd had no idea he'd be driving her home.

God certainly had surprises in store some days, didn't He?

SSS

Mark wasn't being entirely altruistic by offering Miriam a ride home.

He turned the air conditioning up to full blast in his BMW and reveled in being cool for the first time since he'd stepped out of the car hours earlier. Summer was brutal in Lancaster County. He'd felt like he was under a broiler when he was working out in the fields. And his muscles ached after just a couple hours of work.

Miriam opened the door and slid inside. "Oh, my," she breathed. "Air conditioning."

He chuckled. "You don't have that in buggies, do you?"

"*Nee.*"

Mark leaned over to show her how to move the vent near her so that it blew cool air on her face, and felt her tense at the closeness. But when he looked at her, she smiled and thanked him. Had he imagined her reaction?

He started the engine. "Shall I take the long way home?"

She laughed, a full, throaty sound that made him glance at her. Her blue eyes sparkled and her creamy complexion flushed pink. He'd thought she was pretty as a teen, but now realized she'd grown into an attractive woman.

He backed out of the drive, turned the opposite way, and enjoyed her laughter.

"Oh, this feels *wunderbaar.*" She sighed. "Fans just don't do what an air conditioner can. If I had a car, I'd live in it during the summer."

"They make air conditioners for the house, too."

"You're right. How silly of me."

A brief glance showed her cheeks were stained with embarrassment.

He winced. "Sorry, I was teasing you."

"Oh."

"The *Englisch* always go on about how they'd miss television. Or having a telephone inside the house. I think they'd miss their air conditioning in the summer the most."

"Especially if they live in Lancaster County."

"For *schur.*"

"So you remember some Pennsylvania *Dietsch?*"

"Some. If you don't use it, you lose it, and there isn't much opportunity in my day-to-day life."

"John was glad to see you. So you're just here for a day or two?" she asked, remembering what he'd said at lunch.

"I head back in the morning." He slowed and peered at an ice cream stand beside the road. "Wow, that place is still in business?"

"*Ya*, it's the best."

"Do you want a cone? If you don't have the time, I can stop on my way back."

"I'd love a cone."

"Strawberry, right?"

She stared at him. "How did you remember that?"

"A good memory's a must in my line of work." He pulled into the parking lot and left the car running while he got out and bought the cones.

"This is as good as I remember," he told her as he ate his cone.

"Even better when it's not melting all over your hands in the heat," she said.

"I hope my grandfather didn't overdo it in the heat today." Mark finished his cone and wiped his mouth with a paper napkin. "It's too bad my dad didn't decide to stay and help with the farm." He shrugged. "But then who knows where I'd be right now?"

He glanced at her. She'd stopped licking her cone. "Uh, you're dripping." He handed her a napkin from the stack he'd been given.

"I think I've had enough," she said, frowning at it.

"I'll finish it for you. I'm a generous kind of guy."

Miriam grinned, handed it to him, and wiped her hands with the napkin. "So you're happy doing your work?"

He paused. "Sure. Why wouldn't I be? I make good money."

"That doesn't equate with being happy."

"No, it doesn't. But I guess I'm as happy as anyone I know." It sounded lame even to him. Miriam folded her hands and continued to look at him. She'd always had the most direct stare. She still did.

"Didn't someone once say that a person is only as happy as he decides to be?" He finished the cone, wiped his hands, and started the car.

"I'm sorry. I've made you uncomfortable."

"Don't be silly."

"I imagine you're *gut* at your job."

"Because of the car I drive?"

She shook her head. "*Nee*, I think you found something you love and you work hard at it."

Mark winced inwardly. Had his grandfather told her how often he'd said he was too busy to visit because he had a big case?

"I remember how you used to climb up into the hay loft and read those big books when you visited in the summers."

Mark laughed. "I was kind of a nerd."

"Why should reading make you a nerd?"

He couldn't help smiling at how quaint the word sounded the way she said it. There was something about the precise way many of the local Amish spoke that sounded faintly British to him.

"I don't know. My friends were reading comic books and *Play*—" he stopped. "Uh, adult magazines."

"I know the one you mean," she said primly, but he saw her lips twitch. "I've seen it at the store in town. I'm Amish, not blind."

He chuckled and found himself sorry to realize they were approaching her home. He'd always enjoyed talking to her.

"Thanks for everything you did today," he said as he pulled into the drive and stopped the car. "Especially cooking supper."

"I enjoyed it. And the drive and ice cream." She opened the door and heat poured in. "Especially the air conditioning," she said ruefully. With a sigh she got out, then turned back. "Mark? When you talk to your grandfather, please consider what he has to say. Listen with your heart." She closed the door and hurried away before he could ask her what she meant.

Listen with your heart.

Thoughtful, he drove back to the farm and parked beside the barn. His car looked incongruous next to the weathered building.

"*Gut*, you're home," John said when he went inside the house. "Hungry? Miriam's supper is ready."

"Yes, thanks. Sorry it took longer than it should. I was enjoying the air conditioning in the car after such a hot day."

"And talking to Miriam, eh? The two of you always used to have such long conversations."

Mark poured a glass of iced tea and sat at the table. "She wasn't like the girls I knew. She didn't simper or flirt or act silly."

John nodded. "Miriam is a *wunderbaar maedel*."

"I've been worried about you since I got your letter. You've never written me asking me to come help."

"I've been thinking about the farm," he said, staring off into the distance. "I can't run it like I used to. It's time to talk about its future."

"So you're going to sell it?"

John looked shocked. "*Nee*, I don't want to do that. It's been in this family for generations."

"What else can you do? Dad doesn't want it."

"And what about you, Mark?"

"Me? I'm an attorney, not a farmer."

"But you could be."

Mark stared at him, confused. "Could be what? A farmer?"

"*Schur*. I remember how much you enjoyed helping each summer you visited."

"I did. But I've made a life for myself. I'm already trying big cases at the firm. I bought a condo."

John leaned back in his chair and studied him with faded blue eyes. "And are you happy, *Grosssohn*?"

It was the second time he'd been asked that today. He didn't think he was walking around looking unhappy because he wasn't. So why was his grandfather asking him the same question Miriam had?

"Of course."

"There's no 'of course' about it. You are or you're not."

Mark spread his hands. "I don't know what else to say."

John leaned forward. "Say you'll take over the farm, Mark. Say yes to your heritage."

Four

Miriam wondered how the talk John wanted to have with Mark had gone.

She didn't want to intrude on their visit, but she was eager to hear what happened. Had John talked to Mark about his concern about the future of the farm?

And yes, she had to admit that she would enjoy seeing Mark again for purely personal reasons. Her girlhood crush was alive and well, as she'd found out when they went for a drive the day before.

Miriam set out for John's house with a basket of food, but was doomed to disappointment when she saw that Mark's car wasn't parked there.

John raised a hand and waved at her as he sat on the front porch.

"Has Mark gone home?" she asked, trying to sound casual as she climbed the steps to the porch.

He nodded. "Told me he had to get back to work."

She sat down in one of the rockers. "What did you say to him?"

John frowned and shook his head. "I told him I wanted him to take over the farm."

"You did? What did he say?" She felt her heart racing. It would be a dream come true if he did.

John shook his head. "He feels his life is in the city, practicing law." He sighed. "I'm hoping he'll think about it."

"I hope so, too, John."

She watched him gaze out at his fields. It had been another long day of harvesting and he looked so tired.

"I'm *schur* he'll give it a lot of thought. Mark is a responsible person. And he cares about you."

John nodded. "I hope he'll consider the Amish side of his heritage. But what if he doesn't feel he has any here? After all, my *sohn*, Mark's *dat*, didn't."

"It's in God's hands now."

He gave her a gentle smile. "Wise words from the young. But I expected as much from a teacher."

She gave a self-deprecating shrug. "Being a teacher doesn't make me wise. I'm repeating words you've said to me yourself."

John raised his brows. "I did? Well, I wonder how wise I'd be if I had a young man's memory."

A buggy passed by on the road and its occupants waved. They waved back.

Miriam stood. "I should be getting home to help *Mamm* with the *kinner*. Eat the supper I brought you and get some rest, John. I'm *schur* you'll hear from Mark soon."

"*Gut-n-owed*, Miriam. *Danki* again for supper."

"My pleasure, John. Enjoy it."

She walked home, enjoying the scent of honeysuckle climbing fences, and thought about their conversation. She hoped it would be *gut* news for him. But she wondered if Mark could give up the life he had in the *Englisch* world. Few *Englisch* converted to the Amish church and the Plain life.

Fewer still stayed.

John's dream of his *grosssohn* coming home might look impossible, but she'd learned that nothing was impossible for Him.

Helping her *mudder* with baths for the younger *kinner* was a tiring but happy task. When everyone was finally bathed and dressed in light pajamas, they all piled into one bed so Miriam could read a story. Then another. And another.

Afterward, she led each of them to their beds and tucked them in, then went down to the kitchen for a glass of iced tea and a quick look at her lesson plan book.

Her *mudder* settled into a seat at the table. "Listen to that," she said, glancing up at the ceiling.

Miriam did as she directed but didn't hear the pitter patter of little feet. "I don't hear anything."

Sarah smiled. "Exactly. Peace has settled over the Troyer *haus*. Isn't it a *wunderbaar* thing?"

She laughed. "You know you love the chaos."

"And you as well. Here you are after a long day helping me with your *schweschders* and *bruders*, and you're still not done. Already you're looking at lesson plans to help the *kinner* at *schul* in the fall."

"It's true, I'm pretty boring."

"That's not what I was saying at all." She tilted her head and studied her. "But you do need to get out and have some fun."

Her *mudder* had a point. Miriam loved *kinner* but she hadn't been out doing something fun in some time. "Life is busy right now. Maybe I'll go to the singing on Sunday."

"You should. Not maybe, but definitely!" She finished her tea. "I think I'll go take a last check of the *kinner* and see why your *dat* hasn't come in from the barn yet. I suspect he likes the quiet."

Miriam laughed. She thought her *mudder* might be right. He loved his *kinner*, but he always looked a little baffled when they were all gathered at the huge kitchen table and clamoring for attention.

She sighed. She'd said she might go to the singing on Sunday, but did she really want to? This time of year, more and more couples were matching up. As soon as the harvest was over, the weddings would begin. She was only twenty-four and in no way was she considered an old *maedel*, but she hadn't seen anyone romantically in such a long time.

Her thoughts drifted to Mark. She wondered what he was doing right now. She didn't envy the *Englisch*, but she was *schur* he was doing something more interesting with his evening than she was. During the summers when he'd visited, he'd talked about movies, about traveling, about an entire world beyond her own.

Well, if she'd wanted to experience such a life, she'd had a chance. The Amish community here had never discouraged a young person from taking time for *rumschpringe*.

But Miriam hadn't been interested. She enjoyed her life here. And when the church elders had approached her about teaching at the *schul* she and her *schweschders* and *bruders* had attended, she'd been overjoyed. She loved *kinner* and had always been her *mudder's* helper, taking care of her younger siblings.

Now and then she thought about getting married one day and having *kinner* of her own, but she was too busy to date. And none of the men she knew were interested in the outside world at all. They only talked about farming and dairies and weather and whatever vocation they were called to. If they had read a book since *schul*, it was one on rotating crops.

She and Mark, on the other hand, could talk for hours and not one word about this year's harvest would come up. She knew it was silly, even unfair, to compare Amish men to Mark. There was no future for them, but it didn't help her forget how she felt about him. And seeing him again hadn't lessened her feelings for him. In fact, she found herself thinking about him even more now that John had asked him to take over the farm.

She sighed as she climbed the stairs to her bedroom. She had to stop thinking about Mark. Truly, she was beginning to turn into a lovesick *maedel*. Last night she'd even dreamed of him.

She took a cool shower.

For *schur* it had to be the warm weather that was making her feel so flushed.

SSS

It felt good to be back at work.

Mark pulled into his parking space in the garage and walked to the elevator. Lani had warned him he had a heavy schedule lined up for the day, but he was grateful for it. It would keep his mind off his visit to Paradise and his grandfather's emotional request.

"Hold the elevator!"

He punched the stop button and tried not to roll his eyes at the prospect of riding twenty floors in a small space with Chris Parker, another up-and-coming lawyer in the firm.

"So, took a couple days off, huh?" Parker slurped at the cup of coffee in his hand.

"Yeah."

"Good job with the Smith case."

"Thanks." Okay, so he wasn't particularly fond of Parker, but surely he could come up with something more than monosyllabic answers. His schedule was so packed he didn't often get to talk to his colleagues. He flipped through his mental files searching for a topic. "How's the new baby?" What was her name? Elaine? Ellen? Something that started with E.

"Great, great. Got some new pics to share." He handed Mark his coffee to hold, set his briefcase down, and pulled out his cell phone to scroll through them. "Just shot these this morning."

Mark bit back a grin as he looked through the photos on the phone. With thin blonde hair and two chins, the poor kid looked like Parker, not his attractive wife.

"Cute baby," he offered, not knowing what else to say. Babies all looked alike to him.

"Fatherhood's great. You should try it."

"Maybe I should try marriage first."

"Yeah, yeah, you should. How's Tiffany?"

"Fine, fine."

The elevator stopped and the doors slid open. Lani stepped in, her arms loaded with files. "Mark! You're back!" She turned to Parker and leaned over to look at his phone. "So, new photos of Emily?"

Emily. Lani had a knack for remembering such things. She oohed and ahhed over the photos so Mark could go back to thinking about the day's schedule. He checked his Rolex and saw that he had a half hour before his first client appointment.

The elevator stopped at his floor. He handed the cup of coffee back to Parker. "This is my stop."

He got off and Lani followed him to his office. "How was your visit?"

"Don't ask." He set his briefcase on his desk, sat behind it, and watched her settle into a chair before him.

"You're not getting off so easy." She held the files to her chest. "What's up with your grandfather?"

Mark rose and closed his office door, then returned to his chair. "He wants me to take over the family farm."

She burst out laughing, then stopped. "You're serious?"

He nodded. "Dead serious."

"You're the last person I can see as a farmer."

"I spent summers working on the farm." He held up his hands showing her the blister he'd earned the afternoon he'd helped in the fields. "I helped yesterday."

"So, what are you going to do?"

"What can I do? My life is here. I'm not an Amish farmer."

"Maybe you can help him find someone to run it."

Mark pinched the bridge of his nose. "Yeah."

She stood and plopped the files on his desk. "Here you go. A little work for you now that you're back."

He grimaced. "Thanks."

"I'll get you some coffee."

"That'd be great."

From experience he knew she organized the files in order of importance. He opened the first and started his day.

Nine hours later, he saw the last client and closed the last file on his desk. Exhausted, he jotted a note for his billing hours and stood.

"'Night, boss," Lani said as he passed her desk outside his office.

"What are you still doing here?"

She reached into her bottom drawer and pulled out her purse. "Leaving now. I put in some extra time today since I have a doctor appointment tomorrow."

"I told you that you don't have to do that."

"I know."

They got into the elevator and rode down to the ground floor.

"You won't listen to me."

"Nope," she said cheerfully. "Have a good night."

He stopped on the way home at his favorite Chinese restaurant. As he ate General Tso's chicken with chopsticks in front of his wide screen television, he couldn't help thinking it was quite a change from the meal Miriam had prepared for him and his grandfather the night before.

The next few days were just as busy. He took Tiffany out one night and listened to her talk about her job at the museum and the upcoming fundraiser ball.

"My grandfather wants me to take over the farm," he told her as they lingered over dessert at her favorite restaurant.

"You're kidding. Why would you do that? You're an attorney. A successful one," she pointed out.

"He can't run it himself anymore," he said. "He's getting on in years and I can tell his arthritis is getting worse."

She spooned up chocolate mousse. "Well, that's not your problem."

He nearly bobbled his cup of coffee. "Excuse me?"

"You have a very different life than him. He can't expect you to drop everything and become a farmer." She looked up from her dessert. "When did he ask you to do this?"

"A couple days ago."

"So that's why you cancelled going to the gallery opening with me."

"He said he needed to talk to me. When I had trouble contacting him, I drove there to make sure he wasn't ill."

"And he wasn't."

"No. Thank goodness."

"You promised to take me." She pushed the dish aside and her mouth formed a pout. "It wasn't easy to find another escort."

Mark leaned back in his chair and studied her. "So who did you go with?"

"William."

"Did you have a good time?"

"That's not the point. I wanted to go with you."

The server came to top off their coffee. Tiffany gestured him away with a petulant wave of her manicured hand when he approached her side of the table.

Mark frowned. She was what a male friend of his called high maintenance. Her family was wealthy and she'd attended the best schools. The patrons of the museum she worked at were often longtime family friends.

Mark's family had been middle class, and if he hadn't been ambitious as well as a hard-working student who received scholarships, he might never have been able to attend college. His roommate had introduced him to the head of the firm he now worked at, and Mark worked long hours to get noticed by the top partners.

He'd always felt lucky Tiffany had given him a second look.

Now he found himself giving her one. And he wasn't impressed with what he saw. Tonight he saw her as self-centered and snobbish. He turned down her invitation to come inside for a cup of coffee and watched her flounce into her apartment.

Was it because he'd gone for a drive with Miriam just the other day that he found himself thinking about her when he hadn't for a very long time? Or was it the big difference in the two women?

He shrugged and pulled back onto the road and headed home. Out of habit he turned on the news while he stripped off his jacket and tie in his bedroom. A banner ran along the bottom of the screen: BREAKING NEWS!

And there was Maurice Smith being led to a police car by two officers. Mark grabbed the remote and turned up the sound, listening with disbelief as the on-camera reporter told how his client—just found not guilty earlier in the week—was being arrested for murder again.

Five

Early mornings were Miriam's favorite time of day. The house was so quiet she could hear the ticking of the clock hanging on the wall in the kitchen.

She sat at the big wooden table, sipping a cup of tea and reading the latest circle letter. It was long, having traveled to other teachers living in Amish communities in fifteen states. Hannah in Sugar Creek, Ohio, had read about an interesting article about Finland schools where scholars were thriving after homework had been abolished. Amish *kinner* seldom had homework since they had before- and after-school chores.

"*Guder mariye.*" Her *mudder* breezed into the kitchen. "What are you doing?"

"Ruth, a teacher friend in Goshen, sent me the latest circle letter. It's such fun getting new ideas from other Amish teachers around the country."

Her *mudder* smiled and kissed the top of her head. "It's so *gut* that you love your job. But enjoy your summer break." She paused and laughed. "Working with me on harvesting the kitchen garden and canning and preserving. Easy, fun times, *ya?*"

Miriam laughed. "They are. I love how we plant seeds and nurture the plants that grow. It's a little like the way my scholars come in as little *kinner* and grow and grow as eager learners."

"That's true." Sarah walked to the stove to pour herself a mug of hot water. She sat at the table, dunked a tea bag in the mug, and looked thoughtful. "I know it wasn't easy taking over for Anna at *schul*. She was your friend."

"I couldn't have if she hadn't asked me to do it." She sighed. "I still don't understand why she had to die, *Mamm.*"

Sarah laid a hand over hers. "I don't think we're meant to. We're meant to trust Him. Only He knows his reasons."

Miriam sighed. "I know," she said slowly, staring at the window. The darkness of night was fading and pale pink fingers of light began filtering into the room. Dawn always reminded her of the morning she'd sat with Anna after she came home from her last chemo treatment.

"She told me not to feel sad that she was leaving," she said, "'Why wouldn't I be happy?' she asked me. 'It's beautiful here and it's beautiful there. And you get to experience such love in both places.'"

Miriam rose, poured more hot water into her mug, and returned to the table. "And then she asked me to consider teaching her *kinner* at the *schul*. She said she and John Byler had talked about it." She stirred her tea. "So now I can say I had the worst and best time of my life all in the same year."

"Something *gut* came out of it. She gave you a gift so something *gut* came of her passing."

A thump sounded overhead.

"Someone's up." Miriam smiled at her *mudder*.

There was another thump, then they heard footsteps padding lightly down the stairs. Five-year-old Isaac wandered into the kitchen, rubbing his eyes and giving them a sleepy grin. "*Mamm*, I'm *hungerich*."

"And what would you like to eat?"

"Pancakes?"

"I think I could make those in the time it takes you to get dressed and get your *bruders* and *schweschders* up," Miriam said as she set aside the letter.

"Can I have the first one?"

"May I?" Miriam corrected.

Isaac tilted his head and studied her. "You want one too?"

"You know what I mean."

He chuckled. "You do *schul* even when we're home."

"Proper grammar is always important," she said primly. "Well? Shall I make pancakes?"

"*Ya*, you shall!" he cried and ran for the stairs. "Everybody! Wake up, wake up, wake up!"

Sarah put her hands over her ears. "Such a quiet, well-mannered *kind*."

They heard pounding feet and excited shouts. "*Kinner*," she corrected herself.

Miriam smiled. There was nothing she liked better than having a roomful of *kinner*, whether they were her family or her scholars. She reached into a cupboard, got out the biggest mixing bowl, found a wooden spoon, and began measuring ingredients.

Soon she and Emma had the *kinner* lined up at the big table eating pancakes soaked in syrup and wearing big smiles. Their *dat* came in from chores in the barn and settled into the chair at the head of the table. He looked pretty happy himself when Miriam set a plate stacked high with several big pancakes in front of him.

Miriam wished she had been able to get her *mudder* to sit still and eat more than one pancake before she disappeared upstairs to get bed linens for laundering. She ate quickly while keeping an eye on the *kinner*. For once there were no episodes of the boys engaging in sticky fingered mischief. She smiled ruefully. It was early yet.

After breakfast, chores were assigned. Mary washed the breakfast dishes and Emma dried them. Jacob and David followed their *dat* out to the barn. There were many *kinner* but more hands to do the work of the farm. Only the littlest, *boppli* Katie, escaped doing chores. She patted sticky hands on the tray of her high chair and grinned at Miriam.

"You're next for a good washing," Miriam said.

"We can dunk her here in the sink after the dishes are done," Mary joked.

"I'll give her a bath so you two can get started in the kitchen garden. It's going to be a warm day today."

"You mean hot," Emma said. "It's never just warm this time of year in Lancaster County."

"True." Miriam found herself remembering how cool it had been in Mark's air-conditioned car. When he'd leaned over to adjust the vent and she'd turned at that moment and they'd been so close . . .

Suddenly the room seemed warmer. She shook her head to clear her thoughts. Glancing over, she saw that Mary and Emma had finished with the dishes and were gathering up baskets to collect produce from the kitchen garden.

"*Kumm*," she said to Katie as she lifted her from the high chair. "Let's give you that bath."

As she sat beside the tub watching Katie splash, she reflected on how summer break had only started a few weeks ago and she was already longing for fall to come so classes would start.

And on the heels of that thought came the reminder that couples started getting married in late fall.

She wanted to get married. Who didn't? But she was hardly an old *maedel*. Amish couples, like *Englisch* couples, were getting married later these days. It was an especially good idea in her community. After all, there was no divorce here. Amish marriages were forever.

But it had been a long time since she'd dated. It wasn't that she hadn't been asked. She just wasn't interested in any of the young men who asked her out. At some point it seemed that they stopped asking her.

Katie splashed her and brought her back to reality.

"Time to get out," Miriam said. "Your little fingers are beginning to look like prunes."

"*Nee!*" Katie said, pouting.

"*Ya*," Miriam told her firmly, picking up a towel.

Katie tilted her head and gave her a big smile. "Cookie?"

"One." It was impossible to resist the *boppli* of the family.

Lifting her, Miriam wrapped her in the towel and closed her eyes, absorbing the scent and feel of a fresh, clean *kind*.

During the *schul* year her entire day was taken up with someone else's *kinner*. And whatever the time of year, as the eldest, so much of her day revolved around helping with her *schweschders* and *bruders*. She loved it.

But at times like this, when she held a tiny gift from God in her arms, she wanted one of her own.

One day she'd have a *kind* of her own. One day. If only she could find an Amish man as interesting as Mark.

♫♫♫

Mark saw reporters and two film crews at the entrance of the firm the next day. He drove past them and parked in the parking garage.

The ride up to Mark's office was totally silent.

Five people got onto the elevator.

Five people wouldn't meet his gaze.

"Mark! You're here!" Lani exclaimed as soon as Mark entered the firm. She jumped up from her chair, her face pale, her hands shaking. "Mr. Sampson wants to see you right away."

"I'll just bet he does," Mark muttered under his breath. He walked into his office and set his briefcase down on his desk. He turned and nearly ran into Lani, who'd followed him into the room.

"Everyone was talking about Maurice when I came in this morning." She closed the door behind her.

"You're the only one who's spoken to me." He told her about his ride up on the elevator and sighed.

"Did you stop by the jail and see him?"

He shook his head. "There were news people everywhere. I'm going later."

"Do you think he did it?"

"No."

"I don't think he did. Maybe someone had it in for him since he was found not guilty."

Mark sighed. "I just don't know what to think." He ran a hand through his hair. "Well, I guess I'd better go see Sampson and get it over with."

"It'll be all right," she reassured him.

Somehow he didn't think it could be. He made the long walk down the hall, took the stairs instead of the elevator, then walked into the ultra-plush office suite of the head of the firm.

"Go on in," Sampson's assistant said. "He's expecting you."

Sampson was pacing the thick carpet in front of the huge glass window that looked out over the city. He spun around when he heard Mark come in.

"Have you seen the reporters swarming the building? It's a media frenzy!" He took out a handkerchief and dabbed at his forehead. "This is bad, really bad."

"I know."

"This is unprecedented in the history of this firm. Why, we've been here since Philadelphia was established. It's going to cause repercussions for the firm," Sampson said, running a hand through his thinning hair. "We can't have this. We just can't have this."

He looked at Mark for a long moment. "We've never had a client found not guilty go out and murder someone. We're getting dozens of calls. People are saying we got a murderer off to murder again. It's outrageous!"

"How can we be blamed? We can't control our clients."

"We have to create some distance here," Sampson muttered.

"What do you mean?"

"The name of the firm is being impugned." He stopped pacing and stared at Mark. "The television stations have been showing film of you on the courthouse steps after the not guilty verdict. Every time they do they mention the name of the firm. We've got a reputation to maintain."

This wasn't sounding good. "Are you saying you don't want me to represent him again if he asks?"

"It's going to take more than that. I think you need to take a break."

"Are you firing me?"

"No, no, the partners and I just feel you should take some time off."

"But I have a lot of cases coming up. I—"

"Parker, Morelli, and Standish can take them over."

"But I—"

"You're officially taking a leave of absence," Sampson said firmly. "Until further notice."

Mark stared. "But that's unfair."

"That'll be all." He crossed to the window to stare out at the city. Then he spun around. "And you're not to take on that client again under any circumstances!"

Mark turned and strode from the room. When he reached the outer office where Sampson's assistant sat, he saw Bill, one of the security officers, waiting. The man looked embarrassed.

"Sorry, sir, but I'm supposed to escort you from the building."

So Sampson had never intended to discuss anything. He'd been determined to get him out before he had a chance to defend himself.

"It's all right, Bill. I need to get my briefcase from my office."

Bill nodded and they walked down to Mark's office. Lani looked up as they approached and she paled. "What's going on?"

"Sampson decided I need a break."

"For how long?"

"Until the negative publicity about Maurice dies down."

She jumped up and followed him into his office. "He can't blame you for that."

"He's the owner of the firm. He can do anything he wants. He's turning my caseload over to other attorneys."

She laid a hand on his arm. "I'm sorry, Mark. This is a tough break."

"Thanks. I'll keep in touch."

He walked down the hallway with Bill, conscious of the curiosity of those they passed. Once they were in the garage, Bill shook his hand and left him.

Mark supposed it could have been worse. He wasn't leaving with a cardboard box of his possessions from his office. But who knew how long he was going to be on leave?

He stopped at the jail on his way home. This time the news hounds were gone. He went through the routine and got a smirking acknowledgment from one of the guards as he signed in.

"Gonna defend him again?"

"It's up to him," Mark told him briefly.

"Say, did you hear the one about the lawyer who—"

"Heard them all. You gonna let me in to see him?"

"Sure, sure. No need to get your dander up." He checked a clipboard. "You're on the approved list."

Lucky him.

Maurice was dressed again in jail orange. Mark had only seen him in regular clothes during court appearances.

"Mr. Byler! I didn't think you'd come!" Maurice looked up at him through red-rimmed eyes. "Listen, you've gotta get me outta here! I didn't do it!"

He'd said that once and he'd been acquitted. Mark stared at him, unsure what to say.

"I'm telling you, I wasn't anywhere near that guy when he was killed. I barely knew him!"

"But you *did* know him?"

"Yeah, sure. We grew up in the same lousy neighborhood, that's all. That doesn't make me a murderer. I wasn't before. I'm not now. You gotta help me."

Mark sat back in his metal chair. "I can't. My boss doesn't like the publicity from you being arrested again. I've been put on leave and I doubt anyone from the firm will represent you."

Maurice stared at him. "Man, now what am I going to do?"

"I have a friend from law school who might be willing to take your case on a pro bono basis like I did. He's young, but really good. I'll give him a call and have him contact you. If he can't represent you, the court will appoint a public defender." Mark stood. "I ..." He stopped. What could he say? Good luck? How would that sound? "Take care," he said finally.

"Thank you, Mr. Byler. I'm sorry for causing you so much trouble. But I didn't kill that guy. I swear!"

Mark heard the metal door slam behind him and felt the sound reverberate through him.

He headed home and surprised his neighbor in the condo hallway when she saw him unlocking his door.

"You're home awfully early on a work day," she said. "Shush, Lily," she told the yapping poodle at her feet. "Mark's a neighbor, remember?" She glanced up at him and shook her head. "She's usually friendly. Guess she doesn't see you often enough."

"No, I'm not home much." Well, didn't use to be, he thought. But he wasn't telling her that.

When Lily continued to growl, the woman picked her dog up and stared at him with narrowed eyes. "You didn't get fired, did you? I saw the news last night."

He shook his head. "No, ma'am. Just taking a little personal time."

She made a *tsking* sound. "I hope you're not going to help him get off again."

Mark debated telling her the jury had found Marcus not guilty, but when other occupants of the building began to approach, he decided to beat a hasty retreat. "Sorry, I have to go, Mrs. Winkelman. Got a conference call scheduled in a few minutes."

He slipped inside his condo and leaned against the door, feeling like he'd escaped.

Six

Miriam was working in the kitchen garden when she saw the flash of a fancy *Englisch* car drive past on the road in front of the house.

It looked very much like Mark's car—with Mark driving it.

She was seeing things. Mark was in Philadelphia. Maybe she'd had too much sun. "I think it's time for a break," she told her *schweschders*. "Finish filling your baskets and we'll go inside for a bit."

No one argued with her. They quickly finished picking the zucchini, plump red tomatoes, beans, and other vegetables.

Every one of them had berry stained mouths from picking strawberries earlier. She didn't blame them; she'd had a handful or two herself. *Allrecht*, three.

She supervised the prayer of thanks. "Patties on the table," she whispered to Katie, demonstrating with her own hands and smiling when Katie pressed her chubby little hands on her high-chair tray. "Patties on the table" was something all young Amish children learned to do during prayers.

Then she poured lemonade and passed out glasses. Emma brought the cookie jar to the table and began placing cookies on a plate. Emma liked to be artistic, but the *kinner* weren't having any of that. They snatched at the platter. Isaac had one in each hand.

"He just took the last oatmeal raisin," Linda wailed, tears springing into her eyes.

"Looks like it's time for a lesson in manners," Miriam said sternly, crossing her arms over her chest.

"Oh, man," Isaac said. He turned to Linda. "Here, I'll give you one of them if you don't squall like a *boppli*."

"I'm not a *boppli*!" Linda glared at him but took the cookie.

"*Nee*, you're not, and Isaac is going to apologize." Miriam gave him a pointed look.

"Geez, I gave her the cookie," he muttered. But he apologized. It wasn't the most sincere apology, but Miriam let it pass.

"So, let's figure out what we picked today," she said brightly.

Isaac groaned. "Oh, no. She's gonna turn this into a math lesson."

"C'mon, it'll be fun." She didn't want them to lose their skills over the summer. And after all, math was a part of everyday life. "Get your baskets."

She waited until they were lined up in front of her, then handed Isaac a pad of paper and a pencil. "Isaac, since you helped *Daed* in the field, you can write the totals down. Let's do tomatoes first. We'll go around the table and each of you tell Isaac how many tomatoes you picked."

"Are you gonna make them count green beans, too? We'll be here all day!"

"As if you mind sitting here instead of helping *Daed* outside. Hmm," she pretended to consider. "Maybe you should go back outside. One of the others can help make notes."

"I'll do it." Isaac looked at Emma. "How many tomatoes, Emma?"

"Thirteen," she said proudly.

"Ten," said Mary.

"Eleventy-seven," David told them. He chuckled. "Just six. I helped *Daed* for a while."

Isaac marked each down, then they went around the table and gave their totals for zucchini—big numbers. Zucchini was always a bumper crop and turned up in all sorts of recipes. Some cooks even put it into chocolate cake to use it up.

Miriam passed out paper and pencil and the *kinner* proceeded to add up the totals. She smiled when all her scholars gave correct answers. She sent the boys back out to their *dat* and she and the girls worked on canning the tomatoes. It was hot, tiring work, but they'd be grateful for God's bounty when winter came. Their *mudder* took Katie upstairs for a nap, then returned and joined in the work.

"It's such a blessing to have your help," she said to Miriam after the canning was finished and Emma and Mary had left the kitchen.

"You know I don't need thanks. I love helping with the *kinner*."

"Maybe you don't need thanks, but I appreciate how much you do."

"I hope Emma will help you the same way one day." She hesitated. "But she doesn't seem as interested."

"She just needs to be encouraged," Sarah said. "So what if she doesn't do it right the first time? Let her learn. Don't do it for her."

Miriam winced. "Have I discouraged her?"

"A bit." She smiled. "I did it a few times when your *dat* did the dishes or helped with a household chore. He said it made him feel he couldn't do anything right. Emma needs to learn so she can be of help after you marry and start your own family."

"That's a long way away."

"I'm not so *schur* about that. I saw the way Amos looked at you in church last week."

Miriam had noticed. She shrugged. "We're just friends."

"Have you given him a chance to be more?"

Surprised, Miriam looked at her. Her *mudder* didn't often press her like this. Amish parents gave their *kinner* privacy in such matters and Miriam was grateful. She didn't want to share the reason why she wasn't interested in any of the men she knew.

But had she really given Amos a chance? Or any other man? She knew too often she compared men to Mark ...

The day went quickly, and soon it was time to think about supper. The spaghetti sauce they'd cooked and jarred left a heavy, pungent scent in the kitchen that was almost overpowering. Definitely not what anyone who'd worked all day in the heat would want to eat. But hardworking parents and *kinner* wouldn't want just a salad.

"So what shall we have for supper?" Sarah asked, standing at the refrigerator and staring into it with Miriam. There was a baked chicken and two dozen eggs—they always had lots of eggs since they had chickens. Plus tomatoes, carrots, and greens from the garden. And hamburger in the freezer.

"Salads," Sarah decided. Mary and Emma sat at the kitchen table to cut up vegetables as their *mudder* browned hamburger in a skillet on the stove and boiled eggs in a pan.

They cubed the chicken, then mixed it with mayonnaise, celery, and pickle relish and stuffed it into tomatoes. Emma giggled as she placed boiled eggs in the egg slicer and then reversed the egg to chop them. Egg salad sandwiches were popular with the younger *kinner* so she helped make them.

An hour later, the family sat down to supper. In some ways, Amish haystacks were a version of a taco salad, but the Amish placed rice or crackers on the bottom, then heaped lettuce, chopped tomatoes, hamburger, chopped egg, even chopped vegetables on top. The salad ended up looking like a colorful haystack, which was how it had gotten its name. Miriam had eaten many haystacks at Amish fundraisings and special events and loved them.

Sarah sent the *kinner* outside to enjoy big, juicy slices of watermelon before sending them upstairs for their baths. What was better than watermelon in summer and having the juice running down your cheeks after a hot day? Miriam even joined them in a contest to see who could spit a seed the farthest, putting several in her mouth and spitting one several feet off the porch.

"Wow! That one went so far!" Isaac cried.

Miriam spit another just as Emma said, "Hi, Mark!"

She spun around and one of the seeds in her mouth came flying out. It hit Mark's chest and plopped on the ground at his feet.

"Impressive!" he said with a chuckle.

Isaac snickered and the other *kinner* laughed.

Miriam gaped. "Mark! What are you doing here? Is John all right?"

♪♪♪

Mark chuckled as Miriam pulled a tissue from her pocket to wipe red juice from her chin.

She'd always behaved like such a quiet, sedate young woman when she was around him. Now she stood in the midst of her brothers and sisters, all of them with juice dripping from their chins and wearing wide grins.

"Miriam spit the seed the longest," David announced.

"The farthest," she corrected. "I spit it the farthest, not the longest."

"And modest, too," Mark said. He tucked his hands in the pockets of his jeans and rocked back on his heels.

She blushed and turned to the *kinner*. "Time for baths," she said. "Tell *Mamm* I'll be up in a minute. And behave yourselves!"

"Cute kids."

"I like them." She smiled. "Even when they're being little monsters. So, you didn't answer my question." Her hand flew to her throat. "Is John *allrecht*?"

"That's what I came over to ask. He wasn't home when I arrived."

"He told me he had a doctor's appointment this afternoon," she said, relieved. "I spoke to him yesterday when I took him some supper."

"That's good to know." Mark rubbed his temple where a headache had been brewing. "I was worried something else had happened."

"Would you like to come inside and have a glass of iced tea?"

"That sounds good."

They went inside and he sat at the table while she filled two glasses with ice and poured tea from a pitcher.

"Have you had supper?" she asked as she handed him the tea.

He shook his head. "Haven't been hungry much lately."

She nodded sympathetically. "I get that way when it gets warm." Then she shook her head. "I forgot. You have air conditioning."

He smirked. "And not just in my car. But the heat's not why my appetite's been off." He rubbed his temple again and wished for aspirin. "Well, a different kind of heat is responsible."

"I don't understand."

"Neither do I." He sighed and sipped his tea. "Long story."

There was a knock on the door. Miriam excused herself and went to answer it. When she returned, Mark's grandfather was with her.

"I saw your car outside," he said. His eyes sparkled and his cheeks were flushed. "So, you've come home!" He threw his arms around Mark and bear-hugged him.

Mark held up a hand. "It's just for a while. I have some unexpected time off and I thought I'd spend it here. It's a long story."

His grandfather's face fell.

"John, have you eaten supper?" Miriam asked. "I was about to walk over to your house with some food."

"*Nee*, I'm late getting home from my doctor's appointment." He turned to Mark. "Have you eaten?"

Mark shook his head. "I haven't been very hungry lately."

Miriam went to the refrigerator and began pulling out bowls and plastic containers. "Give me a few minutes and you can take supper home with you. We had lots of cold salads and such. *Gut* on a hot day."

"*Danki*, Miriam, that would be *wunderbaar*."

Mark couldn't meet his grandfather's eyes. He wasn't looking forward to telling him why he'd returned to the farm. His hand went to his temple again.

Miriam opened a cabinet. She found a bottle of aspirin and, without commenting, put it on the table in front of him.

He glanced up, thanked her, and washed two tablets down with the tea as he watched her fill the plastic containers and put them in a wicker basket.

"Oh, can't forget the watermelon," she said, giving Mark a smile as she tucked a plastic container of chunks of the fruit in with the food.

When they walked outside Mark looked around, then looked at his grandfather. "Where's your buggy?"

"Driver took me, then dropped me here when I saw your car." He got in the passenger side. "First time I've been in your fancy car."

"That's what Miriam calls it. Do all Amish call them fancy cars?"

John chuckled. "*Nee*. But you have to admit, it's pretty fancy for an *Englisch* car, isn't it?"

"*De rigueur* for an attorney," Mark muttered.

"Eh?"

"Nothing."

The drive was short and silent. Once inside the farm house, Mark set the basket down on the table.

John sat down at the table and looked at him. "*Allrecht*, now tell me what's wrong. You're acting like you have the weight of the world on your shoulders. Nothing can be as bad as you're acting."

Mark sank into a chair and sighed. "Not true." He looked at him. "I guess the news didn't travel this far."

"What news?"

He told him about Maurice and about his boss ordering him to take a leave of absence.

"So you came home, as you should," John said, nodding. "This is where you belong at such a difficult time."

"I appreciate your saying that. I thought I could help you with the harvest instead of sitting around my condo worrying."

"Working with your hands always makes a man feel better," John told him. He looked at his own hands resting on the wooden table. "Well, unless your arthritis is getting worse." He sighed and began unloading the basket.

"I just don't understand what happened," Mark said as he rose to get plates from a cupboard. "I don't believe Maurice killed a man. But it doesn't look good that after the jury found him not guilty, he's arrested for another murder."

"Things will work out."

"I wish I had your faith."

John's gaze was steady and serious. "I do too. It'll come. Sometimes, when we feel tested, we don't think we can meet the challenge. But the strength is in you. I've seen it as you've matured into a man."

"You always saw more in me than I did." Mark studied his hands. "I didn't think I could do anything when I first came here. I was a skinny city kid who'd never seen a farm, who didn't know a corn plant from a weed. You made it seem like something I could do. Something fun."

He'd planted seeds, Mark thought.

"Still, you loved having your nose in one of those big books you borrowed from the library. I can't remember how many times I found you up in the hay loft reading after you did chores."

"All that reading paid off," Mark reminded him. "I was able to do dual enrollment and take college classes while I was in high school and graduate earlier, go to law school sooner."

Funny, he'd often thought his grandfather had understood him more than his own father had, even though they seemed to come from two different worlds. Faith and God weren't mentioned much in his own home growing up. Yet his father had taken the time to drive him to see his grandparents each summer. His parents didn't stay but a night or two, but after Mark asked to stay longer when he was fourteen, he'd been allowed to do so.

His father had been surprised when Mark enjoyed farming and made friends and attended church services. But he'd been relieved when Mark didn't speak of becoming Amish, even after he'd spent summer after summer on the farm.

Mark got plates from the cupboard.

"Get some bread from the bread box and slice us some for sandwiches," his grandfather said.

He sliced the bread and then watched without much interest as his grandfather spooned food onto the plates.

"Miriam's right," John said. "A cold supper's *gut* on a warm evening." He pushed the container of egg salad toward Mark. "You loved this when you were a boy."

"*Grossmudder* made it for me every time I visited."

Finally, more to ease the headache than to appease hunger, he made his own sandwich and found the simple food delicious. He couldn't remember the last time he'd had homemade bread or egg salad. After he finished the sandwich, he found himself making another.

When his grandfather opened the plastic container of watermelon chunks, Mark remembered the seed-spitting contest he'd walked in on at Miriam's house. He'd known her for a long time and never seen her enjoying herself so much. It had been the only bright spot in his day.

What would his grandfather say if he challenged him to a seed-spitting contest? Surely the man would think he'd lost his mind.

So they sat and ate cold watermelon on a warm summer evening and talked of the harvesting work that had been done and what Mark could do during the coming weeks.

It felt like old times when things had been less complicated.

They cleared the table and put away leftovers. Mark watched day turn to dusk as he washed dishes and his grandfather dried them and put them in the cupboard.

"Come outside," John said as he put the last dish away. "There's something I want to show you."

Mark followed him outside and the two of them eased into the rocking chairs on the back porch.

"Look up," his grandfather said simply.

He gazed upward and saw stars winking to life one by one. Soon the sky was filled with hundreds of them—more than he ever saw in the city because of the lights there.

A sense of peace flowed over him, as gentle as the cooling breeze that swept over the nearby fields and brought the scent of honeysuckle.

"Times like this I always remember a passage from the Bible," John said quietly. "'Peace I leave with you, my peace I give unto you: not as the world giveth, give I unto you. Let not your heart be troubled, neither let it be afraid.' I read a lot in the gospel of John because of my name, I'll admit. But this has always comforted me in difficult times. Like after your grandmother died."

He rose and touched Mark's shoulder. "Don't worry or be afraid. Let peace inside you. Trust God."

"I'm trying."

"Don't try. Be. Do."

Mark nodded. "Sleep well."

"You, too. I love you."

Mark squeezed the shaky hand that rested on his shoulder. "I love you, too."

Seven

Curiosity was killing her.

Miriam told herself she wasn't a good person. It was John and Mark's business why Mark had come back so unexpectedly.

But she really wanted to know why Mark was here. Had he decided to do as John wished and take over the farm? She fervently hoped so. But then why had Mark looked so upset? He'd constantly rubbed his temples as if his head hurt. And he'd said he hadn't had much of an appetite for some time.

Something was wrong. She didn't have to be a psychic to sense that. And if Mark had come back to take over the farm, wouldn't he have said something last night? Instead he'd said he and John had to talk and they'd left.

She told herself she'd know soon enough. After all, John shared almost everything with her.

Her *mudder* walked into the kitchen. "*Danki* for making breakfast so I could sleep in a little. Katie kept me up most of the night. I think she's getting another tooth." She yawned. "I hope she sleeps tonight."

"How much sleep have you missed with all of us through the years?" Miriam asked as she took a plate of eggs and bacon she'd left warming in the oven and set it in front of her *mudder*. She poured her a cup of coffee. It was already getting a bit warm, but Miriam knew her *mudder* couldn't get her day started without coffee. When she handed it to her, she received a grateful smile.

"It doesn't matter," Sarah with a tired smile. "All *kinner* are a gift from God." She reached for Miriam's hand. "You look like you have a lot on your mind."

Miriam glanced out the kitchen window to where the girls were busily weeding and gathering produce. Shrugging, she joined her *mudder* at the table.

"Mark came home yesterday."

"John's Mark?"

"*Ya*. He came here when he didn't find John home. John arrived a little later and the two of them left." She traced the rim of her cup with her finger and frowned. "He looked troubled, *Mamm*. Said he and John needed to talk. I'm worried. I think something's wrong. With Mark, I mean. Not John."

"You remember what they say about worry."

"*Ya*." Miriam sighed. "It's arrogant. God knows what he's doing."

"John's a very wise man. If something's wrong, he'll help Mark."

"I know." She finished her tea and then, restless, she stood and got a basket. "I promised I'd go with Fannie Mae and Naomi to help feed the men harvesting with John today." She wrapped a loaf of bread and set it in the basket, added cookies and a frozen pound cake baked earlier in the week. John had said there were two chickens in his refrigerator, so she'd bake them when she got there.

"Do you mind if I take some of the jars of chow chow and pickled beets from the cellar?"

"Of course not."

"I'm sure he'll be giving me some zucchini."

"Gardens are always blessed by zucchini this time of year," her *mudder* joked.

"True. And John's kitchen garden always does so well." She smiled as she gathered food for the basket. "He told me once his kitchen garden grows so well because when he works in it he thinks of his *fraa* and how they planted it together."

"They were so happy together." Sarah finished her breakfast and pushed aside the plate.

"Like you and *Daed*."

"I hope one day you'll meet someone special and be just as happy."

Miriam felt she had, but what *gut* was it when the man was Mark and they could have no future?

"Well, I'll be going over to John's for a few hours."

"Miriam? Don't worry about Mark and John. God has a plan for them and everything will work out."

"I know," she said slowly. "I just wish I knew what it was."

She heard her *mudder's* laugh as she left the room.

Mark's car was parked in John's drive. So he hadn't left. Not that she'd expected him to, but remembering how upset he'd looked the night before, she had no idea why he'd come or how long he'd stay.

She went into the house and found it empty. Apparently she was the first of several women who would help feed the workers today. She set the basket on the kitchen table. The chickens John had mentioned were in the refrigerator, so she preheated the oven and set about preparing them to roast. Then she went outside to harvest produce that had ripened.

An hour later, she used the back of her hand to wipe perspiration from her forehead. Another hot day and it would only get hotter as it wore on.

She glanced at the fields and saw men working. If she was this warm, she couldn't imagine how they must be feeling. She picked up the basket, now full of greens and tomatoes, and went inside. Fannie Mae and Naomi had just arrived and were unpacking some dishes and desserts. She greeted them, washed her hands, and checked on the chickens. Her timing had been *gut*—they were almost ready to come out.

"We saw John's *grosssohn's* car outside," Fannie Mae said as she set a pie on the counter. "So he's here to help with the harvesting as usual?"

"*Ya.*"

"That's *gut*," Naomi said with a nod. She lifted a big bowl of macaroni salad from an insulated bag and carried it to the refrigerator.

Miriam opened the oven, winced at the blast of heat, and pulled the pan with the chickens out. She set it on the top of the stove and turned off the oven. "I think I'll take some cold drinks out to the men."

"*Gut* idea. I brought some monster cookies. We can take them out, too. Something to hold them off until lunch."

"The *kinner* love those when you bring them to *schul.*"

"And so do the big *kinner* we call men," Naomi said with a gusty laugh. She found a plate and arranged them on it.

Miriam poured glasses of iced tea and started outside. Fannie Mae followed her with a pitcher and Naomi carried the cookies. The minute the men saw the women approaching the table set by the field, they started over.

All except for Mark.

She caught a glimpse of him continuing to work in the far reaches of the field.

John caught her glance. "I tried to get him to take a break. He said he'll be along in a minute." He accepted a glass of iced tea from her.

The men took their drinks and cookies and went to sit in the shade of a tree near the house. Fannie Mae and Naomi returned to the house to continue lunch preparations.

"Boy's working hard because he's got some heavy thinking to do," John said quietly, looking at her intently. "He needs a friend."

She nodded. "I hope he'll talk to me."

The men returned to the field and she had no reason to stay outside, so she went back into the house.

$$\mathscr{SSS}$$

Mark drove himself to move down another row and another row. The sun was relentless, but hadn't it always been during harvest? This was just like running a marathon. If you hadn't trained you were going to suffer.

Tomorrow would be better.

He'd watched the other men go for a break and promised them he'd do so soon. It wasn't like he didn't know to stay hydrated. He'd brought a bottle of water out and drunk it, hadn't he?

Another row and he'd take a break. The other men had taken time from their own farms to help his grandfather while he'd been sitting in a cool, air-conditioned office. He knew it was part of community here, but still, he should have been here weeks ago. He'd spent so many summers helping with harvest, but each year work had interfered until he arrived later and left earlier.

Now here he was ... only it hadn't been by choice and he felt bad about that.

So he drove himself.

"Won't get it all done in one day," his grandfather came to tell him. "And you won't get it done if you kill yourself."

"I'll stop soon." He paused to take off the straw hat his grandfather had provided and used a bandanna to wipe the sweat from his forehead. Had he ever sweat this much? "You go in for a bit and I will, too."

The older man hesitated, then nodded. "*Allrecht.* You'll be right behind me?"

"I will be. Tell Miriam I'm looking forward to some of her sun tea."

"Fannie Mae brought her monster cookies."

"Great. I used to love those." He rubbed his temple. Another headache was brewing—a bad one. And while he'd told his grandfather he was looking forward to a drink and cookie, the fact was his stomach was roiling.

He turned back to the team of horses being used to harvest and wished they could use tractors like they used in some other Amish communities.

"Let me take over for you," Abraham said. "You're pushing too hard your first day here."

"I'm fine."

"He's right," Samuel said. "We're used to it. You need to take a break."

Mark started to protest, then realized he was seeing spots before his eyes. He waved his hand at them and frowned. He didn't remember gnats being such a problem in the past. But not only didn't they go away, they were multiplying in front of him, their buzzing sounding louder and louder in his ears.

"Stupid bugs," he complained, waving his hand at them. "Aren't they bothering you?"

"Bugs?"

"Guess I'm going to have to get some bug spray."

He started to walk toward the farmhouse.

And fell flat on his face in the dirt.

SSS

Mark woke and found himself lying on the back porch of the farm house. Miriam's face swam above him and something cool and wonderfully wet was being stroked over his hot face and wrists.

"Miriam?"

"*Ya?*"

"What's going on? What am I doing here?"

"You don't remember why you came to your grandfather's farm? Fannie Mae, I think we need to call the doctor."

"No, no, I remember driving here. Why am I lying here on the porch?"

"You fainted," Fannie Mae said.

"I did not!" he said, appalled. "I must have tripped." He struggled to sit up, but the world spun. Limp, he lay back down.

Miriam wiped his face with the cold, wet cloth. "Abraham and Samuel carried you here. As soon as you're feeling a little better, they'll help you inside to rest."

"They said they tried to get you to take a break," Fannie Mae said tartly.

"Don't fuss at him when he's feeling so poorly," Miriam said.

"Naomi and I will be going then, if you don't need our help."

"*Danki* for the help. I'll see you tomorrow."

Fannie Mae looked at Mark over the rims of her glasses. "You be *schur* to get some rest. Take a day or two to recover. Heat exhaustion can be dangerous. You could have had heat stroke, you know."

"I've learned, believe me." He repressed a shiver as she marched to the kitchen door. How could a woman his own age seem so stern?

She left, the screen door banging behind her.

Miriam pushed a cold glass into his hands. "Here, Mark, drink some water."

He raised up on one elbow, and this time the world didn't tilt. The water felt amazing to his parched throat. "I think I can sit up now."

"*Allrecht*, but take it slow."

Mark felt her arm around his back for support and was touched by her caring. Then his senses swam at her nearness, at the fresh scent of her. She smelled of wildflowers.

"Steady?"

He nodded. Their gazes met, locked, then she looked away and sat back on her heels. "*Gut.* Get your bearings, then we'll see if you feel like you can get up with some help."

Mark decided he'd do best to have Abraham and Samuel when it was time to get to his feet.

"Where's my grandfather?"

"Resting in the downstairs bedroom. I didn't want to worry him unless I had to."

"Good idea." He decided to stand.

Miriam stood quickly. "I don't think you should stand up yet," she cautioned.

"I'm fine, really." But he had to admit his knees were shaky and he didn't mind that her hand went to his elbow as they walked inside.

"Sit and catch your breath before you try to make it upstairs," she urged him. She pushed him into a chair and directed the battery operated fan on his face.

She poured him a glass of iced tea and set it in front of him. "Let's get as much fluid in you as we can. Are you hungry?"

Mark pressed a hand to his stomach and shook his head, which set off another wave of dizziness. He hated weakness, but he was afraid he was about to slide off his chair. "Food's the last thing I want. But thanks." He took a deep breath. "I think I need to lie down for a few minutes. Then I'll see if I can go back out and help."

He stood, bit back the nausea, and was grateful when she hurried to his side to slip her arm around him.

"Don't try the stairs yet." With an air of determination, she guided him from the kitchen to the downstairs bedroom.

"What's going on?"

They stopped and turned. John stood staring at them, his bushy eyebrows raised.

"John, we didn't want to disturb you," Miriam said. "But Mark wouldn't listen to anyone about taking a break, and he got sick. I was helping him to the bedroom."

"You should have called me," he admonished. "He's too heavy for you. Let me help." He put his arm around Mark's waist and the three of them made their way slowly down the hallway.

"I'm not a baby," Mark protested.

"*Nee*, but you know better than to work without a break in this heat," John said, helping him to the bed. "You're not used to it."

"You saying I'm pampered?"

John pushed him down on the bed and lifted his legs onto it. "I've seen you do more than your share. But you shouldn't have overworked your first day here." He laid a hand on Mark's forehead. "You're still awfully warm."

"I'll fetch a cold cloth. And the kitchen fan."

"*Gut. Danki.*" He waited until Miriam left the room. "She's such a *gut maedel.*"

Mark lay on the bed and felt like he was floating on a cloud. He remembered that charged moment when she'd helped him sit up and their gazes had locked. She'd smelled like wildflowers. "An Amish angel," he murmured and drifted off.

Eight

Market day!

It was a day Miriam loved even though it meant a lot of work. Everyone in the family, except *boppli* Katie, got up even earlier than usual to load the spring wagon with fruits and vegetables.

While her *dat* and her *bruders* loaded baskets and boxes, Miriam packed lunches and added plastic bottles filled with frozen water and lemonade. They'd keep the lunches cool and be icy cold to drink once they thawed.

Of course, she, Emma, and Isaac always saved a little money for a shared funnel cake or other special treat. Those special treats made the day seem less like work and tasted so *gut*.

Miriam wanted to take the reins of the spring wagon, but she knew Emma liked to drive it. So she gave her a big smile and hoped they wouldn't encounter too much traffic on the way to the market.

The place was huge and already teeming with activity when they arrived. This time of the year, it was especially popular with locals and tourists. Produce was abundant and reasonably priced, and other vendors, both Amish and *Englisch*, had booths selling baked goods, handmade baskets, clothing, quilts, and all manner of things.

Emma pulled the wagon into the space behind their vendor stall and the three of them quickly unloaded their produce. The sun was just coming up as they finished, so they settled on high stools and waited for their first customers.

And started their day with a big cinnamon roll from a baked goods stall.

People began surging into the market. Some were regular customers, some new. Miriam had always been a people watcher and she loved listening to the different accents and expressions. Sometimes she could guess where they were from and sometimes she couldn't. But it was always fun to watch and listen.

Except when Emma and Isaac were squabbling.

"Emma, it looks like the tomatoes have gotten picked over," Miriam said. "How about you rearrange them? And Isaac, take those boxes out to the wagon and see if Ned needs some water."

They both walked off to do as she said, grumbling but obeying.

She hoped they'd remember why she'd put them to work and not repeat the behavior. But they were *kinner* and she was *schur* that wouldn't last forever.

As the hours passed, they only got busier.

"Be *schur* to drink lots of the water I packed," she told them. "It's getting warm."

"Someone should have told Mark to do that the other day." Emma finished the funnel cake she and her *bruder* were sharing and licked her fingers. Then she caught Miriam's look. She pulled a tissue from her apron pocket and wiped the powdered sugar from her fingers.

"Mark isn't used to the heat."

"Well, I hope he feels better. I like Mark."

Isaac started to wipe his mouth with the back of his hand. Miriam frowned at him, handed him a paper towel, and watched as he used it.

A customer approached, spent ten minutes deciding on her purchases, then bought so much Miriam dispatched her helpers to carry it to the woman's car.

Miriam took a seat, pulled out a bottle of lemonade, and took her first break of the morning. Emma's mention of Mark reminded her that she hadn't been by John's farm house for two days. But the Amish grapevine worked well. She'd heard that Mark had been forced to stay inside and not help harvest. The doctor had told him he had heat exhaustion.

She still didn't know what had made Mark return to the community or why he'd looked so upset. His getting sick that day in the heat hadn't given her a chance to talk to him. She knew she shouldn't worry about him, but she did. He was her friend.

Well, she'd have to swing by John's later today and hope he'd talk to her about whatever was troubling him.

A woman carrying a large tote bag walked up to their stand and looked over the produce.

"So, Mrs. Dotson, you're back from your grandson's wedding. Did you enjoy it?"

The older woman nodded vigorously. "Lovely wedding. The bride looked so lovely in a long, lacy dress. And the flowers. My, my, they were so lovely. She even made sure I had a wrist corsage." She launched into a long monologue detailing every flower, every attendant, and the food. "And this one woman wore a red dress to the wedding. Can you imagine?" She didn't give Miriam time to answer. "I had a red car once. Nice car." And she wandered down that verbal road while she sorted through a basket of tomatoes.

"These are nice and red," aren't they?" Miriam asked when the woman took a breath. "We just picked them yesterday."

"I'll take a pound," she said, nodding.

Miriam weighed the tomatoes, placed them in a paper sack, and helped her put it into her tote. She accepted bills and made change. "Please take a bottle of our blueberry balsamic vinegar. On the house. We just made it the other day."

"Blueberry balsamic vinegar, hmm? Sounds interesting. It's such a lovely shade of blue. That reminds me of some lovely blue flowers I had in my garden once." She gestured as she told the story of her bluebells and Miriam listened politely.

"Mrs. Dotson, did you know the bakery stall has blueberry muffins? I know how you love blueberries. You might want to get some before they sell out."

"I'd best hurry on over and get some." She patted Miriam's hand. "You're such a thoughtful young woman, Miriam."

"Thank you. Have a wonderful day, Mrs. Dotson, and see you next week."

Isaac snickered. "I thought she'd go on forever. 'Your green beans remind me of my lawn,'" he mimicked in a falsetto amazingly like the older woman's voice.

Miriam frowned and shushed him. "One day you'd better hope someone's nice to you when you're old and you tell stories."

"I'm never getting that old," he said confidently.

John was nearly that old. She worried about him and wondered again if Mark was considering taking over the farm.

"I'm going to take a little walk around," she told them. "The two of you are in charge while I'm gone."

"You can leave it to us," Isaac said standing up straight and tipping his straw hat back on his blond hair.

"I'll make sure he behaves himself," Emma said. She loved reminding Isaac she was older than him.

Miriam walked away before she had to referee another dispute.

She enjoyed saying hello to other vendors as she walked along the aisles. A display of sewing supplies caught her eye. She bought a thimble handpainted with tiny flowers for her *mudder's* upcoming birthday, and stopped to look over some bandannas a new vendor was sporting.

"They're filled with a gel that chills you in the heat," he said, picking one up and holding it out to her to inspect. "You tie it loosely on your neck like this." He demonstrated."

It felt cool, she discovered, and remembered how Mark had gotten overheated the other day.

"Quite a bargain this time of year," the man said persuasively. "I'll give you a special vendor's discount."

She pulled out some money. "I'll take a blue one for my friend."

"Excellent choice," he said as he gave her change and slipped her purchase into a bag. "I'll be here next week, so be sure to stop by and let me know how it works for him."

Miriam took the bag from him, smiled, and walked on. She'd been looking for an excuse to stop by John's, and she'd just found it.

$$\mathscr{SSS}$$

Mark answered the knock on the front door and was surprised to find Miriam standing on the porch.

"Come in," he invited, holding the door open.

"I can't, I'm on the way home from a day at the market and I have Emma and Isaac with me."

He looked past her and saw them sitting in the spring wagon. Emma waved at him. Isaac was intently studying something in his cupped hands.

"I have some money for John." Miriam handed him some bills. "I took some of the produce from his kitchen garden with me to the market."

"That was very kind of you." He knew the Amish believed in community, but she certainly seemed to do a lot for his grandfather.

"And I bought this for you." She gave him a bag. "The man said it helps you stay cool. You put it in the refrigerator before you tie it around your neck and go outside."

Mark pulled the bandanna from the bag. "Sounds like a good idea. I'll try it. How much do I owe you?" He dug in his pocket for his wallet.

Miriam frowned." It's a gift."

He started to open his mouth, to tell her not to spend her money on him, but quickly reconsidered. "I'm sorry. I didn't mean to offend."

She nodded. "It's *allrecht*."

"Thank you for thinking of me."

He was rewarded with a warm smile.

"You look better than you did the other day."

"I feel better, thanks."

"You were acting ... driven that day," she said hesitantly. "Like you had the weight of the world on your shoulders. If you'd like to talk about it ..." She trailed off hesitantly.

Her concern touched him. Everyone but Lani from back home was avoiding him, not returning his calls. Even Tiffany.

"I—" Then his attention was pulled away by Emma jumping up in the wagon and fussing at her brother. "Uh, Miriam, I think Isaac is up to something."

Miriam sighed. "He loves to torment Emma and his *schweschders*. Isaac! Stop whatever you're doing!" She turned back to him. "I have to go."

He walked with her to the wagon. "I always envied my friends who had a sister or brother to torment."

"And those of us who have siblings often wish we were only *kinner*. I guess we're not always satisfied, are we?"

Mark leaned on the side of the wagon and looked at Isaac. He'd never been very good with kids. Sometimes when he met a coworker's child, he was just clueless what to do or say. "What's that you have in your hands, buddy?"

"Magic beans," Isaac said, his eyes huge as he held out his hands.

Mark watched the beans jumping in Isaac's palms. "Wow, that's something else. Where'd you get them?"

"A man at the market was selling them."

Miriam peered at them. "How much did you spend on them?"

"Just a dollar."

"So did the man tell you to plant them and they'd grow to be a big beanstalk?"

"He just said they were magic. But I remember you read us the story a couple times. Do you think they'll grow to be a big beanstalk? I can climb up it and get the gold from the giant. Then we wouldn't have to work so hard."

"It's a fairy tale," Miriam said. "You know it wouldn't be right to steal something from someone."

"But didn't the giant steal the money from the boy's *dat*?"

"That doesn't make it right."

"Can I hold them for a minute?" Mark held out his hand.

"*Schur*. Just be careful. Don't drop them."

"I won't." He held the beans in his palm and watched their frenetic jumping. He had a vague memory of such beans from attending a school fair.

"What do you suppose they are?" Miriam whispered.

"I saw these years ago," he said. "Here, take your magic beans, Isaac."

He reached into his pocket for his cell phone, tapped the screen, found a site. "Look, I found a video."

They crowded around him and watched what the video voiceover announced was a pupa—a worm—emerge from the bean. After a few minutes, it became a moth and flew away.

Miriam gasped. "That's amazing. But Isaac, when we get home you have to leave them on the porch. *Mamm* won't let you take them in the house. They're bugs."

He gave a big sigh and shrugged. "*Allrecht.*"

"Mark?"

He turned to Emma. "Yes?"

"Is that how you look things up? On your phone?"

"Yes. Sometimes. You can find all sorts of things on the Internet with it."

"You're smart like Miriam. Oh, I don't mean she looks up things on the phone. But she's always teaching us stuff. Even in summer."

He wasn't sure if it was a compliment, but he had a sudden inspiration. Tapping the screen again, he found a short cartoon video of the fairy tale and handed it to Emma to watch.

She beamed. "Is this the way the *Englisch* tell stories?"

"Sometimes."

"Miriam reads to the *kinner* every night. Both ways are nice." Emma watched the short video then handed him the phone.

"*Danki* for looking all that up," Miriam said as Emma turned to study the beans with her *bruder*. "I would have let him take the beans into the house and then we'd have had a moth flying around. So, he paid a dollar for ... worms that become moths," she said quietly.

"Took advantage of a kid, huh? You want me to go talk to the guy?"

She stared at him, looking surprised. "*Nee.* It was just a dollar, after all."

"The Amish get taken advantage of all the time. It's not right."

Miriam smiled. "Now you sound like a lawyer."

"I am one. You're not going to tell a lawyer joke, are you?"

"I don't know any."

"Oh, that's right. I get so used to people telling them, I didn't think. Of course you wouldn't know any. It's the kind of thing they do in my world. Make jokes about our occupation. They even do it to teachers these days."

"Well, I know the *Englisch* think we're a little naïve, and I suppose we are about the ways of your world." Miriam studied her *bruder*. "But he was entertained for a while, and he's learned a lesson that will serve him in life."

"A science lesson as well."

"True. Not that we teach science in *schul*. But a lesson in nature, shall we say?" She climbed into the wagon. "Tell John I said hello."

"I will. And thank you for selling that produce for him today. I'm sure he appreciates it."

He stood there watching her drive off and found himself frowning. Did his grandfather need money so badly that he sold produce from the kitchen garden? He didn't remember him doing that before. Lost in thought, he wandered back into the house.

His grandfather always had seemed so strong and self-sufficient. He'd gotten used to him being there for him. When he'd visited in the summer, sure, he'd helped. But his visits had grown shorter and shorter in recent years.

He'd been selfish, he told himself as he walked into the kitchen. He placed the money and the gift from Miriam on the table and got a cold drink from the refrigerator. Then he wandered out to the back porch. It was cooling off some.

The screen door creaked. His grandfather walked out.

"How are you feeling?"

"Good. Miriam came by and left some money for the produce she took to the market for you."

"*Gut.*" He settled himself into a chair.

"I don't remember you doing that before."

"We had a bumper crop of some things."

"Everything's okay?"

"*Schur.* Why?"

"If you need money—"

"I just had too much produce and I wasn't willing to ask Miriam and the other women to can it for me, not with all they have to do. And I wouldn't know how to can it myself."

Relieved, Mark grinned. "Women's work?"

"*Ya.* Not that I'd dare say it around them."

"Did you ever think of remarrying?"

John looked out at the fields for a long time. "Never felt the same way about anyone but your *grossmudder*," he said at last.

"She was a special woman, that's for sure."

They sat in companionable silence.

"Getting hungry?" his grandfather eventually asked.

"Yeah, some."

"Used to have a hollow leg, you did."

"You're no piker at the table yourself." Mark stood. "What do you say to a ride into town for some pizza?"

"Who's buying?"

"Me."

"Beat you to the car."

And he did, which showed Mark just how much the heat exhaustion had taken out of him. Of course, he hadn't expected the older man to take off like that either.

"I bet I can still eat more pizza than you."

John just chuckled.

Nine

Miriam didn't really expect Mark to take her up on her offer to talk and rush over, but when two days passed and he didn't appear, she was disappointed nevertheless.

Well, no problem. She regularly visited John with meals and to help with his kitchen garden, so she had a built-in reason to stop by.

She knocked at the front door, then walked in. There were few locked doors in their community. Good thing, too, since her arms were loaded. She set the baskets and totes on the kitchen table, then put a bowl of potato salad in the refrigerator.

A pizza box sat on the top shelf. Just as she suspected, once Mark was here. He loved pizza and had to have it at least once a week when he'd visited before. Was this was the way single *Englisch* men ate?

She pulled out the box and wrapped the leftover slices in aluminum foil. Now she had room to put the things she'd brought on the top shelf. John favored her potato salad so she'd brought a big bowl, along with a ham for sandwiches. Fannie Mae was bringing strawberry-rhubarb pies for dessert.

Naomi walked in a few minutes later. "Warm one again today." She fanned herself with her hand.

Mark came in the back door carrying the big water cooler kept on the table near the fields. He smiled at the women as he set it in the sink and began filling it with cool water from the tap. "We already ran out of water and it's only nine o'clock."

"I'll bring out some pitchers of iced tea and lemonade," Miriam said as she hurried to the refrigerator.

"So did Isaac's moth hatch yet?"

"Yesterday." She chuckled. "Fortunately it was in a box on the back porch instead of in the house. Life *schur* is interesting with *bruders.*"

"You have all those brothers and sisters and teach school, too. I can't imagine being surrounded by so many children."

"I love it," she said simply.

The three of them took drinks out to the field and Naomi passed around a plastic container of oatmeal raisin cookies.

Then Miriam and Naomi got to work weeding and harvesting the kitchen garden.

"I saw the way he was looking at you," Naomi said as she pulled a large weed and tossed it into a pile at her side.

"Who?" Miriam looked up from the strawberries she was picking.

"Mark. John's *grosssohn*. I saw the way he was looking at you."

Miriam swiped the back of her hand over her forehead. "We're friends."

"More than." Naomi tugged at a big weed and won the battle. "Always did seem sweet on you when he came here all those summers."

"We're *just* friends." Miriam wished they were more, but Naomi didn't need to know that.

"Just friends?"

Miriam looked up. "*Gut* friends. That's all."

Naomi gave her a long look, then nodded. "Just as well, I suppose. Nothing could come of it, him being *Englisch* and all." She sat back on her heels, looked off into the distance where the men worked, then resumed pulling at weeds. "How long's he staying? Seems like it's less and less these past summers."

"He has an important job back in Philadelphia. He's a lawyer."

"*Ya*, they're important in the *Englisch* world for *schur*. I heard everyone's always suing everyone else."

They worked for a while.

"Speaking of people not getting along . . ." Naomi began.

"Hmm?"

"Where's Fannie Mae today?"

Miriam couldn't help herself. She giggled as she piled strawberries into her basket. "Shame on us both. She's just not a happy person this time of year."

"I love her, but she does like to avoid working outside in the heat in summer." Naomi sat back on her heels again and rubbed at the small of her back.

"She said she'd be along later with some dessert for lunch."

"*Gut*. In the meantime, I think it's time for a break."

"Sounds *gut* to me." Miriam picked up the basket of strawberries and headed into the house with Naomi.

They poured glasses of ice water and sat at the kitchen table with an eye on the clock. They needed to feed the men their noon meal, and it had to be on time.

"Hope Fannie Mae isn't late," Naomi said, echoing Miriam's thoughts.

"She's often late, but she always shows up when she's promised to."

"True. You know, the reason she's been so unhappy lately is because she's been expecting to marry Abram after the harvest, but now she feels he's hesitating."

"Oh my, I didn't know. I feel bad. I've been so busy, I haven't had much time to talk to her."

Fannie Mae came in a few minutes later loaded with a basket and two tote bags full of plastic containers.

"Well, taking a break, huh? I've been cooking all morning." Her tone was tart, her movements jerky as she unloaded the contents of the basket and totes.

Miriam didn't take offense. She knew why Fannie Mae wasn't being friendly. "We just came in from working in the kitchen garden," she said mildly. "How are you doing, Fannie Mae?"

She looked from one to the other. "So you told her?" she asked Naomi.

"You didn't tell me not to."

Fannie Mae's shoulders slumped. "*Nee*, I didn't. Abram and I are going to talk later."

Miriam hugged her. "We'll pray things work out. We know you love him and he loves you. Listen, he's here today."

"I know."

"Do you want to leave before we serve lunch?"

She stood straighter. "*Nee*. I said I'd help and I will. If we don't resolve this and get married, I'm still going to have to see him at church and such."

They busied themselves preparing lunch, and they'd just gone outside and put everything on the tables when the men came in from the fields to wash their hands and eat. Abram was among the last of the men and he avoided looking at any of them. Miriam noticed Fannie Mae wouldn't look at him.

She exchanged looks with Naomi, who shrugged. No one else noticed. Either the men were too hungry or Abram hadn't shared what was going on with Fannie Mae. No surprise. Amish couples usually kept their relationships private until wedding plans were announced at church. But she, Naomi, and Fannie Mae were close.

Mark smiled at Miriam and she felt her cheeks warm. She tried to act casual but a glance showed her Naomi was watching her.

Heads bent to bless the food, then the men began eating eagerly. There wasn't much talk at the table at such times. Eating to refuel was too important. They'd find time later to discuss the all-important topic of weather—something on everyone's mind at harvest. Many a farmer had lost the time, sweat, and expense of raising crops only to see them ruined by storms or drought.

God was in charge, and the fruits of men's labor were in His hands.

Gradually the men pushed aside their empty plates and looked expectantly at the women, clearly hoping for dessert. They weren't disappointed when Fannie Mae began cutting slices of the strawberry-rhubarb pies she'd brought.

Miriam couldn't help smiling. Fannie Mae had once confided that it was Abram's favorite. Was it Fannie Mae's way of reminding him what he might be missing? Amish men *did* love their food. More than one Amish *maedel* had won the heart of her future *mann* with her cooking.

Mark shook his head when Miriam offered him a slice of pie. "Thanks, but I'm too full."

Soon the pie was gone, the last glass of tea drained, and the men filed out to finish their work. Mark lingered, and as Miriam walked past him to clear the pie plates he caught her eye. "Miriam?"

He glanced at Fannie Mae and Naomi, who were busy at the sink doing dishes. "Would you like to go for a drive later?" he asked quietly.

Her heart leaped. Finally they were going to talk and she could find out what was troubling him. "*Ya*. Love to."

He nodded. "I'll come by around five, if that's all right."

"*Schur.*" She glanced at her friends, making sure they weren't listening. "I'll see you then."

♫♫♫

Mark found himself staring at the contents of his suitcase. He'd been here a week and hadn't yet unpacked.

Unpacking meant staying, and he couldn't handle that.

It wasn't that he minded staying here on the farm for a while. But unpacking had such a final feel to it. Like he was giving up and staying for good.

He chose a pair of cotton slacks and a short-sleeve shirt, his concession to leisure clothing for the summer. They were casual but dressy enough for any restaurant if they stopped for dinner. He hadn't asked Miriam if she would go to dinner, but he figured a long enough drive might make dinner a possibility. And she'd done so much for his grandfather and the men who'd come to help him in the fields. The least he could do was treat her to a meal she didn't have to cook.

After dressing, he stood before the mirror over the bedroom dresser. Working in the fields had given him a tan and he looked more relaxed, less stressed. Enforced vacation was worth something, he guessed. He ran a comb through his hair and frowned. He'd need a haircut soon. He wondered how Giorgio, his stylist, would feel if he went back home at some point and he saw that he'd gotten a haircut from someone else. Once he'd gotten a haircut during vacation, and Giorgio had almost told him not to come back.

He shook his head. Surely he'd be back in Philly before then. Just how long did he have to stay in exile? It had been a couple of days since he'd talked to his friend about what was happening with Maurice's case.

A thought struck him as he walked downstairs. Maybe he should give his private investigator a call. It might be interesting to have him poke around the new case, see if there was anything he could find out. Something just didn't seem right ...

"Well, aren't you all dressed up," his grandfather said.

"Thought I'd go out for a while."

He nodded. "*Gut.* You've worked hard since you came home."

"Can I bring you anything back?"

"Some ice cream would be nice, if it's no trouble."

"No trouble at all. Vanilla?"

"Best there is."

"Will do."

Mark slid into his car, started it, and got the air conditioning running. He'd always enjoyed the comfort, the speed of the car. The status.

Now he thought the air conditioning was the best feature on the luxury sedan. Ever.

He had it cranked up good and cold by the time he got to Miriam's house. He used to think he couldn't get by without his smartphone, his laptop, his widescreen television. Now he wondered if he could live without air conditioning in the summer. Today, when he was working in the field, all he could think about was getting cleaned up and going for an air-conditioned ride.

Miriam's concern touched him. She'd been such a good friend when he visited in the summers. She probably knew him better than anyone apart from his grandfather. So it was only fair to tell her why he was here again.

That reminded him. He hadn't told his parents yet, either. They were off on their latest trip to Europe. His father had gotten about as far away from his Amish roots as he could, putting himself through college, marrying an *Englisch* woman. He had been so successful that he'd taken early retirement and whisked himself and Mark's mother off to Europe twice now.

Mark figured news of his client being arrested again for murder—and his own subsequent forced exile—hadn't reached Europe yet, or he'd have heard from them. He'd give them a call or send them an email in the next day or two.

Miriam must have been watching for his arrival because the front door opened as soon as he pulled into the driveway. She came down the porch steps looking cool and fresh as a daisy. How did she manage that when the day had cooled off considerably but was still warm?

She climbed inside the car and smiled at him. "Right on time." She fastened her seat belt and leaned back in the seat. "This feels *gut*." She turned to him. "So where are we going?"

"No place in particular. To have dinner in a while if you want."

"*Schur.*"

"I should have asked if you were free."

She laughed. "I am. *Mamm's* always pushing me to get out." Then she blushed. "That sounds like I'm pretty boring. A stick in the mud."

He glanced at her, then back at the road. "No. You just like to feel needed. You always did. I remember how you reached out to a gawky *Englisch* kid his first summer here and made friends with him."

She shrugged. "You weren't gawky. You just felt out of place for a little while. But not for long."

"Because you introduced me to everyone."

"And you discovered you had a love for the land like your *grossdaadi*."

"True." Mark sighed. "It's helped a lot to be here this past week. Even if I didn't want to be." He pulled into the parking lot of a restaurant. "Is this okay with you?"

"It's expensive."

"No problem. I'm fine with money." He made a good salary. Okay, an incredible salary. And he didn't spend much. He'd be fine if he had to take a break for a while.

They went inside and were seated quickly. He enjoyed how Miriam's eyes went round, how she gasped quietly as she studied the menu.

"Don't look at the prices. Order what you want. Something you've never tried."

"I always thought a soufflé sounded interesting."

"Then you should have one."

Their server warned them about the wait time for the entrée, so Mark had her choose an appetizer. He ordered one as well. Miriam and her friends had made them a fine lunch, but that had been hours and hours ago and he was hungry.

Mark ordered iced tea since he was driving.

They handed their menus to the server and then they were alone.

"*Allrecht*, are you going to tell me now what's troubling you?"

"I'm *persona non grata* at my firm right now. That means—"

"I know what it means."

"Yes, you're a teacher. I suppose you would." He met her gaze. "A client I defended was found not guilty. Then just days afterward, he was arrested and charged with murder again."

Her hand flew to her mouth and she stared at him. "Oh my. How awful." Then she frowned. "But I don't understand. Why would they be unhappy with you at work? It's not your fault he was arrested again."

"It's an old, established law firm. That's not the kind of attention that the partners want," he explained when her expression didn't clear.

"So what are you going to do?"

"There's not much I can do. I was escorted from the office." He fell silent as their appetizers were served. "The thing is, I felt Maurice was innocent from the moment I met him. The jury acquitted him."

"And this time? Have you talked to him?" She took a bite of her salad and closed her eyes in pleasure.

"I don't believe he did it, but I can't represent him this time." He tasted his ahi tuna and found it surprisingly good.

"But you think he's innocent."

"I don't get to choose my clients, and the firm won't take him on again. Maurice got another attorney. I stopped by the jail before I left town and gave him the name of a buddy of mine who would be willing to take this new case on."

Still, it didn't feel like enough. Mark remembered how grateful Maurice's elderly mother had been the day he was acquitted. She'd called him a saint and had hugged him so hard. He realized Miriam was talking.

"I'm sorry, what?"

"I said, so what are you going to do?"

"I called a private investigator I've used in the past. He's looking into the case."

Miriam beamed. "It's the right thing to do. But I meant, what are *you* going to do? With *your* life?"

"Use my enforced time off to help my grandfather with the harvest."

"And then?"

A trickle of fear he hadn't felt since that first day in court ran down his spine. "Then I guess we'll see."

"Maybe God has something new in mind."

"What could be better than the law?" he asked. "It's all I've ever wanted to do." The server approached with their entrees. "Well, look here, your soufflé has arrived. Let's see if it was worth the wait."

Ten

Miriam gazed at the soufflé—a beautiful golden brown puff in an individual porcelain dish just for her. It smelled divine, warm and cheesy and tempting, almost too perfect to mar by sticking a fork into it. But she did so, carefully, wondering if it would go poof! and collapse. But it didn't. She slipped a bite between her lips and let it melt on her tongue.

"Oh," she gasped, surprised. "It tastes ... it tastes like a cloud. A lovely light cheese-flavored cloud."

Their server hurried over. "Miss? How is it?"

"It's the most wonderful thing I've ever tasted," she told him. "So delicate. It probably sounds silly, but the first thing I thought was it tasted like a cloud."

He beamed at her. "The chef will be so pleased to hear that you like it."

Miriam smiled at him. "It was worth waiting for. I'll remember eating this forever." She ate another bite and sighed as she looked at Mark. "I'm so glad you told me to order what I wanted. Oh, I wasn't thinking. Would you like to try a bite?" Then she blushed. "What am I saying? You've probably eaten it a dozen times."

He grinned. "Not a dozen, but I have enjoyed it a few times. Not here of course. Back home."

She hesitated. It seemed too ... intimate ... to offer him a bite from the fork she was using. So she used a spoon to remove a taste and handed it to him.

"Delicious," he agreed. "But I'm more in the mood for this steak."

"*Gut*," she said. "I'd find it hard to share more of this."

"I bet you could make a soufflé."

"I'm not that *gut* a cook."

"I'll look up a recipe for you on my laptop later."

"The first time I baked a cake, I peeked in the oven too often. And then, just as I was looking one last time, one of my *bruders* startled me running into the kitchen and I slammed the oven door. The cake collapsed." She grinned. "It looked like a pancake."

"My mother tried making a soufflé once and it didn't turn out too badly."

She laughed. "Well, that's a sterling recommendation."

"If you tell her I said that, I'll deny it. She's an amazing cook. We eat everything she cooks with relish."

"She cooks with relish? The stuff you put on hot dogs?"

He laughed. "You know what I mean."

"I'm just being silly." She glanced around the restaurant. It was the most elegant place she'd ever visited. Linen tablecloths, fine china, heavy silver cutlery. Other diners dressed in their best. She'd felt a little self-conscious when they first walked in, but the maître d' had made her feel welcome. The *Englisch* and Amish mixed more in Lancaster County than in other Amish communities, but she suspected few Amish patronized this fancy of a restaurant. And part of that welcome undoubtedly came from his subtle appraisal of Mark. She was Plain, but even though she didn't know much about store-bought clothes—particularly men's— she recognized his clothes were expensive. But it was more than that. He wore an air of confidence she had never seen in the men she knew, or even in the *Englisch* men she saw in the community.

"I wasn't sure I could finish it," she said as she sat back in her chair. "But it tasted lighter than air." She sighed. "This has been *wunderbaar*."

A server whisked away their empty plates.

He grinned. "I think it's about to get better."

"What?"

The server appeared at the table with a tray of the evening's dessert selections. "But the chef has prepared chocolate soufflés for your enjoyment, if you wish," he said, pointing to two dishes on the tray. "I told the chef how much you enjoyed the cheese soufflé, miss."

"Oh my," she breathed as the scent of chocolate wafted up from it. "I would love to try one."

He set it before her with a flourish. "And for you, sir?"

"Looks too good to resist."

Miriam sighed as the scent of warm chocolate wafted up from the dish. She sampled it. "A chocolate cloud. Oh, I am so glad you brought me here. I'll remember this forever."

"I'm glad you're enjoying it."

She nodded, then sobered. "I'm just sorry that you're going through all the trouble with your work."

"I appreciate your listening."

"Mark! Friends don't thank friends for listening."

He stared down at his dessert. "Well, I haven't heard from many of my friends since the firm told me to take some time off."

"Oh, I'm so sorry." Her heart went out to him. "What kind of friends don't stand by you?"

"It's what you get when you spend most of your time at the office." He shook his head and smiled. "Come on, no more talk of it. Things will work out."

He talked about his work in the fields with his grandfather and the other men. She listened as he told a funny story about them surprising a snake and how one of the men had, in his words, "screamed like a girl."

She'd have objected—she was a girl and never screamed when she unexpectedly encountered a snake— but she sensed that he was deliberately trying to change the mood he'd fallen into.

"It's been fun to be back in the fields with the men. I feel like they accept me," he said quietly.

"They do. They've known you for years." She sipped her iced tea. "Everyone asks John about you, you know. How you're doing."

Mark looked surprised. "No, I didn't know." He traced a pattern on the linen tablecloth with his finger. "I do know everyone has helped my grandfather so much. I guess I'll have some time to return the help while I'm here."

"So see, some *gut* will come of this."

He lifted his gaze and stared at her for so long, she shifted uncomfortably. "Do I have chocolate on my face?"

"No."

But he didn't stop looking at her.

"Summer is hard with the harvest and working in the heat to get it done. But it's a *gut* time for coming together, for helping each other and for appreciating God's bounty."

Summer had been her favorite season for years ever since Mark had started spending summers with John.

Being with him this evening had been the stuff of her teenaged *maedel's* fantasies. She told herself she was a young woman now and not to make too much of it. He'd be called back to his job—he was too good at it for them to treat him this way.

John had often told her about his *grosssohn's* work. He did it more with a sense of puzzlement than pride. He didn't quite understand why Mark had chosen the work. After all, the Amish didn't believe in the *Englisch* habit of suing and such. He loved Mark but *hochmut*—pride— was such a basic tenet of the Amish faith. And since he loved the land so much, he wanted Mark to love it and assume its care.

Miriam watched their server discreetly place a leather folder on the table near Mark's plate. Mark opened it, gave the bill a quick glance, tucked his credit card in it, and returned his attention to her. He seemed in no hurry to leave.

She wasn't in any hurry either.

$$\mathcal{SSS}$$

Mark had always thought Miriam was a pretty girl. Pretty in a quiet way.

Tonight she looked more than pretty. The candlelight flickering on the table cast a glow on her creamy skin and made her blue eyes sparkle.

But it wasn't just the candlelight that put that sparkle in her eyes. He'd never seen anyone eat with such pleasure, appreciate it so much. She acted like someone who'd been given a gift with something rare and exotic. Which he supposed a soufflé must seem to her.

It was a gift to see her enjoy something so much that cost him so little.

"I wish I could take some of this home for *Mamm* to try."

"Excuse me, miss, but it won't transport well," the server said with a touch of regret in his tone. "Perhaps I might suggest something else you could take home for her."

"We'll bring her here sometime," Mark said.

"Oh, that would be so *wunderbaar!*" Then her face fell. She glanced around. "But it's so expensive."

"It's the least I can do to show your family appreciation for taking such good care of my *grossdaadi*."

She continued to eat. He found himself watching her as they sipped coffee. She had such a serene way about her. No complaining about bad service from her.

It wasn't fair to compare her to Tiffany. They came from two different worlds. But when he talked with Miriam, he didn't get the sense that her mind was racing ahead to what she wanted to say next. She didn't want to endlessly talk about the next social event and what she'd wear to it. And when he spoke of how it felt to be treated the way he had been by the firm, she'd truly cared.

Tiffany wasn't even returning his phone calls these days.

He sighed.

"Tired?" she asked.

"No, sorry. Just thinking of something." He glanced around and saw that most of the other diners had left. "But it's getting late. I guess we should go."

They walked outside. The temperature had cooled enough to put the windows down so they could enjoy the breeze as they drove home along dark country roads. The scent of honeysuckle drifted into the car.

"Nice night," he said as he glanced at her. "You cool enough? We can put the windows up and turn on the air conditioning, if you want."

"*Nee*, this is perfect. Remember the drives we used to take in the buggy? Before you got a driver's license and a car? Those were fun." She sat up straighter in her seat. "Oh, look at all the fireflies out in the field."

He slowed and glanced at the light show. "We don't see many of those in the city. Or stars. Too many city lights." He chuckled as a different scent wafted in. "Of course, we don't get some of the … pungent country smells, either."

She laughed. "True. But you get used to it."

He had to admit she was right. It hadn't taken long for him to get accustomed to the scents of the country. He just wished he could say he was getting used to the heat. Maybe he'd gotten soft as he'd gotten older.

What was he saying? Age had nothing to do with it. It had to be that he'd gotten used to moving from one air-conditioned space to another in his world.

Now the breeze brought with it the scent of lavender that clung to Miriam's clothing. He knew she didn't wear perfume. He guessed that she must tuck sprigs of the flower in her drawers. It was a charming, old-fashioned habit he remembered she and her mother favored.

He'd take it over the expensive, cloying perfumes worn by so many of the *Englisch* women he knew.

Again, Tiffany came to mind.

Mark shook his head to clear that thought. It was becoming obvious that there was a problem. He'd have to drive into the city and get her to talk to him soon. Very soon.

"Are you *allrecht?*"

"Sure. Why?"

"You sighed."

Had he? "Just thinking it's a pretty night. And that was a delicious dinner. Thanks for going with me."

"Thank you for asking me. I won't ever forget those soufflés."

"It's nice to have something different." He pulled into the driveway of her house.

"Like this break from work is for you?"

He turned off the ignition. "You're right. This is different for me. At least lately. I used to take breaks here in the summer when school was out. I haven't done it much since college."

His cell phone rang. He checked the display. Lani.

"Don't you need to take the call?"

"My assistant. I'll call her later." He rubbed the steering wheel with a finger. "She's the only one who calls me these days."

"Then you should take the call."

He shook his head. "Not now. It'll wait." If there was one thing he'd learned from this mess it was that work—something that had always come first—well, it just couldn't any more. Because when he didn't have it, what *did* he have?

Miriam was a true friend. She'd worried about him, even nagged him until he talked to her. She asked hard questions and made him look deeply at his situation. It hadn't been comfortable sometimes, but he figured that was what made a good friend.

Light spilled out of a front window as someone twitched a curtain aside and looked out. Miriam giggled. "No matter how old you get, parents are still parents."

Mark chuckled. It had been years since he'd pulled up before a girl's house and a front porch light had gone on or a window curtain had been pushed aside so a parent could look out and signal that she should come inside.

Did Miriam's parents think they were out here kissing? He hoped not. He knew she had to marry someone of her faith or be shunned. And he wouldn't tarnish her reputation. Not for anything.

"I guess you should go in."

"*Danki* again. And Mark? Everything will work out. We don't know what God's plan is for us. We just need to believe He knows what's best." She started to get out of the car but turned back. "Why don't you come to church this week?"

"I'll think about it."

"You used to enjoy church."

He nodded.

She got out and went into her house. Mark sat there for a moment before starting the car and backing out of the drive. He took the long way home, finding the drive through the dark country roads soothing.

Finally he headed home. It was a little strange, but he did feel at home here more than where he lived all his life. His father hadn't wanted to stay, but he'd never prevented Mark from spending summers here. Mark wondered how much of a place was in his genes. The farm had been in his family for so many generations. He mused on that. Nature or nurture?

He parked in the drive, locked the car—probably an unnecessary habit here—and went inside. As he climbed the stairs to his bedroom, he remembered how he'd come home late one summer night and avoided the creaky top step. His grandfather had known he'd been out late anyway and had given him a stern talk the next morning. He stepped on it just for old times' sake and grinned when his grandfather called out a greeting.

"Still up?" he asked, pausing at his grandfather's doorway. Then he frowned. "Oh, shoot, I forgot your ice cream."

His grandfather set his book aside. "It's not late. And don't worry about the ice cream."

"Miriam and I went for a drive and dinner. We talked a lot."

"The two of you always enjoyed talking. Once, I thought ..." he trailed off and shrugged. "But I guess it wasn't to be. You wanted to fight for man's justice."

"Yeah. Look where it got me."

He tilted his head to one side. "Where *did* it get you?"

Mark sighed. "I guess I don't know."

"This will always be your home, Mark. Whether you want to stay for *gut* or not."

Emotion swamped him. "Thank you."

"Thanks aren't necessary. You're my *grosssohn* and I love you dearly. Have a *gut nacht*."

"I love you too. Sleep well."

And when he went to bed in the little room where he'd slept so many nights for so many summers, he slept dreamlessly.

Eleven

Miriam drifted up the stairs to her room wearing a smile.

What a wonderful evening out she'd had with Mark.

Well, calling it an "evening out" wasn't exactly accurate. It was a drive and dinner with a friend who was going through some upsetting times. As much as she wanted it to be her fantasy date with the man she'd had a crush on since she was a teen, she had to be stern with herself and not fantasize.

She looked for the little bud vase she'd bought at the dollar store, filled it with water, and set it on her nightstand. The vase *schur* wasn't crystal, and she usually filled it with flowers from the garden or wildflowers that grew near her *schul*. Tonight it held an expensive, beautiful rose.

"Be sure to give the chef our compliments," Mark had told the server. "The lady loved the soufflés."

A few minutes later, the chef himself had appeared at the table, looking so impressive in his white jacket and tall hat. He'd beamed when she told him how she'd enjoyed the soufflé, and told her she should try making one sometime.

"It's really not that difficult," he assured her. "It took me a couple of tries at the culinary school."

She was used to cooking simple things, but since Mark had said he'd find her a recipe, she promised she'd try making one. Now she looked at the rose she'd brought home and put it in the simple vase. Plain and fancy. Just like her in that restaurant.

She undressed and pulled on a summer nightgown. After unpinning her *kapp*, then the tightly bound bun at the nape of her neck, she sat on her bed and brushed her hair. Then she braided it, tying a ribbon at the end. She folded her quilt at the end of the bed and slid between the sheets.

Reaching under her pillow, she pulled out her journal and wrote about the evening, about how it had felt to spend time with Mark and listen to his concern about what was going on in his life. She'd listened and tried to do her best to be his friend.

It had been such fun to be treated to such an elegant supper in such a special restaurant. She'd always remember the amazing soufflé, the service, the ambiance.

There, that was a word she didn't get to use often. *Ambiance*. She retraced it with her pencil and sketched a picture of the rose. Later, she'd press the flower in the journal as a reminder.

A breeze drifted in through the open window, carrying the scent of honeysuckle. It was so quiet she could hear a big bullfrog call to his mate in the creek on the edge of the property.

She paused and wondered what Mark was doing right now. Was he in the bedroom he'd always used when he stayed at his *grossdaadi's* and getting ready for bed?

Living in the country must be so different from his condo in the city. He'd shown her pictures of it on his cell phone once. Property was expensive in Lancaster County, but even more so in Philadelphia. He was so proud he'd been able to buy the condo. She'd been happy for him, but thought the place looked … cold. He'd used an interior decorator and also had the help of the woman who was now his fiancée. Miriam guessed that explained it. Nothing he'd told her about Tiffany had made her think the woman was warm. But she wouldn't criticize the condo or his fiancée. It wouldn't be right.

She tucked the journal under her pillow and reached for the book on her nightstand. Ever since she was a little girl, she'd loved to read for a while before she slept. Usually the day was long and she only made it through a few pages before she drifted off and her book fell onto her chest. Tonight, though, she was wide awake two dozen pages into the book.

And it wasn't because the book was all that interesting.

There was a knock on the door.

"*Kumm.*"

"I saw the light under your door. Reading like usual, hmm?"

Miriam nodded, sat up, and patted the bed, inviting her *mudder* to sit.

Her gaze went to the rose in the bud vase. "Pretty."

"They were on the table at the restaurant Mark took me to. He asked if I could take it home."

"Very thoughtful."

"He's just a friend," she said quickly.

Her *mudder's* brows lifted. "*Ya?*"

"Always has been." Her fingers plucked at the edge of her sheet. "It can't be anything else, right?"

"What's in your heart, *kind?* Do you want to be more than friends?"

Miriam closed her eyes, searched for calm. "*Mamm*, how can I want more? I can't have it."

Her *mudder* gathered her into her arms. "Oh, Miriam, I don't know what to say. I want you to be happy, to be loved. But you're Amish and he's *Englisch*." She sighed as she patted Miriam's back. "I always wondered if he was more than a friend to you."

Miriam sat back. "He doesn't know I have feelings for him. And he won't. He's going through enough right now." She sighed. "*Mamm*, he's here because he's had some trouble at work."

She told her the story and her *mudder* listened sympathetically.

"Well, that is troubling for *schur*," she said when Miriam finished. "What is he going to do?"

"He has a friend who's a private investigator looking into the case."

"That's *gut*. Mark has always been the type of man to think of others. But what is he going to do about his job?"

"He's staying with John and helping him out until he hears from his boss at the firm."

She nodded. "Well, it's sad that this happened to Mark. But John *schur* needed his help right now. And he can help other farmers in the community as well since they help John." She patted Miriam's hand. "God has a plan for everyone."

"But Mark is so upset. I worry about him."

"God knows what's best for every one of his *kinner*."

"I know." Miriam hugged her *mudder* then sat back. "It's just hard to watch while things are working out. But I know they will."

Sarah kissed her forehead and rose. "My smart *dochder*."

She laughed. "Do *mudders* always think their *kinner* are smart?"

"I don't know. I only know that mine are. Not that I would brag," she said quickly, her eyes twinkling. "That would be *hochmut*."

"You've never been prideful."

"And I don't intend to start." She walked to the door, stopped in the doorway, and smiled. "Sweet dreams."

"You, too. Say *gut nacht* to *Daed*."

Miriam lay back against her pillow. Her *mudder* was right. God had a plan for Mark, and even though she was sad that he was unhappy, it really was *gut* to have him back this summer.

Maybe she could think of some way to cheer him up ... She closed her eyes and felt herself drifting off.

When she slept, she dreamed the dreams of a *maedel* in love.

✺✺✺

Mark was helping his grandfather feed the horses the next evening when he remembered something Miriam had said the night before.

"Say, would you mind if I took Whitey out for a buggy ride?"

His grandfather stopped what he was doing and stared at him. "Did I hear you right? You want to go for a buggy ride?"

"Miriam reminded me how we used to go for buggy rides before I got a driver's license and my first car."

"I remember that. You liked Whitey because he was the fastest."

Mark walked over to Whitey's stall and ran a hand over his flank. "I thought it was the coolest thing ever that the Amish often buy retired race horses. I thought we'd go faster than a car. I was a little disappointed to say the least."

He chuckled. "Well, Whitey's slowed down a bit since your teenaged years."

"That's fine. It's not like I have any urgent appointments."

"Still no word from your office?"

"None." He led Whitey from the stall outside to the buggy and began harnessing him. "Anything you need from town?"

"Not a thing. I think I'll have a rest while you're gone."

Mark paused and frowned at his grandfather. "Are you feeling all right?"

"*Schur.* Can't a man take a little rest after all the work we've done this week?"

"Sure." But Mark couldn't help worrying. Maybe he needed to have a talk with his grandfather's doctor.

"Have a *gut* time."

"You're not afraid I'll do something wrong?" he asked as he fumbled with the harness. "What if I can't control Whitey and he takes off and is never seen again? What if I make a fool of myself?"

"Whitey won't bolt, and if you let go of the reins he'll just come back home," his grandfather said calmly. "And you couldn't be a fool if you tried."

Mark doubted that. He frowned. Did Whitey just roll his eyes at him? "Thought this was like riding a bicycle. You supposedly don't forget how to do it ..."

John walked over and showed him how to fasten the harness. He clapped him on the shoulder. "Lighten up."

"Lighten up?"

"That's what the *Englisch* say, right?"

"Yeah. Just wasn't expecting you to say it."

John shrugged. "Strikes me you've been too serious for too long. Maybe God's giving you a break, a chance to relax, smell the roses." He strolled off toward the house.

Roses. That made him think of Miriam and how thrilled she'd looked with the gift of a simple table decoration last night.

Maybe he'd stop by her house and see if she'd like to go for a buggy ride. He got in the buggy and picked up the reins. They brought back the memory of the first time he'd held them. He remembered feeling a mixture of terror and thrill when his grandfather actually suggested that he should drive them into town.

He'd only been fourteen.

No one was allowed to drive a car until they were sixteen, he'd told his grandfather as he tried to hold the reins in hands so sweaty the reins felt slippery. But he'd said the rules were different with buggies. So they went to town and not only survived the trip, but Mark had actually enjoyed it. The pace was slow, but the freedom was huge. Soon he was asking to take the buggy out for errands and whatever excuse he could come up with. And then he'd just taken it out for evening rides with Miriam to talk.

That was the headiest freedom. No one could overhear them talk about their hopes and dreams. Few could see them together and speculate on their relationship. He'd caught some of her fellow Amish watching him when he attended church and speculating when they talked. But unless they passed someone in another buggy or a car and the passengers glanced in, there was a privacy to this quaint vehicle that made it very appealing to him during those long summers he'd spent here.

Miriam didn't know anything about the law or college, but she'd listened avidly to his talk about becoming an attorney and fighting for justice—concepts totally alien to her. God meted justice in her world, not man. But she told him he should study and get good grades and apply for that college called Yale. And when his father thought it was all a crazy pipe dream, Miriam had been the one to urge him to persuade his father he should go.

After all, she said, wasn't persuasion an attorney's best tool?

He chuckled as he remembered her impassioned defense of his dream. She'd done some persuading of her own, convincing her parents to let her attend his graduation ceremony with his grandfather. If she noticed that she got some curious glances in her modest Amish dress, she hadn't shown it. No, he still could remember that brilliant smile of hers beaming at him when they met after the ceremony.

She'd asked so many questions as he took her on a tour of the campus. Thinking about it now as he headed to her house, he wondered if she'd ever wanted to pursue higher education. It wouldn't have been possible for her as an Amish woman—formal schooling ended after the eighth grade and students went on to do apprenticeships for the occupations they wanted to pursue. She'd have had to leave her community for good.

And as much as Miriam loved learning, she'd never leave her family and friends. So she'd done her own studying, reading everything she could put her hands on from the local public library.

Mark pulled into the drive, got out to go to her front door, and wondered if Whitey would still be there when he returned. "Stay," he said, and could have sworn Whitey rolled his eyes again.

Miriam's mother, Sarah, answered the door. "Mark, how nice to see you!"

"Is Miriam home?"

"*Ya*, come in. She's in the kitchen."

He followed her and found Miriam using a washcloth to clean the face of a baby.

She smiled at him. "*Gut-n-owed*. I wasn't expecting you."

"I thought I'd see if you wanted to go for a drive, maybe get an ice cream cone."

"Ice cream!" one of the kids shouted and began racing around the room. "*Mamm*, can we go get ice cream?"

"You weren't invited," Sarah told him gently.

Mark watched the little boy's face fall. His lower lip quivered. When Mark glanced over at Miriam, he saw her biting her lip.

"Can we take the children?" he found himself asking.

"Are you *schur*?" she asked doubtfully. "Do you remember how many *kinner* there are in this family?"

"Nine counting Miriam," he said dryly.

"Very funny." Miriam stuck her tongue out at Mark behind her mother's back.

"Get your brothers and sisters," he told the youngest boy. What was his name? He searched his memory but the kid was already racing for the stairs leading to the bedrooms, shouting at the top of his lungs.

"We're going for ice cream!"

"What is all the racket?" Miriam's father, Daniel, asked as he came into the room. "Hi, Mark."

"Mark invited the *kinner* to go for ice cream," Sarah explained.

"Well, that's very generous."

"The poor man doesn't know what he's getting into," Miriam said, wincing as her *bruders* and *schweschders* came barreling down the stairs. She clapped her hands. "We are *not* going if you behave like that!"

They came to a halt and composed themselves.

"That's better." She winked at Mark. Then she bit her lip. "The buggy's not going to be big enough."

"Oh no!" the *kinner* cried in disappointment.

"We can take the spring wagon," Miriam suggested.

Mark had never driven one, but he didn't suppose it was much different than driving a buggy. The two of them unhitched Whitey and hitched him and one of the family's horses to the wagon used to transport supplies.

"Ready?" Miriam asked brightly.

He wanted to say as ready as he'd ever be, but he wasn't going to give her that satisfaction. "Sure. Sounds like fun. Let's go, guys."

Miriam's stern warning and her schoolmarm expression had them filing out to the wagon and climbing inside. Mark noticed the stream of passengers didn't seem to affect Whitey in the least.

"Everyone in?" Mark asked as he climbed into the driver's seat.

"All accounted for," Miriam told him.

Giggles came from the back.

"Then on with the adventure," he said.

What would his associates at the firm think if they could see him now?

Twelve

Miriam watched Mark drive the wagon. "So, was it like riding a bicycle? Did it come back to you?"

He grinned at her. "Yeah, believe it or not."

A car passed them and he frowned. "Lack of courtesy to buggy and wagon drivers hasn't changed."

"*Nee.*"

"Seems slower going than I remember."

She smiled. "Well, you're used to that fast car of yours."

"Hey, it's not a sports car," he protested. "And I drive the speed limit."

"Always?"

She watched him glance briefly at the back where her *bruders* and *schweschders* were hanging on his every word.

"Always."

She fought to hide her smile, but when he looked her way and grinned, she suspected she wasn't successful.

"Some things never change," he said as he pulled up in front of the ice-cream stand. "I remember when we used to come here."

"It's been here forever," Isaac said.

"He makes it sound like we were around when civilization began," Mark complained as he got out of the wagon. "Hmm. When did they replace the Grecian columns?"

"Mark, help me out!" one of the twins cried as she held out her arms.

He picked her up, set her on the ground beside the wagon, and when he turned to help the other twin, he watched her jump down on her own and scamper off. So, they weren't alike in personality, he mused as he followed the children to the ordering window.

Isaac looked at him. "Can I have a banana split?"

"May I?" Miriam corrected. "And no, you may not. That's way too much for a little boy. You may have a kiddie cone in whatever flavor you want. All of you."

"And sprinkles?"

Miriam watched her *schweschder* stare up at Mark with wide blue eyes and—did she just bat her eyelashes?

"We absolutely have to have sprinkles." Mark got out his wallet.

"I have money, if you need it."

"I think I can afford ice cream for a bunch of kids," he said. "You can even have that root beer float you used to order."

"Big spender," she responded pertly and batted her own eyelashes at him.

They all got their cones and she and Mark their root beer floats, then they headed for one of the wooden picnic tables under the shade of a big oak tree.

"Did you get enough sprinkles?" he asked Sadie.

She nodded and grinned, revealing several missing teeth. "I asked the man for extra and he gave them to me," she told him with satisfaction.

Miriam had watched the man catch Mark's eye as Sadie ordered and Mark had nodded for him to do that.

"You're *gut* with kids," she murmured as she used a napkin to wipe Katie's chin.

"Buying them ice cream doesn't make me good with them. I never know what to say to kids. I always feel awkward when I'm around the children of the people I work with." He frowned. "I suppose some of that came from me being an only child. I got the impression my parents wanted more children, but they didn't have them."

"My parents grew up with your *dat*," she said quietly. "They weren't surprised when he wanted to leave the community." She glanced around at her *bruders* and *schweschders*. They were looking too interested in their ice cream to be paying attention, but it wasn't a *gut* idea to talk about this now.

An *Englisch* woman stopped at their table and smiled. "What a lovely family. Your children are beautiful."

Miriam saw Mark react with surprise. He shot a glance at her and she smiled. "Thank you."

The woman nodded and walked on.

"Can we play on the swings?" Isaac asked.

"May we?"

He sighed and looked at Mark. "She's always a teacher, even when we're not in *schul*."

"I know."

Miriam swatted his arm. "We should always speak correct English."

"But we're Amish."

"We've had this discussion. Do you want to talk about it some more or do you want to go on the swings?"

"May we go on the swings?" he said with exaggerated politeness.

"For a few minutes. I'm *schur* Mark has better things to do with his evening than sit around watching you swing."

Isaac ran off and his siblings joined him, all except for Katie.

"It must be such a trial having your sister be your teacher."

Her mouth turned down as she gathered the crumpled napkins from the table. "*Danki.*"

"I'm only teasing." He took the napkins from her and tossed them in the trash can. "Why haven't you married yet?"

She stared at him. "Well, that's a strange question."

Mark gestured at the children. "You obviously love children."

"And I take care of them every day and teach them as well."

"But don't you want some of your own?"

"Amish women don't marry as young as they used to," she told him defensively. "And I'm hardly an old *maedel*."

"I didn't mean to imply that. I'm just curious, that's all."

"What about you?" she asked. "You're three years older than I am, and *you* haven't married." She watched a flush creep up his neck.

"At least I'm engaged."

She nodded. "Well, yes, of course."

His cell phone rang.

"Maybe that's her now."

He took it out, checked the display. "No, but I need to take the call."

"Go ahead," she said. "I'm going to go push the *kinner* on the swings."

She left him and busied herself with the *kinner*. But she had to admit she was grateful his call didn't take long. They needed to get home so she could give the *kinner* their baths. She made sure there were no sticky faces or fingers before she led them to the wagon and watched as they climbed inside.

"Everything *allrecht*?" she asked Mark as they rode along. "You've been quiet since you got that phone call."

He shrugged. "I was hoping I'd hear some good news by now."

"About your job?"

"Yeah. My paralegal stays in touch." He pulled closer to the shoulder of the road so a car could pass. "I haven't heard anything from the private investigator I hired. Something just doesn't feel right about my former client getting arrested a second time."

He stopped, glanced over his shoulder at his back-seat passengers. "Anyway, we'll talk later."

She nodded. "Little pitchers have big ears."

"Pitchers?" Sadie spoke up. Where's a little pitcher?"

"She means you, big ears," David said with derision dripping from his voice.

"I do not!" she cried. "Miriam, tell him I don't have big ears."

Miriam turned in her seat. "David, say you're sorry."

"Sorry."

She looked over at Mark and mouthed "Sorry."

"It's no problem." He pulled into the driveway.

"*Danki*, Mark!" the children chimed as they climbed out and ran to the house.

Mark laughed and she turned. "Your chin is on the ground. Why are you so shocked? You taught them well."

"I—" she fumbled. "They've never been that polite without prompting."

"Then they deserve ice cream again sometime. With sprinkles."

She laughed. "*Ya*. With sprinkles. *Danki*, Mark."

❦❦❦

Mark listened to the clip-clop of Whitey's hooves on the road as the horse slowly took him home.

No, not home. To the farm. Home was back in Philadelphia. The farm was great, and he was enjoying helping his grandfather and connecting with old friends like Miriam and Samuel, and it had been a welcome respite from job problems. He was glad he'd come here instead of sitting back in his condo.

Summers helping on the farm, spending time with Miriam and the men, had been fun. Sure, there were a lot of differences between them—clothing and language and religion and rules. Oh my, all the rules.

But during those summers, he'd learned how much alike they were under all those differences. Turned out Mark wasn't the only guy who felt shy around girls. Turned out he wasn't the only guy who wondered if he'd ever get good enough at something to make a living. Turned out he wasn't the only one who wondered if he was in the right place in the world.

Some of those summer friends had been gone a few summers when he came—off finding out if they wanted to try the *Englisch* life they asked him about. Most of them found it lacking and returned to their community.

As much as Mark liked it here and was curious about the life, he hadn't ever considered becoming part of it. His father had spoken negatively often enough about why he'd left and besides, Mark liked his life and had a passion for law.

But at times like this—late summer, when the long day had challenged him with hard physical work, when he'd shared supper with his grandfather and enjoyed a peaceful evening like this—he felt the tug of the half of him that was Amish.

His family had farmed this land for generations. Had he learned to love working in the fields because of his grandfather's influence, or had he inherited the memory of it in his very cells? He remembered studying cellular memory in a science class in college. The science textbook had made a case for it, but Mark, always pragmatic, would have liked to see hard evidence for himself.

He glanced down at his hands. They weren't city boy hands now, but were tanned and bore a few calluses.

If his friends could see him now.

Was his Amish heritage one of the reasons he sometimes felt a little distanced from his friends back home? He straddled two worlds in some way, *Englisch* attorney most of the year, Amish *grosssohn* and farmer for a time during harvest.

He passed Samuel's farm and saw his friend sitting on the front porch with his son. They waved to each other as he passed. He thought briefly about stopping for a visit. There was nothing the Amish liked better than visiting or being visited. They weren't stand-offish as some *Englisch* thought, just reserved and more comfortable with their own kind.

And while the Lancaster County Amish mixed with their *Englisch* neighbors more than some of their counterparts in other areas of the country because of business—particularly tourism—there was still a desire to remain separate from the non-Amish. His grandfather had explained why that first summer, quoting the Bible: *Be ye not unequally yoked together with unbelievers: for what fellowship hath righteousness with unrighteousness? And what communion hath light with darkness.*

Funny how that memory came back to him now. Mark pulled into the drive and waved to his grandfather sitting on the porch. After he unharnessed Whitey, led him to his stall, and watered him, he joined his grandfather, settling into a rocking chair with a sigh.

"Found your way home, eh?"

Mark laughed. "Like you said, Whitey knows his way."

John patted his knee. "You, too. Did you have a *gut* drive?"

He nodded. "Took Miriam and her brothers and sisters for ice cream."

"All of them?"

Mark chuckled. "Yes, all of them."

"Something came for you in the mail."

"Really?"

"A package. I had to sign for it. I put it on the kitchen table."

"Maybe it's paperwork from the office." He wasn't sure if that was a good thing or bad. A lassitude swept over him, making him reluctant to see what the package contained.

"Too small for that."

Now his curiosity was aroused. He got up, went inside, and found a padded envelope that had come registered mail. When he opened it, he found a small velvet box and a folded note.

He sank into a chair at the table. No need to open the box. He knew what it contained.

His grandfather walked into the kitchen, saw the box, and laid his hand on Mark's shoulder. "I'm sorry."

Mark lifted his gaze and stared into his grandfather's faded blue eyes. "I'm not surprised. She wouldn't return my calls or see me before I came here."

"I'm sorry."

Mark finally picked up the box and opened it. The diamond—quite a sizeable one—sparkled up at him. He'd spent a lot of time choosing it based on many, many hints from Tiffany about what she wanted. Two carats, Asscher cut, platinum band. He'd spent the recommended portion of his yearly salary on it. She'd acted delighted with it and showed it off at every opportunity when they were out at social events.

He set the box down and picked up the note. Vaguely he registered the sound of his grandfather rummaging in the refrigerator while he scanned Tiffany's neat, precise handwriting.

"Sorry things didn't work out with us," she wrote. "I'm returning the ring. Don't know if you can return it or if you'll want to give it to someone else in the future. Best of luck. Tiffany."

John cleared his throat. "Let's go back out on the porch. Cooler out there."

Mark nodded. "In a minute." Well, it might be lousy to get the news this way, but he had a friend whose girlfriend had texted him that she didn't want to see him anymore. Mark pulled out his cell phone, went into contacts, and deleted Tiffany's name.

Then he followed his grandfather outside.

They sat, rocking, the only sound the creaking of the chairs on the wooden floorboards of the porch. A bird called out from a nearby tree and another answered it. Dusk began falling and stars winked to life.

"My life's a mess," Mark said. "Lost my job. Lost my girl. Geez, it's a country-western song in the making." He blinked, startled when he realized he'd spoken aloud.

John continued to rock in his chair. Mark knew he'd heard him, but when serious matters were involved, his grandfather always gave his words a lot of thought.

"You haven't lost your job, if I understand the word sabbatical correctly," he said at last. "You said that's what your boss told you that you were taking. I know you didn't want to, but you weren't fired."

"Feels like it," Mark grumbled. "Then to get dumped."

"Another choice you didn't get to make for *schur*," John agreed slowly. "Do you feel bad because you love her and don't want to lose her? Or because of the way she did it?"

Mark stopped rocking. "You have a way of getting to the heart of it, don't you?"

"It's easy to say God has a plan for you and always has. Maybe you've always thought what was happening in your life was *your* plan. But it wasn't. Can you trust that He's working on a plan for you now?"

"I don't know," Mark said honestly. "It's not that I don't believe in God."

"*Nee*, just that you don't trust Him?" With that his grandfather got awkwardly to his feet. "Been a long day. I'm turning in." He touched Mark's shoulder. "Get some rest."

With a sigh, Mark followed him inside. He locked the front door—city habits died hard—and made his way to the back of the house to climb the stairs to his bedroom. The day had been long and the work hard, but he was still used to staying up later. He felt restless, his thoughts swirling. He bypassed the stairs, went out the back door, and sat on the steps.

Could he trust that God was working on a plan for him? He stared up at the stars. "It isn't that I don't trust you," he said. The times he'd talked to God, he'd always instinctively looked up to the heavens. "It isn't. Really."

The only sound he heard was the relentless chirp of crickets in the distance.

Time really slowed down here. Buggy rides instead of car rides. Long seasons of planting and nurturing followed by a long, hot season of harvesting. It wouldn't be long before the fields would lie fallow and then be covered with snow.

Would he still be here then?

He sat for a long time, listening to the silence.

Thirteen

Miriam was the first of the women to arrive at John's to help with the harvesting. She set the insulated carrier and two tote bags on the kitchen table.

That was when she saw the small velvet ring box. She'd never seen one in person before, but she knew what it was. Amish couples didn't seal an engagement with a ring or wear wedding bands. An Amish man grew a beard after his marriage. That was the enduring sign to all that he was married.

What a strange thing to find on the table. It had to belong to Mark. But why would he leave it on the table?

She unpacked the food she'd brought and busied herself. But she couldn't help looking at the box. It drew her attention like some forbidden thing. She looked around and then, even though she felt guilty, she reached for it and opened it. Light sparkled off the diamond inside, exploding in a rainbow of color. She'd seen engagement rings on *Englisch* women, but never anything this big, this beautiful.

There was a commotion at the front door. "Miriam?"

She nearly dropped the box. "In the kitchen!"

She shoved the box into her apron pocket and tried to look normal as Naomi walked into the room.

Naomi frowned. "Are you *allrecht*? You look flushed."

"Just a little warm. Let me help you with that," she said, rushing to take a big plastic container from her.

"I'm getting tired of summer for *schur*," Naomi agreed mournfully.

They were busy getting lunch together for the men working in the fields when Mark came in the back door. He greeted them before walking to the sink to fill a glass with water. He turned and leaned against the counter as he drank, and his gaze drifted to the kitchen table.

"We'll be bringing lunch out soon" Miriam said quickly. "Tell the men fifteen minutes."

He nodded. "Okay." He set the glass in the sink and left.

Had he noticed the box wasn't on the table? If he had, wouldn't he have asked where it was? But she couldn't pull it out of her pocket and put it back there without Naomi asking questions.

"I'll be right back. Have to use the bathroom."

Naomi just nodded as she finished placing sandwiches on a platter.

Miriam escaped to the bathroom and splashed some cool water on her burning face. She patted it dry with a hand towel and stared at herself in the mirror. Naomi was right. She did look flushed.

And guilty. The box was burning a hole in her pocket. She pulled it out, opened it, and stared at the ring. Why did Mark have it here if he was still engaged to his fiancée? Why wasn't it on her finger?

She lifted it from its velvet bed and slipped it on her finger. It was snug but oh, so pretty on her hand. She told herself she should feel guilty for putting something that didn't belong to her on her finger.

But just once, she could dream that it was hers ... that Mark was hers. Couldn't she?

Nee! She had to get it off and get back into the kitchen before Naomi wondered why she was taking so long.

She tugged at the ring but it wouldn't come off. Panicked, she reached for the soap and worked at the ring, but her finger must have swollen or something. She worked at it and worked at it until finally, after several minutes, it slid off.

And fell with a clink into the sink. Her heart pounded as she picked it up, dropped it, and watched it roll toward the drain. She bit back a scream and quickly slapped her hand on it before it could slide down. Then she scooped it up, dried it with the hand towel and pushed it into the box.

With the box safely tucked into her pocket, she unlocked the door and returned to the kitchen.

"Everything's ready," Naomi said. "I've already taken the drinks out. Give me a hand with the sandwiches?"

"*Schur.*"

The men began walking over as soon as they saw the women bringing out the cold drinks and food. Today it was so hot, each of the men drank two glasses of cold water before they began helping themselves to sandwiches and cold salads.

There weren't many of these harvest days left. Miriam would miss them even if she wouldn't miss the heat and the hard work. She glanced over at the table where the men sat and talked about whether it would rain before they finished that afternoon. She watched Mark and thought how much more relaxed he looked than when he'd first come here weeks ago.

Her attention was caught by Amos, who sat by Mark. She and Amos had attended *schul* together. He grinned at her and she realized he'd thought she was staring at him, not Mark.

Why shouldn't he, when no one knew about her secret crush on Mark?

She smiled at him, then quickly looked away. It wouldn't do to give him any ideas. Just last month he'd asked if he could give her a ride home after a singing. She wished she felt something for him. He was a nice man, hardworking and considerate. But now she realized her heart belonged to Mark even if he'd never want it.

Evidently Tiffany didn't want Mark. She could think of no other reason why he'd have her engagement ring.

"Pass this to Lovina, would you, Miriam?"

She shifted to hand the platter of sandwiches to her friend sitting on her left and then rested her hand in her lap. She could feel the ring box tucked in her apron pocket, and a flush crept into her cheeks.

Against her will, she found herself glancing again at Mark. What would he think if he found out she was carrying the ring box in her pocket? Maybe she could slip inside and put the box on the kitchen table without anyone seeing her.

"Miriam, you're not eating. Are you *schur* you're *allrecht*? You look flushed again."

Naomi was just too observant. Miriam felt the flush deepen. "I'm not very hungry. I had a big breakfast. Listen, I think I'll go get some more cold water and iced tea for the men."

"I'll help."

"*Nee*, I can manage. You finish your lunch. I'll be right back." She rose, picked up two empty plastic pitchers, and started for the house.

As she passed the men's table, she caught Amos watching her again. She gave him a brief smile and nodded, but quickly broke eye contact. Her glance fell on Mark, but he was busy scooping up a bite of potato salad and didn't see her looking at him.

She set the pitchers on the counter, pulled the ring box from her pocket, and set it on the kitchen table. The door squeaked. She spun and found herself staring up into Mark's face.

"I wondered where that went to," he said, his blue eyes studying her. "Trying it on for size?"

♪♪♪

Mark watched Miriam drop the ring box as if it were a hot potato.

"That's not nice sneaking up on me!" she cried, her hand flying to her throat.

He chuckled. "You're just annoyed because I caught you."

"You didn't catch me doing anything wrong," she told him primly.

"It wasn't on the table earlier. I looked. You have something to do with its disappearance?"

"I saw it and put it someplace safe."

"Yeah?" He studied the twin bright flags of color on her cheeks. She was genuinely embarrassed. He shouldn't tease her.

Aw, why not? If you couldn't tease a friend, who could you tease? And they were friends. Good friends. Family. Practically brother and sister. And what brother didn't tease his sister?

"Guess you can see I'm in the market for a new fiancée," he said as he sauntered into the room. "You interested?" He plucked up the box, snapped it open, and showed her the ring. "Two carats, Asscher cut, platinum band. Want to try it on, see how it looks?"

She put her hands behind her back. "*Nee!*" she cried. "How can you joke about such a thing?"

Mark snapped the lid shut and stuffed the box in his pocket. "You're right. It's not funny. I'm sorry."

She nodded. "Does this mean that Tiffany returned it to you?"

"That's what it means."

"I'm sorry. Really."

Mark pulled off his hat and ran his fingers through his hair. "Thanks. I was sort of expecting it when she wasn't returning my phone calls, but it was a surprise that she sent it in the mail."

"In the mail?"

He nodded.

"Seems to me that a person should do that sort of thing in person. Break things off in person, I mean." Miriam walked to the sink and set a pitcher under the tap. After it was filled, she set it on the table and put another in the sink. She got ice cubes from the refrigerator freezer and dropped them into the pitchers. "Seems pretty coldhearted to do it by mail."

"I had a friend whose fiancée broke up with him by text."

"By text," she repeated. "By sending a message over the phone?"

"Yes."

Miriam shook her head. "That is wrong."

Mark shrugged. "Sometimes people just can't face giving bad news."

"It's cold. Just so cold."

He watched her shiver. An ice cube slipped through her fingers and skittered across the floor. She bent to pick it up and held it in her hand for a moment, studying it.

"I tried it on."

"What?"

She looked at him as she dumped the melting ice cube into the sink. "I tried on the ring. I wondered what it would feel like. *Englisch* women love them so, don't they?"

"Well, some of them do." He shrugged.

Miriam stared at her hands and chuckled. "Tiffany has thinner fingers than I do. It got stuck."

"Tiffany's thin. All over." He frowned. "Too thin."

"Can an *Englisch* woman be too thin? Seems to me they like that."

"Absolutely. I didn't think it was healthy, the way she obsessed over her weight. We argued. Oh well, someone else's problem now."

"I'm sorry. You deserve someone who loves you."

Mark stared at her. "That's the nicest thing you've ever said to me."

Miriam broke their gaze, reaching for a dish towel to wipe the bottom of a pitcher. "Well, I mean it." She carried the pitcher to the table, then returned to the sink to lift the other pitcher and wipe the bottom. "I should get these outside," she said without looking at him. But she didn't move. "You know, I don't even know what she looked like. You never showed me a picture of her."

"No? I thought I had." He pulled his cell phone out and tapped the screen. "Here."

She leaned closer. "She's pretty."

Mark turned the phone so he could study the photo. And then he sent the picture to the phone's trash bin.

"Well," Miriam said. "I guess that means it's over. I'm sorry."

"Thanks." He picked up one of the pitchers. "We should get these outside before everyone goes back to the fields."

His grandfather gave him a curious look when he returned to the table, but he didn't say anything. Miriam walked around pouring more cold water for those who wanted it.

Mark couldn't keep his eyes off her. The way she'd expressed her outrage over the way Tiffany had broken up with him touched him. But there was something more going on. It seemed ... that there was more than friendship in the way she'd told him he deserved more, deserved better. There had been something more emotional, an intensity in those beautiful blue eyes of hers.

No, he was imagining it because he was feeling so down, so rejected.

If he were honest with himself, he had to admit Tiffany had been slipping away from him before he'd been told to take some time off from the job. He'd blamed it on her being involved with planning the wedding but ...

He'd been so busy with work he hadn't noticed as he should have. Too much time, too much attention went into work. His father had done just the same, and Mark had been so determined not to follow in his footsteps. But he'd done it.

After all, his mother never complained. She had her own job, her own interests. And as much as he loved her, he could also admit that she enjoyed the luxuries his father's high paying job brought in. So, too, Tiffany had enjoyed his ability to take her to the popular places she wanted to go.

But in the circles she ran in, there were other men who could do the same.

And they didn't have a cloud hanging over their head the way he did right now.

As if to echo his thoughts, a rumble sounded overhead. Clouds were forming, obscuring the blue sky. Rain, the curse of harvests, was coming. The men took a last, hurried drink, tossed down their paper napkins, and headed back to the fields.

"We'll finish," his grandfather assured him as he got up. "We have a good hour before the rain starts and we're nearly done."

If anyone knew the weather, his grandfather did. But Mark didn't linger. He thanked the women for lunch and followed the other men into the fields.

As always, the work helped chase thoughts of pain and rejection from his mind. The men got in the last of the crop just as the first raindrops hit.

Now thunder boomed instead of rumbling. Rain began pelting down. The men led the horses off the field, hitched up their buggies, and headed for home. Mark heard a loud crash off in the distance just as he reached the barn doors.

"I saw a flash of lightning over yonder, at the King place," John yelled over the noise of the storm as they stood in the door of the barn. "Hope it didn't hit."

But the plume of smoke that rose in the air said that it did. Without speaking, they hitched up the buggy and raced over to the King farm.

Saul and his sons had already led their horses outside to safety and were hosing the barn down when they arrived. A fire truck pulled in and fire fighters directed big hoses that streamed water on the blaze.

But the barn was half-gone before they had the blaze out.

"Old buildings like this go up quick," Mark heard someone say.

"Reckon we know what we'll be doing on Saturday," someone else said.

Mark had been thinking about heading into Philadelphia for a day or two to check on his place, talk to Tiffany, and see how the private investigator was doing.

Well, he was actually just wanting some time in the city. But now he'd be staying here, helping the men to rebuild the barn for the King family.

Much as he'd enjoyed using his weak carpentry skills at a barn raising—something he'd done just once, but had enjoyed—he sighed.

"It's a shame, for *schur*," his grandfather said at his side.

Mark didn't tell him the real reason he'd sighed. "Sure is."

"Well, nothing else we can do here now. Let's head home."

They hadn't fought the fire, but as they climbed into the buggy Mark could smell smoke on their clothes. Both of them were silent when they reached their own barn and unhitched the buggy. The King place wasn't that far away. It could have been their barn that had been hit.

Their gazes locked. "The Lord giveth and the Lord taketh away," John said simply.

Mark hadn't seen or heard anger from the King men as the blaze was fought. He wasn't so sure he could have stood there, stoic, if it had been his property that burned.

Instead, the Kings had taken what had happened with grace and acceptance.

He'd once had the bumper dented on the BMW by a distracted driver and had a fit.

Life here sure was different.

Fourteen

Miriam watched the men building a new barn for the King family and heard Fannie Mae sigh.

She turned to her friend. "Why the sigh?"

"The men get to have the fun." Fannie Mae set a big platter of cold fried chicken down on the wooden table with a thump.

"Fun?"

"They're having a lot more fun climbing around up there hammering than we are preparing the food."

Miriam grinned. "I never thought about it that way. Looks like hard work to me. And I don't much like heights."

She shaded her eyes with her hand and watched Mark climb around on a high beam with ease. He'd helped build a barn just once before, but he seemed to be in his element. He was dressed like the other men, in a plain blue shirt, dark pants, and a wide brimmed straw hat, but she had no trouble picking him out from the other men.

He was a handsome man, so tall and strong, a tool belt slung at his hips like a Western gunslinger. She and Naomi had secretly exchanged a Western romance once that Naomi had bought in town. The hero on the cover was a sheriff holding a woman dressed in a long, old-fashioned gown in a romantic embrace. His face hovered over the woman's as if he was about to kiss her …

Suddenly warm, Miriam waved her hand at her face. "Let's get the rest of the food out here and serve. The men must be getting hungry by now. They've been working for hours."

She wrinkled her nose. The smell of burned wood hung in the humid summer air.

"I'm thankful no one was hurt when lightning struck the barn," Fannie Mae said as they walked back to the house. "Saul says one of the horses nearly trampled him as he ran to get it out."

Miriam cast a last glance at Mark up on the top rafters of the barn, then walked with Fannie Mae back into the house. She was really quite happy with her role as a *maedel* and wouldn't have wanted to be anything else. Women in the community still did most of the caring for *kinner*. They still were most often chosen as teachers in *schul*, although she corresponded with some male Amish teachers. And men didn't get to have *boppli*.

What could be better than that?

The day passed in a busy haze of serving the meal, pouring endless glasses of water and lemonade and tea, and cleaning up afterward. She enjoyed her days teaching more than the days spent in summer "vacation," but both parts of her life had a comforting pattern to them, a seasonal regularity. It was the cycle of life here and she'd never had a desire for the kind of life Mark and other *Englisch* she knew experienced in their world.

Well, that wasn't exactly true. Sometimes she'd wanted to be *Englisch* so she could go to college … see what Mark's world was like.

Did he think she was boring? Sometimes she'd wondered why he talked to her when he had so much more education than she did. After all, he'd gone to college, traveled, met so many different people. But he'd never made her feel she lacked anything.

He didn't linger after the long day was over, but left clutching his cell phone in his hand and wearing a frown as he read the display on his way to his car.

She had the feeling it wasn't good news he was reading.

The next morning, she was back in the kitchen garden, supervising her *schweschders* as they weeded and harvested late summer vegetables for market day. The day went by swiftly as she moved from the garden to canning and preserving vegetables and fruit just hours from the rich soil.

A glance at the kitchen clock had her shifting again to cooking a simple meal and packing it up for John and Mark. Before she left, she went upstairs to her room, splashed water on her face, and toweled it off. Then she changed out of her workday dress into a favorite one of cornflower blue. Her kerchief came off, a freshly pressed *kapp* got pinned on.

She stared at her reflection. She didn't think of her looks often, but when she did at times like now, she thought she looked average. Many

Amish *maedels* had a similar look. After all, their ancestors were strong stock from Germany, Holland, and Switzerland, and settled here in Pennsylvania, met and married others from the same ancestry. Add clothing of a similar pattern and design dictated by the *Ordnung*, the written and unwritten rules of the Amish, and *ya*, there was a similarity of appearance.

She sighed. Oh, well. There was nothing wrong with that. Everyone was here for a common purpose, a common goal of being one, of being a community.

And now she had a purpose: to take supper to John and Mark as she did many afternoons. It was a pleasure to help John since it was harder for him to get around these past months. And it hadn't been an easy thing for him to pick up cooking for himself after his *fraa* died. He hadn't given in to the pressure he'd confessed he felt from the bishop to remarry. Most here felt there were fewer problems if there were married couples, instead of a lot of unattached widows and widowers or young single men and women.

Her fingers stilled on the covering pins she was using to secure her *kapp*. Marriage *schur* wasn't in the imminent future when she didn't even date.

It was her own fault, of course. Not when they had to measure up to Mark. With a sigh, she turned from the mirror and went downstairs.

"I'm taking supper over to John's," she told her mother as she lifted the wicker basket she'd packed.

Sarah turned from the stove and frowned. "Your *dat* just took the buggy. He'll be back in a half hour."

"I can walk. It isn't that heavy." And it was a short walk on a nice day. "I'll be back soon to help you with supper and the *kinner*."

As she walked, she couldn't help noticing how more and more of the fields had been harvested. It wouldn't be long now before the hard work of harvest would be over. Would Mark stay after the need for him passed? Any day his firm could call him back.

The thought of him leaving weighed on her, making her steps slow and the basket heavy.

Sometimes she wished she could go back to those early summers when he'd come to help his grandfather. They'd had long talks catching up on each other's lives since they'd seen each other the previous summer.

Miriam always loved hearing about his studies. The schools he attended were so different from hers in the one room *schul*. He attended classes with students his age, not a mixture of all ages like hers. His day sounded like a whirlwind filled with subjects they didn't even study here, like science, although she was *schur* glad she hadn't ever had to dissect a frog. Why would you want to do that? They were so much fun to watch as they hopped from one lily pad to another and to listen to as they called to each other on warm summer nights when the windows were wide open for the breeze.

And Mark traveled—he'd even gone to France and Italy during holiday break one year.

"My mom insisted we go on a gondola ride in Venice," he'd told her as they sat on a quilt on the grassy slope of a pond at a park.

She'd packed a picnic lunch of the fried chicken she'd learned to make this past year, and it must have turned out pretty *gut* because he'd eaten three pieces. On the other hand, he and all the men who worked so hard in the fields had hearty appetites.

"Tell me about Venice," she'd prompted. "I saw pictures of it in a book I borrowed from the library."

"It's too bad you couldn't go instead of me," he'd said ruefully. "My parents say they want to expose me to history and they say it started in Europe."

"They're right. That's where our ancestors came from, after all. So come on, it must have been a thrill to see something of another country."

"Yeah, it was, even when I couldn't understand the language and when they insisted I try food I'd never seen. Imagine eating octopus and snails and eel. I gotta tell you, it was weird. Just plain weird."

She laughed at the face he made. "*Nee*, I can't imagine."

He made light of those times, but as he got older, she saw that his education and travels had made him into the man he was now: smart, polished, and successful.

Would she have been as interested in reading so much after she graduated if she hadn't wanted to keep up with him when they talked all those summers? Because he was interested in talking to her in a way the local boys weren't. She and Mark talked about more than this small part of the world in which she lived.

Last summer, his visit hasn't been long—his work at the law firm didn't give him much time off—but he'd taken her for a picnic, and that's when he told her about the woman he'd met, fallen in love with, and asked to marry him.

And when he left, the last of her golden summers with the boy she loved had ended.

✒✒✒

Mark sat on the side of his bed and stared at his running shoes. They sat on the floor next to the dresser, silently accusing him.

He hadn't gone for his morning run since the day he'd come here.

The Amish didn't go for morning runs. They got enough exercise working hard every day whether they farmed or worked in other businesses. Running was an *Englisch* habit—one he embraced. He loved the way he felt when he ran and missed it. Sure, he could have kept it up while he was here. But he rose well before the sun was up and worked a day so long and hard that it had taken weeks before he'd adjusted to the manual labor of harvesting.

And he sure hadn't needed or wanted any more exercise at the end of the work day. It wasn't long after supper that he found himself nodding off when he tried to read or talk to his grandfather. He turned in early and fell asleep the instant his head hit the pillow.

So there was no going for a run or even a long walk. But already he could see and feel the difference in his body from the hard physical labor, and he sure hadn't been someone who'd let himself go soft behind a desk.

So he left his shoes there, laced up his work boots, and started out of the room. As he did, his glance fell on the small velvet box on top of the dresser.

What did a man do with an engagement ring? He didn't have any friends who'd gone through a broken engagement and had their ring returned. Did jewelry stores have a return policy? Somehow he doubted it. Rings were bought brand new. He remembered the outrageous amount of money he'd spent. The salesman had been so unctuous with advice on how much to spend—apparently there was a formula based on how much a man made.

He touched the box. He had savings to protect himself, but maybe he should look into selling the ring somewhere. Just exactly where, he had no idea. eBay? Craigslist?

Well, that was a thought for later. For now, it was time to start his day the Amish way. Caring for the horses and other farm animals. Eating a huge breakfast of eggs and bacon. Both of them managed to cook breakfast fairly decently and there would be biscuits or homemade sweet rolls Miriam dropped off periodically. Breakfast here was a meal that was a far cry from the bagel and coffee he usually grabbed from a drive-through on his way to the office.

He still felt he had one foot in the Amish world and one in the *Englisch*, especially when he worked all day as a farmer, then took a drive in his BMW. How long would he be in limbo?

The afternoon they'd finished rebuilding the Kings' barn, he'd gotten a text from Lani, his paralegal. She needed to see him and asked if she could come to Paradise. He prodded her to just tell him what was wrong, but she refused and said she'd be there in the next day or two.

"Mark, you have company!" his grandfather bellowed up the stairs.

He hurried downstairs and his heart sank when he saw Lani. Her eyes were red and swollen from crying. He didn't remember ever seeing her that upset in the years they'd worked together.

"They're reassigning me to another attorney at the firm," she burst out. "It's not right."

He made her come into the house, made her sit down at the kitchen table. He put the kettle on to heat water for tea. Women always fixed tea when they were upset, didn't they?

"I wanted to threaten to quit," she said between sobs. "But I can't. I need my job right now."

"Of course you do." He patted her shoulder awkwardly as he set the cup of tea before her. "Here, drink this and try to calm down."

All the while he was trying to soothe her, his head buzzed with thoughts. The news felt like someone had put nails in his coffin. Was the firm not ever going to let him come back?

"I'm just scared to death you're not coming back." Lani sniffed, voicing his fears.

Mark handed her a paper napkin from the holder on the table and watched her dab at her tears. "You know the boss. He doesn't want anyone to go five minutes without working on a brief or helping a client. I turned in more billable hours than anyone in the firm, and he was always saying I could do more."

Lani balled up the napkin and sat up straighter. "I'm sorry. I wasn't thinking about how you'd feel about this."

"It's perfectly natural," he assured her. "You have a little girl to take care of. When they told me to take some time off, I didn't think it would be for more than two weeks or so. Didn't think how it might affect your job." He frowned. "Lani, do you need some money? I can—"

"No!" She waved her hands in protest. "I've just been moved from one desk to another. I haven't lost my job."

Mark glanced at the kitchen clock. "You need to get home. Who's taking care of Abby?"

"My mom." She stood and they walked outside.

"Text me when you get home."

She kissed him on the cheek. "I will, Daddy. Take care." She glanced around. "It's so lovely here. I can see why you've always loved it."

"Well, I loved it more when I didn't have to stay," he admitted ruefully as he opened the door to her car.

He watched her drive away and found his steps heavy as he returned to the house.

"Miriam's bringing supper over," his grandfather told him as he walked into the kitchen.

"I'm not hungry."

"You feeling sick?"

He shook his head.

Grandfather peered at him, his bushy white eyebrows drawn in a frown. "Your friend bring some bad news?"

"They reassigned her to another attorney. I'm not sure they're going to let me come back." He held up his hand. "I'm not in a good mood right now. I'm going up to my room."

"*Allrecht.*"

He walked into the little room he'd spent so many summers in, threw himself on the bed, and stared up at the ceiling. Life stunk. It just completely stunk. He rubbed his hands over his face. In his wildest dreams, he'd never imagined losing his job.

Minutes ticked by. The room seemed to shrink, the space too small, the walls closing in. He leaped up from the bed, grabbed his car keys, and rushed down the stairs. Air. He needed some air.

"Hey, where's the fire?" his grandfather cried as he rushed through the room. "Miriam just dropped off supper."

"Go ahead without me," he said without stopping. "I'm going for a drive."

"It's fried chicken, your favorite," he heard his grandfather call after him.

Food didn't interest him right now. He kept going. On his way to his car, a clap of thunder startled him into looking up into a darkening sky. Perfect. It matched his mood.

He slid behind the wheel of the car and felt a measure of calm descend. This was familiar territory, where he had some control. A man and his car. He didn't need anything else for the moment. He started it, backed out of the drive, and headed for the open road. A good long drive was what he needed. The country roads hereabout were a pleasure to drive after the traffic clogged roads back in Philadelphia.

A block later the skies opened. He turned on the windshield wipers just in time to see a woman hurrying along the side of the road. Something about her looked familiar. He signaled he was pulling over and hit the button to lower the passenger window. "Miriam?"

She blinked at him. "Mark?"

"Get in."

"I'm wet."

He glanced at the rear view mirror, then back at her. "Doesn't matter, get in before someone hits us."

She did as he asked.

Her clothes and *kapp* were sodden, her dress molded to her slender curves. Beads of moisture sparkled on her long eyelashes. He looked away, too aware.

"What are you doing walking in the rain?" He checked for traffic, then pulled out onto the road.

"It wasn't raining when I set out." She shivered.

Mark flicked off the air conditioning. "Do you want me to turn the heater on?"

"*Nee*, I'm fine."

"Look in the glove compartment. There should be a handkerchief you can dry your face with."

She opened it, found it, and wiped at her face.

He frowned and gave her a long glance. "Were you crying?"

"*Nee*, of course not."

He drove, silent.

"You just passed my *haus*."

"I know. I'll take you there when you tell me what's wrong."

"It's nothing."

"We're friends, Miriam. I'd hope you'd talk to me about something that's troubling you."

She shook her head. "Please, just take me home."

Finally, resigned, he did as she asked.

Fifteen

Mark showed up at her house two days later.

"I thought I'd return this," he said, holding out a bag filled with the plastic containers she'd taken to John's house. "The fried chicken was delicious. I was lucky there was any left after my grandfather got to it first."

Miriam took the bag from him. "I know how he loves it. I'm glad you did too."

Her mother appeared at her side. "Mark, it's *gut* to see you. Is John *allrecht?*"

"Yes, thanks. He's fine."

"*Gut.*" She turned to Miriam. "I'll be in the kitchen finishing lunch."

Miriam smiled. "Would you like to stay for lunch?"

"I didn't drop by to get invited."

"Maybe not, but you're welcome to stay."

"I guess I have time." He followed her into the kitchen.

"*Gut. Mamm,* I invited Mark to have lunch with us."

She gave him a brief glance as she filled glasses with lemonade. "That's nice."

"Have a seat. Would you like some lemonade or iced tea?"

"I haven't had any of your delicious lemonade in ages, Sarah."

Miriam took the glass her *mudder* handed her and set it before Mark. He took a sip. "It's as delicious as I remember."

Sarah nodded, then set the pitcher down. Was it her imagination, or was her *mudder* being uncharacteristically silent?

Mark glanced at his watch, and Miriam realized he was wearing his city clothes. "I'm going back to Philadelphia this afternoon."

She felt the blood drain from her face. "So soon? I thought you'd be here until the harvest was over."

"I won't be gone long. There's some business I need to take care of."

"So you're not going back to stay?"

"Not yet."

"Miriam, call everyone in?"

She forced herself to walk outside and rang the bell, then returned to sit next to Mark. Her throat was dry, so very dry. She sipped lemonade and it eased a little.

The back door crashed open as her *schweschders* and *bruders* piled into the room, chattering a mile a minute. They stopped abruptly when they saw Mark.

"Hi, Mark!" they chorused.

"Hi, to you," he said and he grinned.

Miriam rose automatically to supervise the washing of hands. Her *dat* came in, nodded at Mark, and waited his turn to wash his hands. Soon everyone was seated around the table, heads were bent for the blessing for the meal, then the clamor began. The children fell on the meal like a pack of hungry wolves.

She handed Mark the bowl of potato chips. "Have some before they're all gone."

He took some and passed the bowl on.

A baby's wail echoed down the stairs. Miriam got up. "I'll get Katie," she told her *mudder*. "You eat." She returned with a sleepy looking Katie and put her in the high chair in between her and Mark.

Katie leaned over and gave Mark a big grin.

"Here, Katie, sandwich." Miriam placed a quarter of a sandwich on the plastic tray in front of her.

The toddler picked up the sandwich with both hands and began munching. She turned to Mark and grinned, showing a mouthful of yellow.

Mark laughed and Katie chortled. She held out the sandwich to him, inviting him to take a bite.

"No, thanks. I have my own sandwich," he said, holding it up to show her.

"So you're going to Philadelphia today?" Miriam asked as she wiped Katie's mouth with a paper napkin.

He nodded. "I'll be back tomorrow."

"Will you be returning to your job after harvest?" Daniel asked.

Miriam found herself holding her breath as she waited for his answer.

"I don't know," Mark replied. "My firm is giving me some time off."

"I see." Daniel frowned and helped himself to another sandwich.

"I'm sure John has been happy to have your help," Sarah said. "But it's always nice to get home."

Miriam shot her *mudder* a disbelieving glance. She knew how Miriam felt about Mark. She cast about for something to say. "Have you heard from your parents lately?"

"They're still in Europe. I believe they're visiting France this week."

"John has been grateful for your help," Miriam said. She took a bite of her sandwich and found it tasteless. Was it her imagination, or were both her parents being quieter and less friendly to Mark than they had been in the past? Maybe lunch hadn't been a *gut* idea after all.

"Mark, would you pass the chips, please?" Isaac asked.

"Eat your sandwich first," Sarah told him.

He demolished half of it in two bites, swallowed, then stuffed the remaining half in his mouth. He looked like a chipmunk.

Miriam saw Mark struggling to hide his grin. She sighed and shook her head. What must Mark think of this family?

She got up to clear plates and brought the container of peach ice cream to the table.

"Ice cream?" Sadie asked, her eyes wide.

Katie screamed and clapped her hands. And then, to Miriam's disbelieving eyes, Katie leaned over and patted Mark's arm. He smiled at her.

"Oh my, *nee!*" Miriam cried. "Katie, look what you've done!"

Mark's immaculate white shirt sleeve now bore a baby sized palm print of bright yellow egg salad.

Katie promptly burst into tears and howled. Miriam sprang up, grabbed a dish towel, and wet it with water from the faucet.

"Now, now, don't be upset," Mark told her as she dabbed at the stain. "Miriam, it's no big deal. I'm sure it'll wash out."

She bit her lip. "I hope so. I'm *schur* that's an expensive shirt. But you said you were on your way out of town."

"I'll just go home and grab another shirt."

Miriam lifted Katie from the high chair and carried her to the sink to wash her hands and face.

Mark stood. "Well, I should get going."

She glanced at him. "You're not staying for ice cream?"

He used his paper napkin to wipe at the stain on his shirt. "I'd better not. But thanks for lunch."

"Can I have his ice cream?" Jacob spoke up.

"Why should you get it?" Linda demanded.

"*Kinner!*" Daniel said in a quiet but firm manner.

Miriam wiped Katie's face on a dish towel and followed Mark to the front door. "I'm so sorry—"

"There's nothing to be sorry for," he assured her. He chucked Katie under her fat chin and she chortled at him. "I'm just glad to see you're looking more cheerful than yesterday."

She pasted on a smile and nodded. Little did he know, she thought as she watched him walk to his car.

♪♪♪

"That was a quick trip," his grandfather quipped when he walked into the house.

Mark held out his arm. "If you ever eat lunch at Miriam's, watch out for Katie. She's a toucher."

He stripped off the soiled shirt and walked into the kitchen to run water over it in the sink. "I'm hoping it comes out. This is one of my favorite shirts." He squirted some dish detergent on the stain and scrubbed at it.

"Does this mean you're not going?"

Mark rinsed the sleeve. The stain remained. "No, I'm going. I'll get another shirt and hit the road."

"Let me work on that."

"Thanks. Anything you want me to pick up for you in the city?"

"The city's got nothing I want."

"Okay."

Mark took the stairs two at a time, grabbed a clean shirt, and dragged it on while he descended the stairs.

"Where's the fire?" his grandfather asked as he came into the kitchen.

"I just lost some time, that's all." He finished buttoning the shirt and tucked it into his pants. He started past his grandfather, then stopped to hug him. "I'll be back tomorrow."

"You asked me if I wanted anything from the city," his grandfather said as he stepped back from the embrace.

"Yeah. What should I bring you? A Philly cheese steak sub?"

"You," John said simply. "Just you. Drive safe."

Mark swallowed the lump in his throat. "I will." He touched his shoulder, then walked out of the house.

It felt good to be dressed in regular clothes and tooling along toward the city.

He'd enjoyed farming, but he'd missed the city. He didn't have a plan. Well, not an organized one. He'd check on his condo, get a haircut, and give the private investigator a call.

He'd also call a few of his fellow attorneys, see if he could get a sense of what he should be doing about a job search since it was a distinct possibility he might not be going back to the firm.

Traffic was awful. He grinned, up for the challenge. He wound his way through it to his downtown condo and parked in the garage. His mail box was full. Lani must not have been by for a couple days. He scooped it up and rode up the elevator.

He opened the door to his condo and cool air drifted out. Cool to the point of cold. He'd set the thermostat low before he left. A friend had once told him he'd tried to save on the utility bill by not keeping the air conditioning on at the usual level, and had come home to find his condo smelling mildewy.

"Mark!"

He turned. "Mrs. Winkelman. Hello."

"You're back. I told you things would blow over."

He vaguely remembered her saying that as he had carried his suitcase onto the elevator for the ride down to the garage. He was saved from responding when her cell phone rang and she quickly excused herself to answer it.

Mark tossed the mail on the table in the entryway and winced at his reflection in the ornate brass mirror that hung over it. A haircut was the first order of business. Just that morning he'd noticed how shaggy he'd become, then remembered what day of the week it was … and that had given him an idea. He'd dressed in his city clothes and headed out almost immediately, just stopping briefly at Miriam's.

"I appreciate you getting me in on such short notice," he said as he slid into the stylist's chair.

Giorgio stood for a moment and gaped, then quickly got to work. As he snipped and muttered, Mark asked some careful questions. Giorgio had one very important client who'd recommended him to Mark, and he wanted to know if that man still kept his bi-weekly Wednesday appointment with him—without raising his suspicions, obviously.

A simple, casual question gleaned the information that his former boss was due for an appointment that very afternoon. "*Voila!*" Giorgio announced importantly. "I have worked my magic!"

Mark grinned. "Nice job!"

"Don't stay away so long next time," he admonished, whisking away the protective cape. "And put some conditioner on if you must be out in the sun so much."

Conditioner. Mark bit back a grin. He could just imagine what his grandfather would think if he saw a bottle of hair conditioner in the bathroom.

He walked out to the reception area, handed over his gold card, added a generous tip for Giorgio, and lingered over the display of shampoos and conditioners all packaged in manly colors of navy and burgundy. He picked up a bottle of conditioner, carried it to the receptionist, and paid for it.

As he was wondering what else he'd have to do to stay until the real reason he'd come, his boss walked in. He did a double take.

"Byler. I didn't expect to see you here."

Mark ran a hand over his hair. "Needed a trim."

"Yes, well, that's some tan." Mr. Sampson looked uncomfortable. "Looks like you took some time off in an island paradise."

"Paradise, anyway," he muttered. "Feels good to be back home."

"Yes, well, I'm afraid we're not ready to have you come back yet." He glanced at the door to the salon, clearly eager to avoid more conversation.

"I see." Mark straightened his shoulders. "Well, then, I guess I'll have to consider my options."

"What is that supposed to mean?" Sampson demanded, his eyes narrowing.

"I'm not willing to take time off indefinitely, sir. I'll have to think about this."

"Are you threatening me?"

"I'm just going to consider my options, sir," Mark said evenly. "You have a good day."

He headed for the elevator and pretended not to hear the man splutter behind him. Once he was inside and the doors were closed, he took a deep breath and rolled his shoulders, only now aware of the tension that had built up in them.

Okay, so it wasn't good news like he'd hoped. But knowing was better than the uncertainty he'd been living with.

Lunch had worn off hours ago. Remembering how he'd offered to bring his grandfather a Philly cheese steak sub, he stopped at a favorite restaurant and got one to eat at an outside table. Tourists and locals passed by. He'd lived here long enough to recognize which was which. Both moved with purpose, but the tourists usually had maps and a schedule to keep of all the important landmarks—Liberty Bell, Independence Hall, Betsy Ross House, Carpenter's Hall, Penn's Landing.

Sometimes he wondered why his father had settled here when he left the Amish community in Paradise. Was it because Philadelphia had represented freedom to him the way it did to so many in the country?

Right now, he felt pretty alone in the midst of so many people. And if he were honest, he'd felt that way a number of times before the case that had sent him back to Paradise. Life here had become a treadmill of overwork and sterile relationships that hadn't made him happy.

In Paradise, he'd felt welcomed not only by his grandfather, but by people he saw only for a short time each summer. Even when they knew why he'd returned from his big time career in the big city, they hadn't judged him or distanced themselves the way his boss had done.

His sandwich sat half-eaten on the table before him as he thought of that welcome—and of a woman who'd never wavered in showing him understanding, compassion, and deep friendship. He frowned when he thought about how upset she'd been the other day when he found her walking in the rain.

Had she been upset about a man? He suddenly found himself eager to return to Paradise and insist she tell him what was wrong. He cared about her, cared more than he'd realized.

Maybe he wouldn't wait until morning to start back to Paradise.

Sixteen

"There you are."

Miriam glanced up as her *mudder* walked out onto the front porch. "Did you need me?"

"*Nee*, the *kinner* have been asleep for some time now." She sank down into the rocking chair next to Miriam's.

Miriam watched as a car approached on the road in front of the house. When it passed, she tried not to sigh.

"Expecting someone?"

"Hmm?" Miriam looked at her *mudder*.

"You paid a lot of attention to that car."

She shrugged. "Just enjoying the breeze."

"I don't want you to be disappointed if he doesn't come back."

"He said he would."

"Sometimes people can't do what they promise."

Her words stung. "He said he'd be back in a day or two, and he will. He's always done what he said he would." Miriam paused. "*Mamm*, do you and *Daed* have a problem with Mark?"

Sarah's rocker stopped. "Why would you ask such a thing?"

"It seemed to me you both were ... different with him at lunch yesterday."

Sarah nodded and rocked, staring out at the gathering dusk. "He's facing a lot of change right now. We don't want to see you hurt."

"How can I be hurt?"

"We know you care for him."

Now Miriam wished she hadn't said anything.

"It worries us."

"He's a friend. He can't be more. Even if he asked me to marry him—and he's not going to do that—I would never leave my family. My community."

"That doesn't mean you can't be hurt by him."

134

The screen door creaked and Daniel walked out.

"Daniel, Miriam and I are talking about Mark."

His steps halted for a moment, then he resumed walking over to the rocker next to his *fraa's*. He settled into the chair, rested his head on its back, and stretched out his long legs.

"Our *dochder* asked me if we had a problem with Mark."

"*Ya?*"

"*Ya*," she said firmly, as if urging him to speak.

He lifted his head and looked at Miriam. "Your *mudder* worries."

"I know. But there's nothing to worry about," Miriam insisted.

"Try telling *her* that," he said simply, resting his head on the back of the chair again.

She smiled and reached for her *mudder's* hand. "You can't protect me from hurt."

"You should have seen her when you started taking your first steps."

Sarah swatted her hand at him. "Go on now. You know you worried, too."

"*Daed*, I told *Mamm* she doesn't need to be concerned about Mark. We're friends. And he could really use our love and support right now. His whole life has been turned upside down."

"That's when God's working the most in someone's life."

Miriam stared at her *dat*.

Sarah chuckled. "He doesn't talk much, but when he does, he has something to say, doesn't he?"

"*Ya*. And I know it's true. But this has been so hard on Mark."

"Maybe you need to learn you can't protect him from hurt, eh?"

A car pulled into the drive. "Looks like we have a visitor," Daniel said.

He came back! was all Miriam could think.

Sarah stood and held out a hand to her *mann*. "Looks like *she* has a visitor." They went into the house.

Mark stepped onto the porch. "I didn't mean to chase them away."

Miriam laughed. "I think they're just giving us some privacy."

He sat in one of the chairs. "Really? I got the hint they weren't happy with me when I came for lunch yesterday."

"Parents worry."

"What are they worried about?"

She felt warmth rushing into her cheeks and hoped the growing dark hid her blush.

"Miriam?"

"They're worried that we're becoming more than friends."

"I see."

"I never said we were," she rushed to say. "I wouldn't do that."

"No, I'm sure you didn't." He leaned back in his chair.

Silence stretched between them.

"Do you want me to talk to them?" he asked finally.

"*Nee*, I told them we're just friends." She searched for a way to explain. "It's not that they don't like you, really."

"But I can see their concern. A lot of marriages come out of good friendships, and I'm sure not very good marriage material right now, am I? Unemployed and *Englisch*."

"It's the *Englisch* part."

"Ah, I see."

"Lavina Troyer married an *Englisch* man last year. Her family's shunned her ever since."

"Sometimes I forget how backward things can be here."

"Backward?" she asked, indignant.

He held up a hand. "Sorry. That didn't come out right. Let's just say particular to your church."

"You know, plenty of other religions don't approve of their members marrying those of another faith."

"Yeah." A car passed on the road in front of the house, radio blaring in the silence of the night. "They're not going to tell you that you can't see me, are they?"

"*Nee*. They wouldn't do that. So, tell me about your trip."

"I'd rather talk about you."

"Me?"

"Yeah. I worried about you while I was gone. You were so upset the other day and you wouldn't tell me why. We've always been there for each other. You've certainly listened to an awful lot of what's going on with my life right now. So why aren't you telling me what's bothering you?"

She'd hoped he'd forgotten about that day. "You're making a mountain out of a mole hill."

"I don't think so. If it was nothing, then there's no reason why you can't just tell me and be done with it."

"You're relentless, you know that?"

"I do," he said with a grin.

"And you're proud of it?"

He leaned over to stare at her. "It makes me a good attorney. And a good friend."

There had to be some way to get him off her back. She frowned and thought hard. And then it came to her.

"You were right. The other day you asked me if I was upset about a man. I was. I am."

"I knew it!" He leaned back and set the chair rocking with his foot. "So who is this turkey who upset you? Tell me and I'll go have a word with him."

The situation was so absurd, she burst out laughing. "Don't be ridiculous!"

"I'm not being ridiculous. I don't like some guy making you upset."

"*Ya*, well, it happens."

He stopped rocking and turned to her again, looking serious. "You were crying. This guy means something to you."

"Yeah. And I'm not talking to you about him. Now let's change the subject. How was your trip?"

SSS

So she was dating.

Mark ran a hand through his newly shorn hair. Why was he surprised? She'd always been pretty, in a quiet way, and so intelligent. Every summer he'd come back here, he'd wondered why she didn't seem to have a boyfriend. Sure, Amish couples kept things quiet, but he thought he'd have known.

A memory came to him. Earlier this summer, he'd asked her if she was seeing anyone. She'd said no. So that meant she either wasn't telling the truth or she'd just recently started seeing him.

Hmm.

He found himself wondering who she was seeing. It would be someone she'd known for years, grown up with, worshipped alongside in church, worked on community events with.

Not like the relationships most *Englisch* couples had before they married.

Married. If she were seeing someone, that might mean she was getting married. Weddings began as soon as harvest was over.

"Are you getting married?" he blurted out.

"What? *Nee!*"

"Is that why you were upset? Because he doesn't want to get married?"

She threw up her hands. "If you're going to keep this up, I'm going inside."

"All right, all right." He subsided.

"I appreciate you caring," she said, "but I would rather talk about your trip."

"I wouldn't. It didn't go well. Bloodsucker," he muttered.

"Excuse me?"

"Mosquito just got me."

"Come on, let's go inside. Have you eaten?"

"I had lunch before I got on the road."

She stood. "Then you haven't had supper. John ate with us earlier. *Kumm.*"

"It's getting late."

"It can't be more than seven."

Mark touched the dial on his watch. "Seven-fifteen. Almost bedtime in these parts."

"I think I can manage to stay awake while I serve you some leftovers."

He grabbed her hand. "You're sure your parents will be okay with this?"

"I'm *schur*."

They went inside, and Sarah and Daniel glanced up from the books they were reading in the living room and nodded.

"Have a seat," Miriam said as she went to the refrigerator. "How does a cold supper sound?"

"Wonderful. Don't fuss. You've probably had a long day." He noted row upon row of jams, jellies, and preserves on the kitchen counter near him.

"They're all long during harvest time. But we'll be grateful this winter."

He'd only been to Paradise a few times in winter. He and his parents had come for Christmas, but the visits had been short and, as he remembered, a bit uncomfortable. His father really didn't enjoy returning to the community, but he hadn't stood in the way of Mark getting to know his Amish grandparents.

"You're being quiet," Miriam said, breaking into his thoughts.

"Sorry, I'm probably not good company." He scratched the mosquito bite on his arm.

She set a plate with a huge red tomato stuffed with chicken salad before him, then went to a cupboard, pulled out a first aid kit, and brought it to the table. "Here," she said, producing a tube of ointment. "Put this on that mosquito bite."

"Thanks." He unscrewed the top and squeezed some of the ointment on the bite.

"Lemonade or iced tea?"

"Lemonade."

She poured two glasses and joined him at the table. "So tell me about your trip."

Mark stared at the mosquito bite as he remembered his encounter with his boss. "Bloodsucker," he said again. "That's what my boss is."

"That's not a nice way to talk about him."

"People don't tend to say nice things about attorneys. Even other attorneys. Anyway, he sure was happy to know me when I was a top producer in the firm."

"Producer?"

"Made the most money. But now he says they're not ready to have me come back."

"Oh, I'm so sorry." She traced the condensation on her glass of lemonade.

"He didn't like it when I said I was going to have to look into my options." He stabbed his fork at the ripe tomato and it oozed red juice on the plate.

"What does that mean?"

"That's what he asked me." Mark grinned at the memory and poked at the tomato some more before trying the chicken salad. "This is good."

"*Nee*, really, what does looking into your options mean?"

"Everything from threatening to sue to looking for another job." He hadn't felt that hungry, but now that he'd started eating, he discovered he was ravenous.

"You don't have to look for another job. You have the farm here."

"I'll keep helping here until I find another job." When she was silent, he looked up from his plate. "What? You know this isn't permanent. We've talked about it."

She nodded.

He felt like a heel every time the subject came up. "Thanks for supper. It was good."

"It's nice to have something cold when it's been so hot. We have pie."

"That's quite an incentive to stay," he quipped, but she didn't smile. "I'd love some."

"You didn't ask what kind." She got up and took his empty plate to the sink.

"It's pie. And either you or your mother made it. That's all I need to know." He smiled with satisfaction when she set a big slice of fresh strawberry icebox pie before him.

The day was looking up.

"It really bothers me that I worked so hard, made the firm so much money, and I get treated this way."

"I'm sorry he hurt you."

"Yeah, well, I'm a big boy. It's time to stop feeling sorry for myself and get proactive. Take some kind of action." He finished the pie and sat back, satisfied. "I feel a little better. I didn't realize I was hungry until I started eating."

"Sometimes food helps."

"And pie."

She managed a smile. "I'll give you a piece to take home. Don't let John try to talk you into giving it to him. He had two pieces when he ate with us."

"John does love your pies."

Miriam cut a slice and put it in a plastic container. "I enjoy taking him food. He's always so appreciative." She sealed the edges on the container, looking thoughtful. "John's been like a grandfather to me since my *mamm's dat* died. I only had *Grossdaadi* since my *dat* lost his own *dat* when he was a little boy."

That was one thing they'd had in common growing up. Mark had only one grandfather as well. Maybe that was why he'd been so interested in spending time with him on the farm. Well, that and it was so different from his city life. What boy didn't love the adventure, the freedom, of spending the summer on a farm instead of the hot, crowded confines of the city and all its restrictions?

Sure, there were a lot of rules here on a farm in an Amish community. But most of them didn't apply to him since he wasn't Amish.

It was rather ironic that he'd gone into a career that dealt with people being accused of breaking rules, sometimes the biggest rule of all—thou shalt not kill.

Miriam walked with him to the door. Her parents looked up from their books and said good night.

"I hope things look a little brighter in the morning," she said when they stepped out onto the porch.

"My mother used to always think things would be better in the morning," he said, remembering. "Is that a woman thing?"

She laughed. "I don't know." Her brow furrowed. "It fits with what you went through today, though, don't you think?"

"What do you mean?"

"'For his anger endureth but a moment; in his favor is life: weeping may endure for a night, but joy cometh in the morning.'"

Her words stayed with him long into the night, when he lay in his narrow bed in the plain bedroom of his grandfather's farm house. And wondered how he'd feel when he woke in the morning.

Seventeen

Joy. Pure joy. Miriam woke and as she lay there watching thin fingers of dawn light filter into the room she smiled.

Mark was back.

Schur, he'd said he'd be back and he'd never promised something and not done it. But she'd been worried. What if his boss had welcomed him back? Of course he'd have wanted to stay. And she wouldn't have blamed him.

She hated that the man had hurt Mark, but oh, how happy she was that Mark would be here for a while longer. She hugged her pillow and sighed.

Then she thought about Mark. How was he feeling this morning? Before he'd left last night she'd told him she hoped he'd feel better the next day.

Now, as she felt joy, she remembered the psalm she'd quoted to him.

She threw back the sheets, fairly jumped out of bed, and dressed. She was downstairs, flipping pancakes on the stove, when her *mudder* walked into the room yawning.

"Well, you're up early." Sarah said as she walked to the stove to pour a cup of coffee from the percolator. She tilted her head and studied her. "And looking pretty happy. I can guess why."

"*Ya.*"

Sarah sat at the table. "He came back, but we don't know for how long."

"*Nee.*" Miriam flipped pancakes onto a plate and set it on the stove. She poured more batter into the pan before she turned to her *mudder*. "I know he'll be leaving again. But it's nice to have him here for as long as he can stay. It's *gut* for John and I think it's *gut* for Mark, too. He's worked so hard for such a long time and not been able to visit as much as in the past."

"I just don't want you to be hurt."

"I know. But I'm not going to be. Honest." Liar! she chided herself. *You've already been hurt by loving a man you can't have.*

She stared at the bubbles forming around the edges of the pancakes, then, judging it time to flip them over, did so expertly with the spatula. "Want to eat now?" she asked her *mudder*.

Feet hit the floor above them. They heard a scuffle, a cry of outrage, a toilet flush.

"I think I'll wait," Sarah said with a rueful grin.

Kinner ran down the stairs dressed in thin summer pajamas and nightgowns, hair mussed.

"No breakfast looking like that," Miriam teased. "You know the rules."

They turned to look at their *mudder*.

"You know the rules," she echoed.

Pouting, they filed out of the room and ran back up the stairs, pushing and shoving as they went.

"My *kinner* are so well behaved," Sarah said as she watched them go.

Miriam just laughed. "Well, at least I'm well behaved."

Daniel came in the back door. "You're well behaved? Since when?"

"*Daed!*"

He washed his hands at the sink, then looked over Miriam's shoulder. "Hmm. Pancakes. Maybe you're *allrecht* after all."

She laughed as she stacked several pancakes on a plate.

"*Danki*," he said, reaching for the plate.

"*Nee*, these are for *Mamm*. She was here first."

He sank into his chair at the head of the table and pulled a long face as he watched his *fraa* pour syrup on her pancakes. Then he brightened as Miriam set a plate with an even higher stack of pancakes before him. He ate quickly, then went back outside to do chores.

The *kinner* came down the stairs with a noisy clatter and found their seats. Miriam served them and monitored how much syrup was poured so there wouldn't be a lake on any plate.

She shook Jacob's shoulder. "What?" he muttered sleepily. "I'm awake."

"Barely."

"There's one in every family," Sarah observed. "My youngest *bruder* was like that in the morning."

Jacob shoved a bite of pancake into his mouth and his eyes closed in bliss. Miriam watched him carefully. He'd fallen asleep eating more than once. She vividly remembered the time he'd drifted off and his face had landed in his bowl of oatmeal.

Once again, she wondered how Mark had he felt when he woke this morning.

Pancakes were a favorite breakfast here in the Troyer house, and this morning was no exception. Miriam was kept busy moving from stove to table and back again, but finally the hungry *kinner* were full.

"Sit and eat," Sarah insisted.

Miriam did as she was told, and enjoyed her pancakes with an unusually good appetite. Her mind drifted as she planned what she'd make for supper for John and Mark. She couldn't wait to see him again. Mark, that is.

"So I guess we'll get started weeding the garden and then do some canning," her *mudder* said as she supervised her *dochders* doing the washing up.

"Mmm hmm."

"We might be able to can a hundred jars today."

"Mmm hmm."

"Then we can scrub all the floors."

Miriam glanced up. "Huh? Scrub all the floors?"

"So you're back from whatever planet you visited?"

She chuckled. "*Ya.* Just thinking." She picked up her plate, took it to the sink, and looked out the kitchen window. "Looks like another warm one."

The *kinner* went outside to do chores and Miriam washed up her plate and fork.

Daniel came in the back door looking grim. "I'm going over to Abraham Miller's. His *fraa* left a message on the machine in the phone shanty. He needs my help today." He put his hands on his hips. "The Millers were hurt last night when their buggy was run off the road."

Sarah's hand flew to her throat. "*Mein Gott!* Are they *allrecht?*"

"Abraham's arm was broken, but Lovina and their *kinner* just got a bunch of bumps and bruises. But he won't be able to do his chores or any harvesting. I called some of the men to help."

"We'll get some food together and meet you there," Sarah said.

Miriam dried her plate and fork and put them away. She and her *mudder* worked quickly to put together sandwiches and snacks. The men would need food to sustain them during a long day helping their neighbor.

"Why would anyone want to hurt the Millers?"

Sarah shook her head. "Let's not get ahead of ourselves. It may have been an accident."

Miriam wanted to say that's not the way her *dat* had made it sound, but she subsided. They'd know soon enough when they got to the Miller farm.

SSS

John set a cup of coffee before Mark. "So, I'm glad you're back."

"Thanks." He wasn't really happy to be here, but it seemed unkind to say so when his grandfather was beaming at him. He took a sip of coffee.

"So, it's back to work." He spooned scrambled eggs onto plates and set them on the table. "Miriam brought cinnamon rolls over yesterday. I managed not to eat them all." He pushed the basket of rolls toward Mark.

Mark bit into one and rolled his eyes. "Must have been hard. I can't say I could have done the same for you if I'd gotten them first."

"Some man is going to be lucky to get her for a *fraa*."

"Seems to me you've told me that before."

He just smiled. "Bears repeating." He shoveled a bite of eggs into his mouth.

There was a knock on the back door a moment before Samuel stuck his head in. "*Guder mariye.*"

"Samuel, *kumm*," John invited. "Have some coffee."

He shook his head. "*Nee, danki.* I came to ask if you and Mark could help at the Millers today. Abraham broke his arm. His buggy got run off the road."

"*Schur.* Is the family *allrecht?*"

"Will be. But he won't be able to do his chores or any field work for a while."

"We'll be there as soon as we finish eating."

Samuel left, and Mark and his grandfather hurriedly finished their breakfast, grabbed their straw hats, and headed out to hitch up the buggy.

This was community, Mark thought. Dropping everything to help a neighbor in need. He barely knew his neighbors back in Philly, and those he did know had never asked for his help.

Abraham was sitting on his back porch when they arrived. He looked wan and in pain, but insisted on greeting those who came to help.

"What happened?" John asked as they stepped up onto the porch. "Samuel said there was an accident with your buggy."

"It was no accident." Lovina walked out onto the porch. "It was no accident."

"Lovina!"

She burst into a spate of Pennsylvania *Dietsch* so fast Mark couldn't decipher it. He glanced at his grandfather, but he just shook his head, signaling silence.

Mark saw movement behind Lovina. Miriam stood watching her friend and looked visibly upset.

Abraham's *fraa* turned on her heel and went back into the house. Miriam cast Mark a look he couldn't interpret before she followed Lovina.

A group of men had arrived and chores were divvied up. They set about working to get as much done as possible before the heat intensified.

Miriam came out with several other women to serve the men cold drinks and cookies.

"I need to talk to you," she whispered, glancing over her shoulder so that she wasn't overheard.

"Sure. What's up?"

"Later. I'll give you a ride home?"

He nodded and went back to work, wondering what the mystery was.

The men were quieter than they'd been during other days harvesting and doing chores. Mark could see that the incident had affected them.

Buggy accidents were more common in Lancaster County than some other Amish areas because of so much tourism traffic. What brought prosperity to the area often brought car-buggy encounters that sometimes proved fatal to the buggy occupants.

The Miller family had sustained injuries and property damage, but it could have been worse.

"Lovina says it was no accident," Miriam said the minute they got inside the buggy after the work day. "They were run off the road by a couple of *Englisch* teenagers she thinks had been drinking."

"Did they contact the police?"

"Have you learned nothing about us?"

"Okay, dumb question."

Miriam stared into the distance, her expression grim. "Their buggy was badly damaged. Their horse was seriously injured and may have to be put down. Do you have any idea how much buggy repairs cost? How expensive vet bills can be?" She took a deep, shaky breath. "And that's not the worst of it. This wasn't the first time this same group of teenagers harassed them on the road."

"I'm sorry." Mark waited, unsure how to proceed. "Why are you telling me this, Miriam?" he asked her finally.

"We don't press charges," she told him. "That's man's law, not God's."

"I'd be broke if we did that back in Philly," he joked, then bit his tongue at the look she gave him. "Sorry."

"Right now I'm having trouble with it," she admitted. "Things have been rough for the Millers this year. Very rough. I don't want to betray their privacy but this ..." she trailed off. "Lovina looks so worried. She's not just concerned about the buggy and the injuries. She's worried the teenagers won't stop."

"So what do you want me to do?"

"Talk to Abraham. You're good at talking."

"But if they won't press charges, what will that accomplish?"

She bit her lip. "Maybe you can persuade him to let you talk to the teenagers who did this, get them to pay for the buggy repairs and the medical bills for Abraham and the horse. I mean, talking's not pressing charges or suing, right?"

He nodded. "It's what most attorneys do. They don't all immediately go to court. My specialty is where we do, though."

She pulled into the drive of John's farm house then turned to him. "So you'll think about it?"

Mark gazed into her eyes. Her concern for her friends, her passion to help them, touched him. "I'll think about it."

His grandfather was already home and dozing in the recliner in the living room. Mark tiptoed past him and went out to the barn to do evening chores.

What a change in daily routine, he couldn't help thinking. Back home, he'd park his car and not think about it again until morning. Here there were actual animals that depended on them for food and water and care.

On the other hand, he'd never had a neigh or a nuzzle from his car in thanks for caring for it. He chuckled as he fed his grandfather's horses some quartered apples.

He thought about what Miriam had said about the Millers and their horse being gravely injured. Horses powered buggies here and helped with the farming. A farm couldn't survive without its livestock, and like she'd said, the vet bills would be a burden.

When he returned to the house, his grandfather was still snoozing. Mark was exhausted and he wasn't anywhere near the old man's age. He went upstairs, showered, and dressed in clean clothes. Then he poked in the refrigerator for something for supper. He felt too tired to eat, but knew a man couldn't expect to work his body without refueling it.

"Dozed off for a few minutes there," his grandfather said when he wandered into the kitchen a little while later.

He'd been sleeping for an hour, but Mark decided not to point that out. "You want to eat now or after you clean up?"

John sighed. "I suppose I should shower first. No point putting you off your appetite catching a sniff of me downwind as you eat."

He chuckled. "I don't think anything will put me off some food. Hurry up or nothing may be left by the time you come back down." He watched him trudge up the stairs and worried about how old he was looking.

Back home, Mark would have picked up takeout on the way home or called his favorite Italian restaurant for delivery. And he'd have eaten alone in front of the television set or before his computer as he worked.

Tonight there was just enough leftover cold chicken from the previous night's meal. Miriam and other women from the community left jars of chow chow, bread and butter, summer squash, and pickled baby beets. John sliced the loaf of bread and they sat down to the simple but filling cold supper.

"*Danki* for doing the chores," John said as he helped himself to a couple of thick slices of ripe tomato. "I was tuckered out when I came home."

"No thanks needed. " Mark sliced chicken and passed the platter to him. "Miriam wants me to talk to Abraham about the accident. If you can really call it that."

"*Ya?*"

He nodded and related what she'd said. John listened as he ate.

"You thinking about setting up shop here in Lancaster County?"

Mark started to shake his head, then stopped. It would be a way to be closer to his grandfather and help with the farm. And he didn't have a job right now …

"No. Mr. Miller won't want to have me sue or help him press charges anyway, from what I know of your ways. But Miriam thinks I could put pressure on the teenagers to make restitution and reform their ways."

"Humph." John finished eating and pushed his plate aside. "It's going to take some persuading."

"I'm good at that."

"You are," he acknowledged. "I'm pretty *gut* at it, too."

"You thinking of talking to Abraham about it?"

"*Nee.*" John went to the refrigerator and drew out a plastic container. "I'm thinking you should give a tired old man the piece of strawberry icebox pie you brought home last night."

Mark chuckled and leaned forward to rest his elbows on the table. "Let's hear you present your case."

Eighteen

"I spoke to Mark about what happened," Miriam told Lovina as they worked in Lovina's kitchen a few days later.

She didn't like the way Lovina looked today. If anything, she looked paler and more tired than she had the day after the accident.

Lovina paused in the act of grating a head of cabbage for cole slaw. "What did he say?"

"He told me he'd think about talking to Abraham."

"*Gut!*" Lovina went back to grating the cabbage. "It's not right what happened. We weren't doing anything to those teenagers when they ran us off the road. I heard them laughing as they did it." She stopped suddenly, pressed her hand against her mouth.

"What's the matter?"

Lovina held out her hand and showed two scraped knuckles. "I wasn't paying attention. The grater got me." She walked to the sink, rinsed the small cut off, patted it dry with a paper towel, then applied a bandage to her abraded knuckle.

When she returned to the table, she sank into a chair and burst into tears.

"Lovina! Oh my, please, don't cry." Miriam rushed to her side and hugged her. "Everything will work out."

But Lovina just sobbed harder. Miriam patted her back and let her cry it out. When finally her friend's tears subsided, Miriam handed her some paper napkins from the napkin holder on the table.

"I lost the *boppli* I was carrying the night of the accident," Lovina said through trembling lips. "I was three months along. I'm grateful that I still have my three *kinner*, but I lost my precious little *boppli* I carried under my heart for such a brief time."

Miriam's own heart broke at her words. "Oh, my, Lovina, I am so sorry."

The kitchen door opened and Mark appeared. He took in the scene and looked at Miriam. She shook her head. He backed out and quietly shut the door.

"Abraham says we have to forgive. I say, why can't the ones responsible pay for what they've done?" She reached into her apron pocket and withdrew a ragged piece of paper. "I got the license plate number that night." She held the paper out with shaking fingers. "Please, give this to Mark."

Miriam took the paper and put it in the pocket of her apron. "I will. Lovina, please, go lie down and let me finish here. You need to rest. You need to stay strong for your family."

Lovina's sigh was weary. "A few minutes only. The other women will be along soon."

"Do you want me to get Abraham?"

"*Nee, danki.*" She rose and climbed the stairs to her bedroom.

She listened to her friend's slow, steady footsteps and her heart ached. Then, because the men would be needing a meal, she reached for a paper napkin and wiped her own eyes.

Women crowded into the kitchen a few minutes later, bearing containers of food. Their smiles faded when Miriam quietly told them that Lovina was upstairs resting. She didn't say why—that was Lovina's personal business—but the women nodded and said they were glad she was resting.

"She looked so pale and shaky the other day," Miriam's *mudder* said. "Are the *kinner allrecht?*"

Miriam nodded. "They're spending the day with one of their *grossmudders.*"

"And Abraham?"

"He's sitting on the back porch supervising."

The women bustled about preparing the meal, chatting quietly, long years of experience putting them at ease in the kitchen of another woman.

The atmosphere was quiet as the meal was served at the long wooden table beneath the shade of a tree in the back yard. Miriam wasn't sure if it was because of the reason they had gathered, or because everyone was just so tired this time of year.

Lovina joined them and sat, pale but steady, eating little. Her *mann* ate awkwardly since he was right-handed and that was the arm he'd broken.

Mark met Miriam's gaze and raised his brow. She lifted her shoulders, dropped them in a wordless gesture of frustration.

Miriam lingered after the meal was served, cleaning Lovina's kitchen until it sparkled, then washing a load of clothes. Her *mudder* put together a couple of casseroles and tucked them into the refrigerator freezer.

"Ready to go home?" her *mudder* asked after hanging the wash out.

"I want to do another load. I'll get a ride home with Mark."

"*Allrecht.* See you later."

Miriam hung up the second load of wash and waved to Mark as he left the field. "Can I get a ride home with you?"

"Sure. But I'm going to try to talk to Abraham as soon as the other men have gone. My grandfather said he'd get a ride home and leave me the buggy."

"Good luck."

He nodded. "Thanks."

She checked the first load of laundry she'd hung and found it dry. On such a warm day it didn't take long, especially the little garments the Miller *kinner* wore. She said a silent prayer of thanks as she folded the small shirts and pants and dresses, all lovingly made by their *mudder*. It would have been so sad if God had called them home. Next year she'd have the oldest *kind* as a student at *schul*, God willing.

When she walked toward the house, she saw Abraham and Mark engaged in an intense discussion. Abraham sat stiffly, frowning, as Mark sat forward in his rocking chair, speaking passionately. She didn't know what he was saying, but from Abraham's expression and his body language, it didn't appear Mark was convincing him.

Well, the Amish belief in God's law, not man's, had been a part of the faith probably since the very beginning. It might take a long time to convince Abraham. But if anyone could do it, Mark could.

After what Lovina had told her about losing her *boppli* today, Miriam was even more *schur* that Mark should talk to Abraham.

Lovina was sitting at the kitchen table mending when she walked in. "*Danki* for all the help," she said quietly when Miriam set the basket down.

"Why didn't you try to get some more rest?"

Lovina shrugged. "The *kinner* will be home soon. And it helps to keep my hands busy."

"*Mamm* put together some casseroles. What else can I do to help?"

"You've done more than enough."

Miriam walked to the kitchen window. "Mark's out there talking to Abraham. I wish I could hear what they're saying."

Lovina smiled slightly. "Me, too. But knowing Abraham as I do, I can well imagine. He's saying *nee, nee, nee.*"

The three of them had grown up together, although Lovina and Abraham were two years older than she was. "You're probably right. But we have to try to convince him."

"Abraham is stubborn, but he's a *gut* man."

"He is that."

"Mark is a *gut* man, too."

Miriam met Lovina's gaze. "*Ya,* he is."

"I can tell you care about him very much."

Miriam fixed two glasses of ice water. "Is it that obvious?"

"Only to someone who knows you well." Lovina knotted her thread, clipped it with scissors, and set the dress down. "Does he know?"

"*Nee,* thank goodness. He thinks I'm interested in someone else."

"Men are clueless."

She laughed and sipped her water. "Thank goodness," she said fervently. "It would be so awful if he knew."

"If who knew what?" Mark asked as he walked in the back door.

Miriam nearly dropped her glass. "If Abraham knew what Lovina was making him for Christmas."

"Christmas? Isn't it a little early to be talking about Christmas?" He helped himself to a glass of ice water.

"It's never too early," Lovina said quickly. "We make our gifts and it'll take a long time for me to knit the sweater I want to make him." She glanced at the door. "Shhh," she hissed. "Here he comes."

Abraham walked into the room, gave them all a nod, and proceeded into the living room without speaking.

"*Danki* for talking to him," Lovina told Mark.

"He won't be mad at you, will he?" Miriam asked, worried that Mark looked so grim.

"I told him you didn't ask me to," he said. "Because you didn't. He doesn't need to know Miriam did. I just told him I wanted to help. He said no, but I asked him to think about it." He sighed. "I hope he will."

"Well, it's done. " Lovina picked up another dress to mend.

Mark turned to Miriam. "Ready to go?"

"I should see if the clothes on the line are dry."

"My *mudder* will do that later," Lovina said. "You two go on."

"*Allrecht.* Try not to overdo."

The back door opened and the *kinner* walked in followed by their *grossmudder*.

They were quiet. Too quiet. Two of them—the oldest and youngest—wore bandages from the accident.

Lovina sprang up and gathered them in a hug. "I'm so glad you're home. Did you have a *gut* time?"

"We made cookies," the smallest girl said, holding up a plastic container. "We brought home some for *Daed*."

"He's in the living room. Why don't you take them to him?"

Miriam bid them a quick good-bye and hurried out to John's buggy. She barely made it there before she burst into tears.

♪♪♪

Mark heard a choking sound coming from Miriam as he followed her to the buggy.

Was she crying? He climbed into the buggy and winced when he saw that yes, indeed, she was crying. Like most men, he approached a woman in tears cautiously. "What's wrong?"

"Just get us out of here, quickly. Please?" She fumbled in her purse and pulled out a tissue.

"Okay." He did as she asked, careful to watch for traffic as he pulled out of the drive.

They traveled down the road, the only sound the clip-clop of the horse's hooves on the road and Miriam's helpless weeping.

Finally, her sobs subsided. She took a shuddering breath, blew her nose, and stared out at the passing scenery.

"Rough day, huh?" It wasn't sparkling dialogue, but it was the best he could do. He'd seen her in tears before, but never this gut level despair.

"*Ya.*" Miriam balled up the tissue in her hands. "It was one thing to see Abraham hurt, to … talk to Lovina about that night. But seeing the *kinner* so quiet, knowing that they could have been hurt more—or worse—I—" she broke off, lifting her hands and letting them fall into her lap. "Next year I'll have their oldest in my classroom."

She reached into her apron pocket for the slip of paper and handed it to him. "Lovina wrote down the license plate number that night. She said it was a fancy SUV. She doesn't know what kind."

"This should help. I'll give my private investigator a call, see what he can dig up."

"Has he been able to find out anything for you on that man back in Philadelphia?"

Mark frowned and shook his head. "He thought he had a lead the other day, but it didn't turn out to be anything. We both feel Maurice is innocent."

She touched his arm and made him look at her. "I'm sorry, maybe I shouldn't have brought it up."

He shrugged. "It's okay. It's not like it's not on my mind, you know?" He pulled into the driveway of her house. "Maybe I'll be able to help Abraham and his family. That's why I went into law."

She smiled. "I know. Have a *gut* evening."

"You, too."

As he drove home, he thought about what he'd said. He'd gone into law to help people, but at some point his advisor had talked him into criminal law. Now he couldn't help wondering how different his life might have been if he'd gone into some other specialty. He wouldn't have had such a high public profile, which mean he wouldn't now be on the outs with his firm because of bad publicity. Then again, he wouldn't have had the high standard of living he'd enjoyed, either.

But as he unhitched the buggy and put the horse up for the night, he remembered the night not long after the trial had ended when he'd asked himself whether he'd made a living or a life.

He walked slowly into the house.

John straightened from looking into the refrigerator. "There you are. I was about to eat supper without you. You didn't stop somewhere on the way home to eat, did you?"

"No. I stayed to talk to Abraham. Listen, go ahead and eat. I think I'll take a shower first."

"Sit. It's just us two men. You can shower after. You look tired."

"I am." Mark sank into a chair and bent his head for the blessing of the meal.

"I didn't get a chance to talk to Abraham today. How is he doing?"

"The arm's giving him quite a bit of pain still. I can relate. Remember I broke my left arm when I was ten?"

"I remember."

Mark helped himself to food. "Help me understand something. Abraham doesn't want to press charges."

"That must be hard for a lawyer to hear, isn't it?"

He saw the humor in his grandfather's eyes. "Yeah. I told Miriam I'd be broke if the *Englisch* felt that way." He took a sip of ice water. "But Abraham doesn't have to press charges. Some teenagers deliberately ran him and his family off the road, injured them, and caused property damage."

"I'm aware of what happened."

"He can approach those who did it and demand they pay monetary damages," Mark said. "I know that, too." John began buttering a slice of bread.

"But he says he doesn't want to do it. Or have me do it."

John's knife stilled. "You offered?"

"Yes."

"I see."

"Is that a problem?"

John set the bread on his plate. "You know we believe in God's law, not man's."

"Asking a man to make something right isn't going against God's law."

"Interesting argument. But it's up to Him to settle such matters."

Mark pushed aside his plate. "It's hard for me to see a wrong and not try to make things right. To leave everything up to God."

"But He's in charge of everything in our lives."

That stopped Mark. He hadn't let God be in charge of his life in a long time. Maybe ever. He'd always figured he would take care of himself, and let God take care of bigger issues, of other people who needed Him more.

"I can see you're struggling with this."

"You bet. If nothing else, if these teenagers don't face the consequences of their actions, they could hurt someone else, do more damage. Maybe even do worse."

"And you think that, if we leave it to God, they'll never face those consequences?"

"I don't think we should have to wait around for them. Or have good people like Abraham and his family suffer financially and physically in the meantime."

"And what about you?" John picked up the piece of bread and bit into it.

"What about me?"

"Are you tired of waiting around for Him to resolve the problem in your life?"

Mark chuckled. "You know the answer to that."

"Ask yourself if you want to help Abraham and his family because it's the right thing for them, or the right thing for you."

"How can it be the right thing for me?"

"I think you really want to help because you have a good heart. But it might not be the right thing for Abraham and his family."

They cleared the table, washed the dishes, and walked out to the barn to do the last check of the animals before bed.

"Well, I'm going to read for a while," John said.

"I think I'll take that shower and hit the sack. Had a long day today and I'm sure tomorrow will be one as well."

John gave him a pat on the shoulder as he headed toward the living room.

Mark climbed the stairs. He would read for a while, too ... on his computer. He needed to contact his private investigator and do some research. There had to be a way to help Abraham that was compatible with Amish law.

He just had to find it.

Nineteen

Miriam didn't need the calendar to know summer was finally fading . . . or rather, melting away.

When she walked outside one morning, she felt a small drop in temperature and a lessening of humidity in the air. Every *dochder* of a farmer was in tune to the weather.

She was looking forward to a new school year. There was nothing better than seeing those bright, shining faces on her scholars, whether they were new to her *schul* or returning for another year. She loved planning lessons and seeing young faces light up when they understood a new lesson. It was a joy to watch the older *kinner* help the younger ones. And it was such fun to go out onto the small playground next to the *schul* and join in ball games or other sports during recess.

Soon she'd be surrounded by *kinner* for much of her day, trusted to carry forward their academic and spiritual education. Here in her community, she was not only allowed but encouraged to bring prayer and church teachings into her *schul* room. She'd be forever thankful to John for her teaching job.

She was seated at the kitchen table, chin in hand, papers spread in front of her, when her *dat* walked in.

"Now there's something I don't see often," he said as he walked to the kitchen sink to wash his hands. "Miriam the whirlwind actually sitting still."

She laughed. "I have my quiet, still moments."

"Not often." Daniel said as he dried his hands on a dishtowel. "You're a busy little bee, for *schur*. Always have been." He gestured at her papers. "Looking forward to *schul* starting, eh?"

"Mmm. And I bet you and *Mamm* are looking forward to having some peace and quiet during the day."

Sarah came into the kitchen and went straight for the coffee Miriam had made. She looked at her *mann* and, when he nodded, poured him a cup, too.

"Miriam thinks we're looking forward to having some peace and quiet when *schul* starts."

"*Nee*, your *dat* and I walk around complaining it's too quiet those first few weeks," Sarah said. "But part of being a parent is learning to watch your *kinner* grow to be independent. What's that saying about giving them roots and wings?"

Miriam smiled. "It's a *gut* saying. You do that as parents and I have to do that as a teacher." Her smile faded. "The Miller *kinner* came home just as I was leaving the other day. It broke my heart to see how quiet they were, how bruised."

Sarah sat at the table and patted her hand. "*Kinner* bounce back quickly. They'll be fine."

"Their oldest will be attending *schul* for the first time this year. I couldn't help thinking things could have turned out very differently."

"But they didn't," her *dat* said quietly.

She sighed. "I know. It's just hard to see people you care about suffering."

"Faith isn't easy. I don't think it's meant to be."

"Have you always been so wise?"

She chuckled and shook her head. "*Nee*. Your *dat* will tell you so."

"*Nee*, I won't," he disagreed. "She's the wisest, most beautiful woman I know."

"Oh, go on now," she said, blushing.

Miriam loved the way her parents loved each other. She hoped God had something just as *wunderbaar* planned for her. It wouldn't matter how long she had to wait, so long as God brought her someone like her *dat*, someone who would love her like he loved her *mudder*.

Well, *nee*, she didn't want to wait too long. And if she was honest, she still wished that man could be Mark.

She jerked to attention when the timer on the oven dinged. "Biscuits are done. *Dat*, do you want your eggs scrambled or fried?"

"Whatever's easiest," he said.

"You always say that."

"*Ya*," he said with a grin. "So why do you keep asking?"

She served him two of the golden brown biscuits and pushed the dish of butter and jar of blackberry jam closer to his plate. Then she brought the basket of eggs to the stove and began cracking them into a big bowl. She beat them and poured them into the cast iron skillet she'd been heating on the stove.

As she worked, Miriam gazed out the window as the sunrise spread light over the sweeping expanse of fields. The view filled her with peace and joy.

Daniel finished his breakfast and returned to his chores in the barn.

Little feet began pattering down the stairs—bare feet for summer. Soon the weather would force her and the *kinner* to don shoes for *schul*, but for now it was so *gut* to have the freedom of bare feet, to feel the grass and warm earth beneath her toes.

She remembered how appalled Mark had been the first summer he'd visited and seen the Amish *kinner* running around barefooted. Couldn't their family afford shoes? he'd asked. He knew they had a lot of children, but shoes were important, kept them from getting hurt.

Then he'd looked down and seen her bare toes. He'd turned red and stammered while she laughed. Before summer was over, he'd gone without shoes himself when he wasn't working in the fields.

Miriam served the eggs, helped butter biscuits and wipe chins when purple jam dripped on them, and turned the meal into a lesson. She'd used two eggs for each of them to make the scrambled eggs they ate. How many eggs had she used in total?

Isaac rolled his eyes. "*Schul's* starting soon. Can't we do this then?"

She ruffled his blond hair and it stood up in little spiky tufts that reminded her of a chick's downy head. "What if you forget your multiplication tables before then?"

"I won't forget."

"*Allrecht*, then. Prove it." Miriam poured more coffee into her *mudder's* cup.

Isaac scrunched his forehead, looked thoughtful.

"Twenty-eight!" Emma piped up.

"I was gonna say that!" he cried. "That's not fair, Miriam! You asked me."

"I asked all of you. Katie could have answered if she wanted."

He snorted. "Like she could! You're being silly." He made a face at Katie and she giggled and slapped her hands on the plastic tray of her high chair, scattering biscuit crumbs.

"I thought we could drive into town later today for some supplies," Sarah said. "I thought I'd get some fabric to make a few new dresses and shirts for the *kinner.*"

"Can we come?" Emma asked.

"*Schur.*"

"I'll stay and help *Daed,*" Isaac said. "I don't want to look at stuff like that."

"Me, too," said Jacob. "I'll stay."

"It's nice to have a kind of girl's day out," Miriam said as they rode into town. "Even if it's just for a few hours." She glanced into the back seat. "Katie's asleep."

"She always falls asleep when we go for a ride." Sarah said and she smiled. "You, on the other hand, were always awake and ready to jump into action."

"*Daed* called me a busy bee."

They passed the Miller farm. Miriam felt her spirits sink.

"Don't be sad. Things will work out. You know they will."

Miriam turned and forced herself to smile. "*Ya.*"

✍✍✍

Mark rubbed his forehead. A headache was beginning to form. He shut down his laptop and rose to set it on the dresser.

Lou had come through with the name and address of the teenaged driver who had hit the Miller buggy. He hadn't found any other information about any crimes the kid had committed, but that didn't surprise Mark. Juvenile records were protected from the public.

Of course, there was a good reason. Teens were considered immature and deserving of a chance to learn from their mistakes. By keeping their juvenile records secret, they had a chance to go into adulthood without a criminal record.

Mark thought that was fine, so long as the crimes were minor in nature. The buggy situation hadn't been. It had been a deliberate act that had caused injuries to humans and animals as well as to valuable, necessary farm property. And the whole thing could have been worse. As Miriam had pointed out, the Miller children had been traumatized, and both they and their parents could easily have been killed.

And so far, the teen hadn't even been arrested for his crime. Something had to be done. He'd given Abraham a couple of days to think about their conversation. He figured it was time for them to talk again.

There was a rap on his bedroom door. His grandfather stuck his head in. "Church tomorrow at the Zooks' house. Thought you might like to go."

It was on the tip of his tongue to say no, but he hadn't attended a service since he came, and this might give him an opportunity to talk to Abraham.

"I might. I'll let you know in the morning?"

"*Schur*. Sleep well."

"You, too."

Dawn came earlier on Sunday than other days of the week. Or at least it seemed to do so this morning. And his grandfather seemed to make more noise than he did on other days. Did he do that so that Mark would get up and join him for church?

He lay there in bed for a long moment, remembering Sundays back in his world. He'd get up late, meet Tiffany for brunch at the country club her parents belonged to, and spend the afternoon in the VIP box at some pro sports team event or playing racquetball with his buddies.

Then he got up.

His grandfather was important to him, and if he wanted Mark to go to church with him today, it was the least he could do. In any event, while the services were long, he'd enjoyed himself in years past.

He remembered visiting the Zook home many times, but this was the first he'd been in it for a church service. There was something very intimate and simple about a church service in a family's home. Perhaps it was one of the reasons the family, the community, was stronger here.

As he and his grandfather found seats in the men's section of the temporary benches brought into the Zook home, Mark was welcomed by the men he'd been working with this summer. A flurry of motion made him glance over at the women's section. Miriam smiled and nodded.

It took Mark a moment to recognize the sober looking man who walked to the front of the room. Was that really Samuel Troyer dressed in Sunday best and about to lead the service as lay minister? Mark had joined him on some adventures looking for a beer on a hot summer night when Samuel was on his *rumschpringe*. Fortunately, they'd never gotten in serious trouble. Mark knew what damage an arrest could do to his chances of getting into law school, and Samuel was deeply afraid of what his mother could do to him.

Mark had met Mrs. Troyer, and she could scare any boy straight.

A few minutes later, Abraham came in and took a seat. His arm was still in a cast and sling. Dark shadows lay under his eyes and his mouth was bracketed by lines of pain. He avoided Mark's gaze.

Well, that was fine. He was looking forward to beating down that resistance. He'd won over many a jury whose nonverbal body language had signaled an uphill battle to prove his client's innocence.

The assemblage quieted and Samuel began. Mark had always liked the Amish choice of lay ministers more than the paid ministers in the church his parents had attended. It seemed to him that the message of faith was more humble, more sincere, coming from a peer than from some man of the cloth who held himself above his congregation.

Samuel spoke of gratitude for God's abundance as the harvest grew to a close.

Mark winced at the reminder of how long he'd been here.

"You *allrecht*?" his grandfather leaned close to ask.

He nodded, keeping his eyes on Samuel.

The hymn singing soothed him as it always had. Voices raised in praise—pure and simple, without musical accompaniment—touched him in a way no other had.

When the service ended, he remained in his seat, weighed down by a flood of mixed emotions.

"Did you fall asleep, *sohn?*" John teased.

"No, no, of course not. Just thinking." He got up and helped turn the benches into seating for the light meal the women would soon serve.

"Mark, so *gut* to see you join us this morning," Samuel said, holding out his hand and grinning. "Did I surprise you by leading the service?"

"A bit," Mark admitted.

The tips of Samuel's ears turned red. Mark chuckled and leaned closer. "Don't worry, what happened during that one summer is our little secret," he murmured.

"*Gut.*"

He watched Abraham quietly slip out of the room, and an idea came to him.

Maybe Samuel could help him persuade Abraham to accept his help in getting restitution for the buggy and the medical expenses.

"Listen, Samuel, do you think we could talk outside for a few minutes later?"

"*Schur.*"

Mark settled down with one of his favorite after-church treats— "church spread," a mixture of peanut butter and marshmallow spread on home-baked bread. "I remember *Grossmudder* used to give this to me," he said, slipping into Pennsylvania *Dietsch.*

John nodded and his faded blue eyes warmed. "She knew it was one of your favorites."

"And her ginger cookies."

"*Ya.* I miss those."

"I didn't know you missed those." Miriam approached with a tray filled with glasses of iced tea. "I'll make you some."

"*Ach*, you're a *gut maedel*," John said. "You do too much for me."

"It's a pleasure," she said simply. "Mark? Some iced tea?"

Mark accepted a glass gratefully. The church spread was rich and stuck to the roof of his mouth. He finished the light meal and took his plate and glass to the kitchen, then caught Samuel's eye and jerked his head in the direction of the front of the house. Samuel met him there.

"You wanted to talk?"

Mark guided him toward the rocking chairs and they sat. "I spoke with Abraham the other day," he began without preamble. "I'd like to help him get restitution for the damage to the buggy and the medical expenses."

Samuel set the rocking chair in motion with his foot and stroked his beard. "You know it's not our way to press charges."

"Of course I do. But there are ways to get a guilty party to pay for the consequences of his actions."

"We look to God for justice, not to man's law."

No matter what argument Mark came up with, Samuel remained as unconvinced as Abraham.

"I was hoping you'd help me talk to Abraham about it."

Samuel stopped rocking and shook his head. "But I will talk to you about why we Amish feel this way, if you like," he said gently.

"No," Mark said with a sigh. "Thank you. I have my grandfather for that."

"A *wunderbaar* man to talk to about it," Samuel said with great seriousness. "I've learned much about faith from John." He paused. "And I think you have, too, *ya*?"

"*Ya*," Mark said, and realized for the second time that afternoon he'd slipped into the language he'd learned at his grandfather's knee.

Samuel went back into the house. His grandfather came out a short time later. "Ready to go home?"

Mark stood. "I'll get the buggy."

John sat in a rocking chair and grinned. " And I'll let you do that."

Twenty

It was Miriam's favorite day of the year. Even better than Christmas. Well, maybe not better than Christmas.

She adored the first day of *schul*.

No need to set her alarm. She woke an hour early and fairly jumped out of bed. For weeks, she'd reviewed her lesson plans and spent hours cleaning her small one room classroom. Her *bruders* and *schweschders* traveled to the *schul* with her, of course, and knowing they wouldn't want to be there as early as she liked, she made pancakes—the family favorite—before calling them downstairs.

Their clothes had been laid out the night before, lunches packed, and they'd been persuaded to go to bed early by her promise to read them an extra story.

Now she stood on the front steps of the *schul* and watched *kinner* making their way up the road carrying their lunch boxes and chattering madly.

They filed inside, giving her bright smiles and a cheerful, "*Guder mariye*, Miriam!"

Once the last scholar had stepped inside, Miriam shut the door and walked to the front of the room. The blackboard was scrubbed clean and bore the date and a quote from the Bible. A banner with the alphabet in block and cursive letters was pinned above it for the younger scholars. The wood burning stove under one window sat cold and empty for now. It wouldn't be long before she'd fill it with wood and it would burn cheerfully, warming the room and the occasional foil-wrapped sandwich a scholar set on top of it at lunchtime.

She began the day with a prayer, then started the *kinner* on their lessons. It was a challenge teaching all grades, but one she relished. Older scholars often helped younger ones with arithmetic or reading, which reinforced their own understanding. Here, too, scholars learned to get along with not only *kinner* from other families, but with their own siblings.

And how special was it that she taught her own *bruders* and *schweschders*?

"Recess!" she called, and made sure she was out of the way of the door. Her first week teaching, she hadn't remembered to do that and had nearly been mowed down. Amish *kinner* worked hard and played hard. They were always eager to get outside when the weather was *gut*.

The weather was so gorgeous this time of the year. Crisp enough for sweaters but not too cold for playing outside. She enjoyed being out with them and did her best to hide her own regret when they had to go back inside.

The day ended too soon. She didn't assign homework on the first day, but didn't often anyway. Amish *kinner* started and ended their day with chores on the farm.

She had chores when she got home, too, helping her *mudder* with the *kinner*. But she lingered at *schul*, straightening the desks into orderly rows, wiping down the blackboard and writing the next day's Bible quote, date, and lessons. Her *bruders* and *schweschders* walked home with other *kinner* so she could stay and finish her work.

It felt so *gut* to be back here with work that centered her and made her feel useful. That was most important to her—being useful.

She wondered what Mark had done that day. Had he heard from any of the firms he'd written to looking for a new job? It was still hard for him to not do the work he'd trained for, even though he was such a help to his grandfather.

Today could be the day he'd hear and be gone from her life . . .

She forced away the thought, locked the door to the *schul*, and started home.

Fall didn't just signal the beginning of *schul*. Weddings began to be performed. One of the first was Fannie Mae's, and Miriam served as one of her attendants.

Fannie Mae glowed all during the daylong festivities. Miriam had begun to wonder if she would ever marry the man she'd loved most of her life. Abram had been so determined that they start off right with their own place, but finally she'd convinced him that she didn't mind living with his parents until they could afford one. After all, so many couples did that here. Since they were good friends, Fannie Mae had told Miriam of the conversation with him.

Busy with her duties as one of the *newehockers*, Miriam didn't notice Mark at first. She was startled when she carried a tray to one of the tables and found him seated there with his grandfather.

He grinned at her. "You look surprised to see me."

"I am," she said, setting a glass of iced tea before him.

"I was invited."

"Well, of course you were," she replied. "You're part of the community after all. Hello, John. You're looking handsome today."

"Hey, what about me?" Mark demanded, his eyes alight with mischief.

"You look nice, too," she said quickly, feeling her face redden.

"Nice?" he said, acting indignant. "Nice?"

His laughter followed her as she moved on, serving others at the table. Did he notice how the other *maedels* here stole glances at him? He was taller than most of the men here, with darker hair, and he had that air of confidence that was so attractive. And she was sure that he was even more attractive to the other *maedels* because he was *Englisch* and therefore more than a little forbidden to them. She knew they were curious about whether he was going to stay. If he did, he'd inherit one of the most prosperous farms in the county.

She carried the empty tray back to the kitchen, and as she passed his table, he winked at her, teasing and irrepressible as always.

The day was long, but weddings were always so much fun for a community that had worked hard. They enjoyed any reason to get together, but especially one that saw two people in love joined in marriage. Wedding days started early with the ceremony in the bride's house followed by a bountiful noon meal. Baked chicken and *roasht* were always the star of the meal. Her *dat* always asked her *mudder* to prepare anything but chicken or turkey for Thanksgiving because so much baked chicken and *roasht* was eaten at the many weddings after the harvest. Creamed celery was a special feature here in Lancaster County, one Miriam liked.

She sat and pretended to eat after she finished serving. It wasn't her nature to feel envy, but she felt a little let down today. She kept telling herself she wasn't an old *maedel*, but still, *maedels* younger than her were getting married.

"Not hungry?"

She looked up. Mark stood before her. "*Nee*, I had a big breakfast." She hoped she didn't blush at the fib.

He sat in the empty chair beside her. "If this were an *Englisch* wedding, I'd ask you to dance."

"I wouldn't know how."

"It's easy."

She couldn't imagine being held so close to a man, dancing with him. Now she *did* feel herself blushing.

If he noticed, he didn't show it. Instead he watched the *kinner* playing a game.

"I can't believe a wedding lasts all day here," he said. "The only time I was a guest at a wedding that lasted all day, it was one I was invited to by a friend whose family is Greek." He leaned back in his chair. "Boy, there was some great dancing at that one. Everyone dances, no matter how old or young, in a big circle, with lots of enthusiasm. Had my first taste of ouzo. Had lots of ouzo." He grimaced. "I found out it's more … potent … than anything I've had before. My friend had a wedding videographer. I kind of made a fool of myself dancing."

"I can't imagine you making a fool of yourself."

"If you ever meet Paul, he'll insist on showing the video to you."

She laughed. "Sounds like you enjoyed yourself."

"Perhaps too much."

"You need to do that sometimes. You've always been a very serious man."

"Says a very serious woman."

She shrugged. "Maybe. It wouldn't do for the teacher to be silly."

Fannie Mae and her *mann* rose from the *eck*, the corner of the table where the new couple sat, and walked around and visited with their guests. Before Miriam knew it, it was time to serve the evening meal.

"I'm stuffed," Mark groaned when she brought a basket of rolls to his table.

"Me, too," said John and he patted his stomach. "I think it's time for me to be getting on home."

Miriam's mood had lightened during the day, but now she felt her mood shifting.

Always a newehocker, never a bride. She carried the empty tray to the kitchen. How soon could she leave without being rude?

A few minutes later, Sadie walked up to her looking upset. "Miriam, I feel sick."

Miriam put the back of her hand to her sister's forehead the way she'd always seen her *mudder* do. "You feel warm. Let's go tell *Mamm* we're going home."

"Something wrong?" Mark appeared at her side.

"I don't feel well," Sadie replied.

"I'm going to tell *Mamm* I'm taking her home."

"I'll get my car and drive you."

"*Nee*, there's no need—"

But he was already gone.

Miriam put her arm around Sadie's shoulders and led her to her *mudder*.

♫♫♫

"I like your car, Mark."

He glanced at Sadie in the rear view mirror and smiled. "Thank you. I like it, too."

"This is nice, but you really didn't have to do it," Miriam said.

"Are you feeling okay?"

"Me? Of course. I'm fine."

"You seemed quiet at the wedding."

She shrugged. "I'm just a little tired, that's all. It was a busy week."

"Mark? I hafta throw up!"

He quickly checked traffic, pulled over, and helped Sadie out of the car. He led her to the passenger side as Miriam hurried out of her seat. Sadie threw up, and when she finished, she began crying.

"Here, bathe her face with this." Mark handed Miriam a handkerchief he'd dampened with the bottle of water he kept in the car. "Do you want me to drive you to the emergency room?"

"*Nee*, she's just running a little fever. Probably ate too much candy at the wedding. She'll be fine. I'll get her home, give her some Tylenol, and tuck her into bed."

"I can't get in the car!" Sadie wailed when Miriam began leading her back to it. "What if I need to throw up again?"

"Don't worry about it," Mark reassured her. He looked at Miriam. "Get in the back seat with her. I'll see what I have in the trunk."

He found a blanket he'd tucked in there the time he'd taken Tiffany for a picnic. Talk about a bust. She complained about the heat (a moderate eighty degrees). Bugs bothered her (a ladybug and a butterfly). And she barely ate any of at the gourmet food he'd picked up.

Shaking his head at the memory, Mark carried the blanket to the back seat and tucked it around Sadie. "There. That'll keep you warm, and if you need to throw up and I can't stop in time, you can just use this, sweetie." He glanced at Miriam. "Don't worry about the car. It can be cleaned."

She nodded and smiled.

The remainder of the ride home was uneventful. All three of them were grateful for that. He carried Sadie inside and up to bed, then returned to the front porch

"I'll stick around for a few minutes in case you need anything," he told Miriam.

"There's no need. We have Tylenol."

"I'm sticking around," he said firmly.

Miriam went back inside, and Mark helped himself to a rocking chair, his thoughts once again turning to Tiffany. It wasn't just the blanket that had reminded him of her today. Did weddings remind people of their own relationships? Especially the failed ones?

Miriam had said she was tired from her week, but she was the most energetic woman he knew. Maybe she'd been thinking of relationships today, too. So many of her friends were married.

"She's already asleep," Miriam said when she returned. "I checked her temperature and it's only slightly above normal." She sat in the rocking chair beside him. "*Danki* for staying, but it wasn't necessary."

He shrugged. "I didn't mind. It was a lovely wedding, but I was ready to go home. To tell the truth, I'm not a big fan of weddings right now."

"I guess not," she said slowly. "When were you supposed to get married?"

"After the first of the year."

"Today's wedding must be very different from the *Englisch* ones. I've seen the bridal magazines. Ours are pretty simple compared to the ones in them."

"Simple, maybe, but there was something special about the ceremony," Mark said. "It was the way it should be. Two people pledging their love before friends and family. Prayers said for them. Voices raised in song. The important things were there. All the rest, the expensive rings, the fancy flowers, satin runners, photographers … they're just trappings."

He looked at her. "But then, I'm a guy. Most of us don't care much about that sort of stuff. Well, except for wedding cake. Now that's something we guys care about, you know?"

Miriam smiled. "Did you have a piece of cake today?"

"Two. It was very good cake."

Twilight fell. Buggies began rolling past on the road before the house.

"People are going home from the wedding," Miriam commented.

"I guess I should go and help my grandfather with the evening chores. He seems to tire more these days, like his arthritis is bothering him."

"It's been *gut* you've been here."

"I don't know how much help I've been, but I've enjoyed it." And Mark meant it. He stood. "Hope Sadie feels better."

And you, too, he wanted to add. *There's something faintly sad about you today and I'm afraid to ask you more about it. Some things are just too personal even between such good friends.*

Instead, he said goodbye, headed home, and wondered if he'd done the right thing.

Twenty-One

Miriam pulled a plastic container from the wicker picnic basket and set it on the quilt Mark had spread on the grass beside the pond. "So the talk with Abraham didn't go well? I'm so sorry."

Mark sighed and shook his head. "You have nothing to apologize for."

"But I asked you to talk to Abraham. I fear I've just added to the frustration you've felt since you came here."

He stretched out his legs. "I knew what I was up against. I'm not a complete newcomer to this community. I was just hoping I could help the family somehow."

"I'm ... conflicted about this." She handed him a container of cold fried chicken. "I grew up saying 'God's will,' but I am a teacher and I teach consequences. What will happen if there are no consequences to the actions of these young men?"

Mark chose a golden brown leg and bit in. "Granddad said eventually they'll have consequences. That God sees to it." He swallowed. "I swear, you could be rich if you sold your fried chicken."

"You exaggerate," Miriam replied. But it was worth standing in the still-warm kitchen the night before to make the chicken. It wouldn't be a picnic without fried chicken. Or potato salad made from her *mudder's* recipe. She fixed her own plate. "So, I guess that's it."

He shook his head. "I have the name and address of the driver. I'm going to pay a little visit to him."

"You are?"

"Nothing says I can't let this young man know that I know what he did. Intimidate him a little, make him wonder what I'll do."

Miriam stared at him. She'd often wished she had a chance to see him in the courtroom. Now she saw a glint in his eyes, heard a cold purpose in his voice.

She wouldn't want to face him if she'd done wrong.

"I believe in our system of justice, of looking out for the victim. I

175

want justice for the family. If Abraham won't prosecute, I can still put the squeeze on this … guy."

She had the feeling he wanted to use a more colorful word than "guy," but had cleaned up his language for her. Undoubtedly he thought she was an innocent Amish *maedel* who'd faint at a bad word.

"When are you going to do this?"

He laughed. "You sound like you'd like to be there." He chose another piece of chicken. "And no, you can't."

She pouted. "Not even if I let you have my share of this strawberry shortcake?"

Mark gazed at the dish she held out. "Nope. Sorry."

Miriam portioned out the shortcake, holding out the bigger piece to him.

"Bribes won't work."

She laughed and handed it to him. "You're no fun."

"Speaking of fun, I saw something on the way here that might be fun."

"What is it?"

"It's a surprise. We'll go as soon as you finish eating, slowpoke."

Typical man, she thought. He'd already demolished his serving.

She handed him the remainder of her shortcake and threw the plastic containers into the picnic basket. "Ready."

He drove them to a pumpkin patch attraction an *Englisch* family had run on their farm for many years. All sizes of pumpkins were available for sale, as were apple cider, dried cornstalks, and hay bales for fall decorations.

"Look, a maze!" a child cried as he ran past them.

"I've never done one of these," Mark said. "I always had to go back home before they set this up."

"Why would you want to get lost in a corn maze?"

He grinned. "I don't intend to get lost. Bet I can make it to the end faster than you."

"You are so competitive!" Miriam laughed.

"Chicken?"

She pulled some bills from her purse. "I'm paying. And when I finish first, you have to do something I want."

"Deal."

As they waited in line to pay for the popular activity, she cast a surreptitious look at him. The time spent working in the fields had bronzed his skin, streaked his hair, and honed his already athletic body. He stood more relaxed and at ease than she'd seen him since the day he'd arrived.

And she wasn't the only woman noticing.

"See you!" he said and was suddenly gone, streaking down a path cut into the corn field.

Miriam knew it wasn't speed that would win. Taking the time to think before heading down a path was the best plan.

But it took no time at all for her to realize she was hopelessly lost. Every cornstalk looked the same as the last one. If only she had some crumbs to toss down on the path like Hansel and Gretel.

She stopped and waved a hand at her face, wishing for a cooling breeze. The path seemed to narrow. Cornstalks pressed in on each side of her. The air grew musty. Her chest hurt when she tried to breathe. Her heart pounded.

This wasn't fun. She wanted out. Now!

A little girl ran past, shouting for her mother.

Miriam wanted to do the same.

She trudged on, and when she came to a fork in the cornstalks, she thought of the Frost poem and wondered which path to take.

What would have happened if she had pursued her interest in higher education? She'd envied Mark for being able to go to college. What would it have been like to study in the classrooms with others and discuss great ideas, great literature? To have the freedoms the *Englisch* enjoyed? To be near Mark? To discuss thoughts and hopes and dreams with him, not just during the summer? She'd have been near him because he'd offered to ask his parents to let her stay at their house while she attended college.

It would have meant giving up everything she knew and loved—her family, her home, her community. That's what it would've been like.

So she read and studied library books. Just because she didn't attend *schul* beyond the eighth grade as the Amish had for generations didn't mean education ended. So many were voracious readers. And no one loved to talk more than the Amish. If one had a listening ear, one could learn a lot.

At this moment, Miriam wished she'd listened to her *dat* more about how to study the sun and the shadows it cast in order to tell time and direction.

She wiped perspiration dripping down her face. It was so hot here in the maze.

Someone yelled a row over, and for a long moment she longed to do the same. Surely if Mark heard her, he'd come to her rescue.

Nee, she told herself sternly. *You're not a* kind. *You can figure this out. It doesn't matter if you're first. Just get out.*

She trudged on. A ribbon fluttered on a cornstalk. Had she seen it before? Her dress clung to her. She longed for a glass of water.

She was going to make Mark pay for this if she made it out alive. And if she won, she was going to make him do something he really wouldn't like ... maybe shoveling out the horse stalls in the barn. Or killing and cleaning a chicken for supper.

Or maybe she'd make him take the *kinner* someplace one day. All of them. *That* would be the perfect punishment. Oh, they were *gut* kinner, but running after them for a few hours should test that easy charm and patience of his.

She came to another fork in the cornstalks and sent up a prayer. *Please*, Gott, *get me out of here!*

Tears filled her eyes. She blinked furiously, determined not to cry. Then, because her vision was blurred, she tripped on a root and fell flat. She sat up, but when she tried to stand, she cried out in pain.

She'd had enough. "Mark? Mark? Can you hear me?"

But all she heard was the rustling of the cornstalks as the wind swept through them.

Mark was getting a kick out of the maze. Figuring it out was turning out to be no effort at all for his analytical mind. He was going to win this one.

Too bad it wasn't as easy to figure out the twists and turns of his life lately. Sometimes he felt like Job.

Okay, so that was being melodramatic. He hadn't faced the trials and tribulations of the biblical Job.

He'd get another job. He had a home here with a grandfather he loved, a dear friend like Miriam, and other friends in the community. And he enjoyed farming. Always had. It must run in the genes. If his father hadn't chosen to leave this place, he'd have even grown up here, likely married Miriam.

He came to a screeching halt. What? Married Miriam? Where had that come from?

"Hey, mister!" a kid cried as he veered around him and ran ahead of him on the path. "Watch out!"

"Sorry!"

Mark began walking again, but slower. The thought had never occurred to him before. But the fact was, in the Amish community, couples grew up together, became friends, and then often those friendships matured into marriages. Surprisingly strong, enduring marriages. Sure, the prohibition against divorce kept some couples together, but it was only a small part of it from what he'd witnessed. Amish couples were close because they knew each other so well before marriage, and if they weren't compatible, they didn't marry. They often worked together as partners managing a farm or running a business, and they shared child care and embraced their elderly family living with them.

He'd become engaged after mere months. How well could anyone know someone in that amount of time? Was it any wonder it had fallen apart at the first sign of a problem?

Up ahead lay two paths. He considered for a moment, gazed up at the sun, down at how the cornstalks threw a shadow, and thought about what grandfather had taught him. He turned right.

The day was growing warm. He'd worn a cotton short sleeved T-shirt and khaki pants, and wondered how Miriam was faring in her traditional modest dress. It couldn't be very cool. He stepped up the pace, eager to get out of the sun and get a cold drink. Maybe some ice cream on the way home? Yeah, he'd console her after her loss with ice cream.

He took the next turn and suddenly was free of the maze. Miriam was nowhere in sight. He grinned and sat on a nearby bale of hay.

Fifteen minutes later, he was still sitting waiting. He frowned. He'd teased her, but she had a pretty good sense of direction. Everyone they'd stood in line with had emerged several minutes ago.

He flagged down one of the employees. "Have you seen a young Amish woman come out?"

The man shook his head. "Want me to go in and look for her?"

If he knew anything about Miriam, she'd hate that. Mark glanced at his watch and shook his head. "I'll give her a few more minutes."

He pulled out his cell phone, checked for texts. In the old days there would have been dozens. Today there were just two. He read the one from Lou— and it was his usual cheery note saying he hoped to dig up something soon.

Mark sure hoped so, or he'd be digging deep into his savings.

Lani left a text that was more upbeat than her last one. The attorney she'd been assigned to "isn't you but he's okay." That was a relief. She wasn't just his paralegal and assistant—make that former assistant. She was a good friend and a hard-working single mother, and he didn't like her being unhappy or worrying if she had a job.

He checked the time again and frowned. What on earth was taking Miriam so long? The employee he'd spoken to before was nowhere to be seen, so Mark wandered around to the front and approached the woman who took the admission.

"My friend hasn't come out. I'm getting worried about her."

"No problem. We'll find her. I'll get my oldest to look for her. Hey, Bill, we've got a lost one. The lady who came in with this man. Young Amish woman."

A shaggy headed teenager nodded and loped off into the maze.

"Bill will find her real quick. You're looking warm. Want a root beer? Made from a recipe an Amish friend of mine gave me."

Concerned, Mark looked over her shoulder. "I should go find her."

"Give Bill a minute. Don't need two of you lost."

She was right. Business seemed slow and she looked anxious as she watched the road. He dug out his wallet. He bought a half gallon of apple cider, an apple pie, apple butter, and a bag of just-picked apples to take home to his grandfather.

Minutes ticked by. As he waited, Mark stared at the nearby fields and found his mind wandering. His thoughts went straight back to the disconcerting epiphany he'd had in the middle of the maze. The one that had stopped him dead in his tracks.

If his father hadn't left the community and raised him in Philadelphia, he would have grown up here and could very likely have married Miriam. What would it have been like to marry her?

More minutes ticked by. "I'm going in."

He started into the maze, calling Miriam's name, but there was no answer. He turned right, then left, called her name again. Then suddenly she was there, limping toward him.

"Miriam!" Mark rushed forward and caught her as she fell into his arms. "Are you hurt?"

"I tripped and hurt my ankle."

She looked tired and hot and frazzled. She pushed at the strands of hair that escaped her *kapp* and stared at him. "Why are you looking at me like that?"

He shook his head. For the first time in his life, he was speechless. He thrust the root beer at her and she took it, looking grateful. She took a long sip, sighed, then turned to the teenager. "Thank you, Bill. If it wasn't for you, I might have been in there forever."

"No prob," the kid said, grinning.

She turned to Mark. "Well, I guess you're going to gloat."

"Me?" he said, finding his voice at last. "I never gloat."

"Hah! You love winning."

She knew him so well. "Sure. But I wouldn't think of it now."

When she tried to put weight on her injured foot and winced, Mark swept her up in his arms.

"What are you doing?"

"Isn't it obvious?"

"You don't need to carry me!"

"It's no prob." He winked and started for the car. She was light as a feather.

"Bill, please put this bag in the car for the nice people," the woman said behind him.

"Sure thing." The kid grabbed Mark's bag, hurried ahead of them to put it in the back seat, then opened the passenger side door for Miriam.

"Oh, wait, Mark! I wanted to get a bag of apples."

"I can get those for you," the teenager said.

Mark helped her into the car, then turned to the teenager and handed him some money. "Will this cover it?"

"Yup. Be right back."

When he returned and put the apples in the back seat, Mark handed him a ten dollar bill. "Thanks for all the help."

"Hey, man, I was happy to help. You don't have to tip me."

Mark gave him a level stare. "Yes, I do. Thank you." He turned and saw Miriam wincing in pain. Crouching down, he touched her ankle and frowned. "It's pretty swollen. I think I should take you to the emergency room."

"*Nee*, it's just twisted." She fanned her face with her hand. "Just take me home and *Mamm* will fix it."

He rounded the hood and slid into the driver's seat. The minute he started the car, he turned the air conditioning up to full blast.

"Oh, I love you," she said with a heartfelt sigh.

He jerked his head to stare at her. She was leaning close to the vent to cool her face.

Miriam opened her eyes. "Something wrong?"

"No." He pulled out onto the road and headed home. He had a lot to think about.

Twenty-Two

The second the words escaped her lips, Miriam blushed. "I'm sorry."

Mark glanced over. "Sorry? For what?"

"I didn't mean to say I loved you. I've obviously embarrassed you."

"You didn't embarrass me. Attorneys can't be embarrassed."

She laughed and leaned back in her seat. "You're just joking to try to make me feel less foolish."

"Is it foolish to say you love someone?"

She rolled her eyes. "You're making this worse. I meant it like, I love you, you know just what to do to make me feel better. Like turning on the air conditioning right away when I'm about to pass out from the heat."

"So you love me for my air conditioning."

"And the root beer. I really enjoyed the root beer. I was so thirsty."

She had to keep this light. If he ever discovered just how much she'd meant those accidental words, he'd start stammering and feeling sorry for her. She wouldn't be able to bear it. She just wouldn't.

"I love you as a friend, of course. A very *gut* friend."

"I was worried about you today," he said, staring ahead. "You were in there for a very long time."

"I know."

"I'm sorry that I dared you."

She shrugged. "You couldn't know I'd get lost."

"You're so capable. The most capable woman I know. I really did think you'd make it out of there quickly. Not as quickly as me but …" He turned to her, his eyes alight with mischief.

Then he sobered. "In the middle of the maze, I had a thought that stopped me in my tracks."

"About what?"

"You."

"Me?"

"Do you ever think about what might have happened if my dad had stayed here? If I'd grown up here?"

"What do you mean?"

"I never thought about it before. So much would be different if Dad had stayed here. I'm not saying I'm not glad he left since he didn't like it. But my life would have been so different. You know?" He hesitated, almost seemed to be about to say something, then stopped.

Oh yes, life would have been so different. Sometimes Miriam wondered if they'd have gotten married. ... *Schur,* she'd fantasized about what might have happened.

"Miriam?"

"I was just thinking. *Ya,* you're right. So many things would be different." She smiled. "You probably would have been a farmer. And the farm would pass to you. And John would be a happy man now."

"You're probably right. If I hadn't grown up in Philadelphia, I might not have become an *Englisch* attorney." He shook his head. "An unemployed *Englisch* attorney."

She shifted in her seat, trying to get comfortable. Her ankle hurt so much.

"You sure we shouldn't swing by the ER?"

"*Nee,* once I get some ice on it, I'm sure it'll be fine."

"Your parents are going to kill me," he muttered.

"They are not. I tripped, that's all."

A few minutes later he pulled into her drive. Miriam reached for her door, but before she could open it he grasped her arm. "Don't you dare move. Wait until I get around the car to help you."

She threw up her hands. "*Allrecht!*" She hoped he wouldn't touch her ankle again. His touch had made her shiver earlier. Fortunately he hadn't noticed ...

Then he was opening the door and reaching for her. "*Nee!*" she protested, batting away his hands.

He ignored her, scooped her up, and carried her up the porch steps.

"Remember what you said about my parents killing you?"

He gave her a wary look. "Yeah."

"Well, don't let *Daed* see you carrying me. Put me down."

He did as she asked, and she was sorry she'd had to. But a *maedel* just wasn't supposed to allow a single man to touch her that way.

And nothing made her sorrier. It had felt so *wunderbaar* to be cradled in those strong male arms.

She hobbled inside, Mark hard on her heels. Her *dat* was sitting in his recliner in the living room and he jumped up instantly.

"What happened?" he demanded.

"Just a silly accident. Where's *Mamm?*"

"In the kitchen." He followed them.

"*Mamm*, I twisted my ankle." Miriam sank into a chair. Mark pulled up a second one and lifted her foot onto it.

Sarah hurried over and slipped her shoe off as gently as she could, but it hurt a lot. "How did this happen?"

"I tripped on a root when I was going through the cornfield maze at the Henderson farm."

"Looks like a nasty sprain," her *mudder* said. "Let's get some ice on it."

Miriam glanced at Mark. "I had a *gut* time," she said.

He shuffled his feet, clearly uncomfortable as her father continued to stand there, silent. "Well, if you're sure you don't want me to drive you to the emergency room."

"She'll be fine," Sarah said as she placed a bag of ice wrapped in a dish towel on Miriam's foot.

"I'll be going then. Hope you feel better." Mark started to leave, then turned back. "Almost forgot the apples. I'll get them."

When he returned, he set the apples on the table.

"I thought the *kinner* and I could make caramel apples this week," Miriam told her *mudder*.

"I'll hide my knitting needles."

Miriam laughed. "Last year," she explained to Mark, "we ran out of sticks for the apples, so Jacob borrowed *Mamm's* bamboo knitting needles when I wasn't looking."

Mark chuckled. "Well, see you later."

She watched him go, then turned to her parents. "It really wasn't his fault. I just turned my ankle when I didn't see a root in the maze."

"I don't approve of you going to such an activity." He shook his head. "Halloween nonsense. Guess this was Mark's idea."

"It's just a maze where Mrs. Henderson sells her baked goods and such this time of year. Not a haunted house."

Daniel harrumphed and left the room.

Sarah set a glass of ice water in front of her, then sat down at the table. "We've talked about this before, Miriam. It's not a *gut* idea to keep doing things with him. He's not Amish."

Miriam sipped the water, then looked at her *mudder*. "He said something interesting today, *Mamm*. He asked me if I'd ever thought about what would have happened if his *dat* hadn't left here. If he—Mark, I mean—had grown up here." She shifted the ice bag on her foot. The ice was helping a lot. "I think Mark would have become a farmer, like John, maybe be inheriting it from his *dat* if he'd stayed." She thought about how Mark had hesitated, almost seemed to be about to say something and stopped. "And I wonder if I wouldn't have ended up marrying Mark."

"But his *dat* didn't stay, *kind*, and Mark is *Englisch*."

"I know, *Mamm*," Miriam said with a heavy sigh. "I know."

$$\mathcal{SSS}$$

"Hey, can I help you, dude?"

Mark turned from examining the SUV to the tall, gangly teenager walking out of the swanky home in a neighborhood of mini-mansions. "Yeah. You Jason Durham?"

"Who wants to know?"

Mark studied the teen, noting the wary look, the defensive posturing. Major attitude with a side of privilege.

"Me." He gestured at the dent in the bumper. "What caused this?"

"You the insurance adjuster or something?"

"Ah." Mark tilted down his sunglasses and pierced the kid with a hard look. "So you claimed this on your insurance?"

"That's none of your business if you're not the insurance adjuster."

"Did you happen to tell him you hit a buggy?"

The kid turned pale. "I'm not talking to you."

"Okay, then, maybe I'll talk to your parents. Bet they don't know the truth."

The kid's gaze slid past him to Mark's BMW.

"You a lawyer or something?"

"Or something." Mark gave him a feral grin.

"I don't have to talk to you. You haven't read me my rights."

"That's the cops. Maybe you'd like to avoid this going to court. Leaving the scene of an accident with injuries is a felony. The friend who was with you is an accessory, too."

A nervous tic flickered at the corner of the guy's mouth.

"The Amish don't do that. They don't go to the police or the courts. What are you saying, you're like that show about the Amish mob or something?"

"You have quite an imagination."

He backed up and nearly tripped on a sprinkler head on the lush green lawn. "Look, it was an accident."

"No, it wasn't. It was deliberate and you and your friend left the scene with injuries and property damage."

A car pulled into the drive behind them. Now the kid looked panicked. "My parents don't know. Keep quiet and I'll work a deal with you. Promise." He wiped at the sweat on his upper lip.

Mark stuck his hands in his pockets and rocked back on his heels. He watched as an attractive woman in her forties got out of another SUV and approached them.

"Hello," she said, giving him an appraising look. "Jason, who's your friend?"

"I just stopped to ask directions to the Amish community," Mark said. "I'm in town for a couple of days on business, decided to take in the sights."

"I see." She glanced at his BMW. "Well, after you tell him how to get there, Jason, we need to have a talk. The school called me today." She marched into the house.

Jason let out a sigh of relief. "Thanks, man."

"I'm having a chat with your mother in five minutes if I don't like what you have to say."

"Look, I don't need any hassle with the cops."

"No, you don't. And a struggling family doesn't need to scrape up money to fix their buggy or replace their horse if it doesn't live. The father has a broken arm and the children have bruises."

Jason swallowed again. "So how much are we talking?"

Mark had done the research. He'd asked Abraham how much the repairs cost, talked to the vet. The Amish community had pitched in to help Abraham with the medical costs, but Mark wanted that reimbursed as well as the vet bills. He named a figure.

The kid paled again and gulped. "I don't have that kind of cash."

Mark pulled out his cell phone.

"Hey, hold on! Jeez, I didn't say I couldn't get it!"

"How?"

He shoved his hands in his pockets, stared at his feet, and mumbled.

"I didn't catch that, pal."

"I said I'll sell some of my stuff." His jaw tightened as he glared at Mark. "I need two days."

Mark pulled a business card from his pocket and scribbled on it. "Get a cashier's check—not a personal one—made out to this name." He fixed him with his best intimidating stare. "I'll be back in two days, same time. Be here."

Jason nodded and trudged toward the house.

Mark watched him. It was the first time he'd used his legal skills on a minor. He searched his conscience. Nope, he didn't feel a drop of sympathy for Jason. Miriam had said Lovina heard the teens laughing as they drove off.

He'd seen those sad, too-quiet kids with their bruises, and didn't want to think about what might have happened if they'd been more seriously hurt. When a car and a buggy clashed, it was almost always bad for the occupants of the buggy.

Miriam had said there should be consequences.

He'd sure suffered consequences when he'd done something wrong growing up. How well he remembered his own mother disciplining him and calling it tough love.

The law called it justice.

SSS

He showed up at the appointed time two days later. The front door opened before he knocked, and the check was thrust at him.

But Mark had another idea. "Come with me. The offer to settle this includes your delivering this personally."

They stared at each other for a long moment. Then Jason grabbed his keys from a hook by the door. "Fine. But I'm taking my own car."

Mark glanced in the rear view mirror as he drove. Jason followed him dutifully. He pulled into the Millers' drive, parked, and watched as Jason's SUV pulled in beside him.

Abraham sat on the porch. Mark climbed the steps with Jason and introduced him.

"Jason here has something he wants to give you." With that, Mark stepped back.

Jason handed Abraham the check. Abraham's eyes widened.

"It's to fix your buggy, pay for the medical bills," Jason said, reddening.

"I see." Abraham studied the check.

"Look, he said that's what I needed to give you." Jason jerked his head toward Mark.

Abraham lifted his gaze. "Did he tell you that you had to?"

The screen door opened. "Mark? I thought I heard cars." Lovina glanced at the SUV and paled. "That's the car that hit us." She put her hand to her throat as she turned to stare at Jason. "Why are you here?"

Abraham held out the check to her. "He brought this. I was just asking Mark if he made him do it."

"*Mein Gott!*" Lovina gasped.

"*Mamm?* What's wrong?"

The Miller children stepped out of the house and clung to their mother's skirts.

"Nothing's wrong," Lovina said. "This man came to see us."

One of the two girls looked at the SUV. "That's the bad car! It hurt us!"

Jason edged toward the stairs, but Mark grasped him by the arm. "They were in the buggy that day."

"I didn't know," Jason sputtered. "I didn't know. Sorry."

"Don't say that to me." He indicated the Miller family now gathered around Abraham's chair.

Jason closed his eyes, nodded. He opened them and turned to the family. "I'm sorry."

The smallest girl walked over to him and grinned. "You want a cookie? *Mamm* makes *gut* cookies."

"I—" He looked at Mark. "I guess so. Yeah, I like cookies. My mom never makes them."

"You can have two," she promised him. She looked at her *mudder*. "Right, *Mamm*?"

"He *schur* can. Take him into the kitchen and all of you can have some," Lovina said, her eyes on Mark.

The children took Jason's hands and led him into the house.

As soon as they were out of earshot, Lovina turned to Mark. "Did you make him do this?"

"I just encouraged him to do the right thing." Mark turned to Abraham. "I wanted him to see what he'd done. At first it was just about getting you the money. Then I realized he needed to see the consequences of his actions." He glanced at the front door. "Would you deny this young man the chance to do the right thing by you? To learn from his mistake?"

Lovina looked at her *mann*. "*Kinner* need to learn such things, Abraham," she said quietly.

"*Mamm*," said one of the children as they returned to the porch. "I put some cookies in a bag for Jason. Is that *allrecht*?"

Lovina touched her face. "Of course."

"Well, I better go," Jason said. "My mom will pitch a fit if I haven't finished my homework by the time she gets home."

"Bye, Jason!" the children chorused.

"Bye!" He looked at Abraham and Lovina. "Thanks. I hope you feel better, Mr. Miller."

Abraham stood and held out his good hand. "Abraham. And this is Lovina. You stop by anytime and say hello."

Jason gulped and nodded. Then he rushed off to his vehicle.

"I hope he's learned something," Mark said. "I think he's been raised to have everything and hasn't thought about what he's doing, thought about other people. Hung with the wrong crowd."

Lovina smiled. "So are you trying to be a teacher like Miriam, Mark?"

He chuckled. "I hadn't thought about it that way."

"Ruth, are there any cookies left?" Lovina asked her daughter.

The child nodded.

"Then please put some in a bag for Mark."

Ruth raced off to do what her *mudder* told her.

"That's the first time she hasn't looked sad since the accident," Lovina told Mark. "*Danki.*"

Twenty-Three

"Miriam!"

At the sound of her name, Miriam turned from watering the flowers in the front yard and saw Lovina hurrying toward her.

Alarmed, she stood. "What is it? Are you *allrecht*?"

Lovina burst into tears. "You can't imagine what just happened!"

Miriam took her arm and led her to one of the rocking chairs on the porch. "Here, sit down. You're shaking. Is something wrong with Abraham? One of the *kinner*?"

"Mark brought that teenager who hit the buggy to our house." She pulled a tissue from her apron pocket and dabbed at her streaming eyes. "Miriam, he got him to give us a check to fix the buggy and pay for the medical expenses."

Her heart leaped. "He did?"

Lovina nodded. "He had him apologize, too. You know, he seemed really sorry. I think Mark had a good talk with him, made him see he'd done wrong." She chuckled. "I told Mark maybe he was trying to be a teacher like you."

Miriam sank into the chair beside her. "When did this happen?"

"Just a little while ago." Lovina tucked the tissue back into her apron pocket. "Abraham didn't want to take the check at first. He was afraid Mark had forced Jason. But he said he didn't. Jason, I mean." She sighed and leaned back into the chair. "Oh, this means we can get the buggy fixed and pay the vet and the hospital expenses."

A car pulled into the drive.

"There's our hero now," Miriam murmured.

"I should go so the two of you can talk," Lovina said and she jumped to her feet.

"Don't go," she said, but she couldn't take her eyes off Mark as he crossed the lawn with long strides.

Lovina chuckled. "See you later."

"*Allrecht.*" She watched Lovina stop, talk with Mark for a moment, and whatever she said made him smile.

How she loved that smile. She hadn't seen it much since he came here so upset about his job in the city.

Mark climbed the steps and sat down in the chair Lovina had vacated.

"I heard the good news. *Danki* for helping them. I knew you could."

Mark shrugged. "I didn't do much. I don't think Jason's a bad kid. He made a big mistake, but hopefully he's learned something from it." He looked out at the surrounding fields. "I went to college with some kids like him. They grow up with a lot of privilege, have parents who indulge them. Sometimes they don't realize there can be consequences to what they do." He stopped, turned to her, and grinned. "There's that word you love."

Miriam stared at him. It hit her hard at that moment. She loved him. Really loved him. He was a decent, caring man, one who did his best to help his *grossdaadi*, his friends in the community, a family in pain and need.

"Miriam?"

She realized he was staring at her, looking puzzled. "*Ya.* I'm sorry, I was just thinking about how happy Lovina was. She had a ... rougher time with this than you can know. The money can't make everything better, but it helps ease a lot of the worry for both of them."

"I got cookies for payment." He grinned. "I've never gotten cookies for my services before."

Miriam laughed. "Where are these cookies?"

"I ate three on the way over here."

"Lovina bakes *gut* cookies. I should find some way to thank you for what you did for them."

"You've already baked me plenty of cookies. And pies."

"Those were for you and John, and well before you agreed to help Abraham and Lovina."

"It's called *pro bono.*"

"Pro what?"

"*Pro bono.* Attorneys often help people who can't afford their services. I haven't done enough of it for some time. I worked too many hours. But maybe I'll think about doing some since I have some time on my hands."

193

Mark rocked for a few minutes in comfortable silence. "You know what was better than the cookies? Abraham and Lovina's youngest girl smiled. It felt so good to see her smile after the kids were so sad and quiet that day we were there together. I wish you'd been there to see it."

"Me, too."

He had such a *gut* heart. Who couldn't love a man who cared about *kinner* that way? Emotion swamped her. She stared at her hands folded in her lap and struggled for composure, for something to say to break the silence before he realized how she was feeling. He'd always understood her better than anyone except her *mudder*.

A buggy rolled past. Inspiration struck. She took a deep breath, plunged ahead.

"Saul told me the other day that he doesn't understand a letter he got about a permit he wants from the city." She looked at him. "Maybe you could help?"

"Are you trying to keep me busy?" he asked.

"Can't have you twiddling your thumbs after harvest is over," she shot back, feeling calmer. "Got to keep boys busy so they don't get into mischief."

He shot her a sharp glance. "Have you been talking to Samuel?"

"Should I?"

"No!" he said emphatically.

Miriam laughed. "I know the two of you sometimes went looking for trouble."

"I'll take the Fifth."

"I know what that means. No self-incrimination. But I don't think lawyers know how to keep their mouths shut, do they?"

He groaned. "Here come the bad lawyer jokes. I thought you said you didn't know any."

"I don't. I only know you."

He clapped a hand to his chest. "Oh, now you wound me. I'm a bad lawyer?"

Her jaw dropped. "Oh my, *nee*, I didn't mean that."

Mark touched her hand. "I know. I'm just teasing."

His touch sent a tingle all the way up her arm. Did he feel it, too?

Something shimmered in the air, an awareness even more powerful than she'd felt the other day. She leaned toward him, her gaze on his mouth …

The screen door creaked open, the sound echoing in the stillness like a gunshot. They sprang apart and Miriam jerked around to see who was coming out onto the porch.

She breathed a sigh of relief when she saw Isaac.

"Miriam, *Mamm* says see if Mark wants to stay for supper."

So her *mudder* knew he was out here with her. Did that mean she'd looked out the window, seen them about to kiss, and sent Isaac to interrupt them?

Mark stood quickly. "Tell her thank you, but I need to get home."

"*Allrecht.*" He went back inside, letting the door slam behind him.

"Miriam—"

"I have to go help *Mamm*. *Danki* for stopping by." She escaped like the chicken she felt herself to be.

$\mathscr{SSS}$

"Stupid, stupid, stupid," Mark muttered under his breath all the way home. What was the matter with him?

He couldn't act on his attraction to Miriam. He just couldn't. It wouldn't be fair to her when he returned home. And wouldn't it be a betrayal of their friendship?

She lived in a community where her innocence was protected, her relationships prescribed. Her future was traditional, predictable. Amish married Amish almost exclusively. There were few *Englisch* who converted to the Amish faith in order to marry, and the adjustment was hard.

And few Amish left the church to marry an *Englischer*. To do so meant being shunned by their community, family, and friends. He could never do that to Miriam. She loved her family and her school children so much.

He was in quite a mood when he got home, and was grateful to find the house empty. The best thing to do when he was in a bad mood was to avoid other people, so he went up to his room. He took his laptop from the dresser and sat down on the bed to check his email. There was nothing important. No responses to the four resumes he'd sent out several days ago to the top law firms in Philadelphia. Well, it was too early really to expect a response.

But it didn't mean he had to sit and wait. He opened the "Job Search" folder on his desktop and scanned the list of firms he wanted to apply to. Selecting the names of four more, he revised his cover letter to tailor it to each specific firm, then submitted them by email with his resume attached.

Then he reached out to two men he'd attended college with, asking if there were any vacancies at their firms. The thought that they already knew about his situation made Mark uncomfortable. It was easier to approach firms with which he wasn't acquainted. His finger lingered over the send button a moment before tapping it. Done. If they responded in the negative … well, he'd be no worse off.

And maybe, just maybe, he'd get a positive response.

There was a rap on the door frame and his grandfather poked his head in. "You hungry?"

"A little."

"Let's have some supper."

"Okay. I'll be right down."

He shut down the laptop and put it back on the dresser. His mood felt a little lighter as he descended the stairs. Doing something felt like progress. He made a mental note to charge the laptop and his cell phone in his car later. Thank goodness they were on the edge of the Amish community and he could piggyback on their *Englisch* neighbor's WiFi.

His grandfather had his head in the refrigerator. "Got some leftover baked chicken, bread, and butter summer squash, macaroni salad, some ripe tomatoes to slice."

"Sounds good." Mark glanced at the plastic container on the kitchen countertop. "What's that?"

John carried the cold chicken and a couple of containers from the refrigerator to the table and set them down. "Pie. Waneta, Lovina's *mudder*, dropped it off a little while ago. Told me what you did for her *dochder* and Abraham."

"She didn't need to do that." He shrugged. "Least I could do."

John gestured to the loaf of bread on the counter. "Bring that over and slice it for us. Well, you managed to do it in a way that didn't involve the police or the court. So it's a *gut* thing." He reached into a cupboard and brought plates to the table, then sat.

"Lovina said you brought the young man who hit them with his car, and he apologized. Sounds like a fine way to settle things. Maybe the boy will learn from the experience."

"That's what I hope." Mark searched for a way to change the subject. "Miriam's already decided I should help someone else. Said Saul doesn't understand some permit issue with the county. So I'm going over there tomorrow to see what's up. I figure it's just some legalese I can explain."

"You do know that," John acknowledged soberly.

They bent their heads to say thanks for the meal, then ate in silence for a few minutes.

"Glad you attended services on Sunday. Been a long time since you've done that."

"I've always enjoyed it. Mom got Dad to attend church, you know."

"*Nee*, I didn't."

"They settled on a Methodist church. Mom grew up Catholic, but that was too strict for Dad."

"He was always chafing about the rules of the *Ordnung* here." His grandfather stopped eating and stared into the distance. "He had to find a different path for himself, I guess." He looked at Mark. "And then he led you that way until they came for a visit and you wanted to come for the summer."

"I guess I've always walked both paths." *And felt divided.* But he didn't say it. He didn't want to upset John. Besides, it wasn't a bad thing to have experienced two such different cultures. He hoped that made him more sensitive to people, made him think along different lines. Outside the box, some might say. Odd expression, that.

He buttered a slice of bread and bit into it. Some days he felt he could make a meal out of just bread and butter, it was so good here.

His appetite picked up with the simple meal, surprising him.

"Got room for pie?"

"When don't I?"

John chuckled. "Never met a man, Amish or *Englisch*, who could turn down an Amish woman's pie. This one's blackberry."

One of his favorites. Had Waneta known that or was it just because the berries were in season now?

If work wasn't so hard here, he'd have had to worry about gaining weight. It was one of the things he was going to miss when he went back to Philadelphia.

He debated telling his grandfather about the resumes he'd submitted, and decided against it. Better to wait until he had some news.

"So you're going to help Saul?"

"I'll look over the permit situation for him. See if I have any advice for him."

"Thought you did criminal law."

"We get basic training before we specialize."

"I see." He polished off his piece of pie and cut another for himself.

Mark restrained himself from a second helping. After all, he'd had those cookies earlier.

They worked together to clear the table. Back home, it would have been a quick thing to stick the dirty plates in a dishwasher. But Mark didn't mind. He was learning not to rush, to do simple chores, to "be in the moment," as *Englischers* put it.

Then it was time for a last walk out to the barn to check on the animals. Mark had come to think of it as a parent tucking in their children for the night. Certainly his grandfather treated the animals like his children.

The days were long and hard. How did his grandfather do it? Mark was much younger, and thoroughly exhausted at the end of each day. And while it was true that men in the community helped each other with farming chores, they couldn't fully run Grandfather's farm on top of their own farms. His grandfather didn't want to put the farm up for sale, but what else could be done? One way or the other, it was about to pass out of the Byler family after generations.

"Something wrong?"

Mark jerked to attention. "What?"

"You're being quiet."

"Just thinking."

They headed back to the house. A big house. Much too big for just the two of them—make that one of them, since Mark was only visiting.

"Why didn't you get married again?"

John turned to stare at him. "Where did that come from?"

"I don't know. I was just looking at this house and thinking it was big for one man."

"It is." He gestured at the rocking chairs on the back porch. They sat. "Never found another woman I wanted to marry, I guess." He grinned. "A few nice women came by after a while, bringing food, saying they were concerned I wasn't eating right. You know how it is."

"No. *Englisch* women don't cook like Amish women."

John chuckled. "There's something to be said for traditional roles."

Remembering that Waneta was a widow, Mark turned to him. "Was that pie Waneta brought by for me or for you?"

"Today she said it was for you."

"I see."

"The bishop finally gave up on me." He chuckled. "He'd rather not have single men in his community. I think he was hoping I'd marry Waneta or one of the other widows." He glanced at Mark. "But I'm still not ready."

"*Grossmudder's* been gone for ten years."

"And like I said, I'm not ready yet." He rose and patted Mark's shoulder. "Well, these old bones want their bed. I'll see you in the morning."

"Sleep well."

He sat there thinking about what his grandfather had said. Funny how they were far apart in age but both of them unmarried. It seemed the Byler men were going to be single for a while yet.

Twenty-Four

She'd never considered herself a foolish, romantic *maedel*.

So why was she daydreaming about almost kissing Mark?

And how was she going to avoid temptation when she saw him on a near-daily basis?

Miriam yanked a weed and threw it on the pile to her right. She had to think about something else or she'd go crazy.

"I think it's time for a break," her *mudder* said.

"In a minute. I'm almost finished."

"There isn't another weed in sight," Sarah said. "I do believe they've run off to hide."

Miriam sat back and sighed. "You're right." She stood, brushed dirt from her skirt.

"Do you want to talk about it?" her *mudder* asked, slipping her arm around her waist as they walked to the house.

"Talk about pulling weeds?" Miriam forced herself to smile.

Her mudder just looked at her until Miriam looked away. "I'm *all-recht*. I'm just working something through in my head."

"And you have a *gut* head," Sarah said quietly. "When you want to talk, I'm here."

Miriam stopped and so her *mudder* had to as well. She turned and put her head on her shoulder. "Oh, *Mamm*, your *dochder* doesn't have a *gut* head. She's just fallen head over heels over a man she can't be with."

Sarah patted her back. "We don't always love wisely."

"You did. Why can't I be like you?"

She turned her and guided her toward the house. "Because God created you to be the special Miriam that you are. " She opened the back door. "He doesn't make two exactly the same."

"Except those Zook twins" Miriam gave a mock shudder.

"And He doesn't make mistakes."

"Well, God doesn't, but I sure do."

"Falling in love with Mark might be unwise, but would you call it a mistake?"

Shocked, Miriam stared at her *mudder*. "You don't?"

"It's not my job to judge." Sarah said, stroking her cheek. "It's my job to love you."

They fixed glasses of iced tea and sat at the kitchen table.

"You sound surprised about loving him. It's not a far walk from loving a friend to loving him as more than that."

Miriam nodded. "I think I need to avoid seeing him until he goes home."

"That won't be easy."

"I'm still going to cook and bake for him and John, but I'll see if I can just drop things off and not get into any conversations or … situations … with Mark while there."

Sarah nodded. "That's a *gut* plan." She rose and looked out the kitchen window. "Let's fix lunch, then why don't you go to Lovina's to see what help you can give today? We've done most of the harvesting and canning of the kitchen garden."

"You're *schur* you don't need me here?"

"*Nee*. I'll be fine."

So Miriam spent the afternoon at Abraham and Lovina's farm. Lovina looked better. The dark circles under her eyes were gone, and she looked cheerful when she greeted Miriam at the door.

"Abraham's gone to pick up the buggy," she said. "It's all repaired, and the vet said Star is well enough to pull it."

The house was quiet.

"Where are the *kinner*?"

"They went with their *dat*. They should be home soon."

"Then let's see how much we can get done before they get home."

They did laundry and hung it on the clothesline, worked in the kitchen garden, and cooked supper.

Miriam insisted Lovina sit and take a break, and was glad she did when, just a few minutes later, they heard the buggy roll into the driveway on its way to the barn. A few minutes later *kinner* burst into the kitchen grinning. "*Mamm!* We're home!"

"So I hear." Lovina peered closely at the *kinner*. "What's that on your face?"

"We got ice cream!"

Abraham followed them inside.

"You gave them ice cream this close to supper?"

He nodded and grinned, unabashed. "It was a special occasion. Mark treated them."

Lovina picked up a paper napkin and dabbed at a spot on Abraham's shirt. "Looks like you had some ice cream, too."

Mark stepped inside. "Hey, Jason and I are leaving." He glanced over and saw Miriam. "Didn't know you were here."

"I'm helping Lovina."

"Need a ride?"

She shook her head. "*Nee, danki.*" Better to walk to the moon and back to avoid being with him right now.

"*Danki* for helping us get the buggy," Abraham said.

"My pleasure."

He left and Abraham took the *kinner* with him to help with outside chores.

"Jason came by?"

Lovina nodded. "He came with Mark. Said he wanted to help. I think Mark has had a good influence on him. I told Mark maybe he's trying to be a teacher like you."

Miriam shrugged. "He told me you said that. I'm just a teacher. He's had all that college, been a successful attorney."

"It's a *gut* thing to be a teacher. Where would anyone be without teachers?"

"Or *mudders.*"

Now it was Lovina's turn to look modest. "You'll be a *wunderbaar mudder* one day."

"If I ever get married," she muttered.

"You will."

Miriam was saved from responding when one of the *kinner* ran into the kitchen.

"*Mamm*, we're all *hungerich*. When's supper?"

"Tell everyone to come in and wash up now." She turned to Miriam. "Will you stay for supper?"

"*Nee, danki.* I should get home and help *Mamm*."

Lovina hugged her. "*Danki* for the help. I'll see you at church next Sunday."

Miriam grabbed her purse and sweater and escaped just as the *kinner* came rushing in the back door. She walked out the front door, started down the porch steps. And stopped dead in her tracks when she saw Mark parked in the drive.

❧❧❧

Mark looked up from the email on his smartphone as he leaned against his car.

Miriam was staring at him in shock.

"Hi." He straightened.

"I thought you'd left."

He held up his phone. "Checking my email. I got some good news. I've been called for some interviews."

"Interviews?"

"For a job."

"Oh, I see."

A brisk fall breeze blew through the trees in the yard, scattering leaves down. Miriam shivered and drew her sweater closer.

"Get in. I'll give you a ride home."

"*Nee*, I can walk."

Mark rounded the hood and held open the passenger door. "Come on, Miriam. Get in. I promise I won't touch you." *Or almost kiss you*, he wanted to add but didn't dare. She already looked like a doe ready to bolt.

She hesitated a moment, then did as he asked.

"So I guess you're happy?"

He nodded and started the car. "I was beginning to wonder if anyone would call."

"Why wouldn't they?" She buckled her seat belt. "You're a good lawyer."

"The bad publicity," he said shortly as he pulled out onto the road. "It's a big deal in my line of work."

Silence stretched between them. He tapped his fingers on the steering wheel and wondered if someone from her background would ever understand the problem. They were at her driveway before he could frame what he wanted to say.

"I may stay in town a day or two."

"And if you get the job?"

"I'll come back to take care of some things."

"Some things?"

He pulled into the driveway. "It's obvious my grandfather needs help with the farm, more help than the community can or should have to do for him." He'd seen how much pain his grandfather was in, how tired. Several times he'd found him sleeping in his recliner, his *Budget* newspaper spread open, unread, on his chest.

"We take care of our own."

"I'd feel better if he had some hired help. Something."

"Well, that's between the two of you."

He turned to look at her. "I'm glad he's had you to look out for him, take him meals and things."

"I love John. He's been like a *grossdaadi* to me." Miriam bent her head and stared at her hands folded on her lap. "I'll never be able to repay him for helping me get my teaching job."

"I'm sure he'd say no thanks needed. He simply recognized your talent." He gave her a rueful smile. "I'm glad I could help Abraham and his family. Lovina said it was the first time her youngest smiled since the accident."

"That's nice to hear."

"Who knows. It might have made Jason think about things. He was going in a wrong direction. He has a chance to turn that around."

She nodded. "We're all teachers in a way, aren't we? I always figured

God put us on earth with others because we're supposed to learn from each other."

"I've learned a lot from you." Mark reached across the space between them to touch her hand.

"You ... you promised not to touch me." She raised her gaze to his and stared, her troubled expression preventing him from saying more.

He withdrew his hand and rested it on the steering wheel. "Anyway, I'll be back in a day or two unless something comes up."

"*Allrecht*." She fumbled with her seatbelt, then the door handle.

Mark reached to help her with the handle, but as he did she jerked her head around, startled at his nearness. Their faces were just inches apart. They stared at each other and his gaze dropped to her mouth.

He couldn't help it. He couldn't. He kissed her.

Miriam drew back, pressing her fingers against her lips. "*Nee*," she whispered. "We can't."

"I'm sorry."

She looked at him, trembling. "You're sorry because you kissed me?"

He dragged a hand through his hair, then decided to tell the truth. "No. I'm only sorry I broke my promise not to touch you. Twice."

She closed her eyes, shook her head. And then she was out of the car before he could grasp her arm and stop her. She ran up the steps to her house and disappeared inside.

Great. There probably wasn't anyone more innocent than a young Amish woman. They even called them *maedels* here, for goodness' sakes.

He sighed and shook his head, debated whether he should try to apologize. Before he could get out of his car, his cell phone rang.

"Mark? It's Saul. I was wondering when we could get together so you could look at the permit paperwork."

He pinched the bridge of his nose with his fingers. He'd been so caught up in his good news he'd forgotten he'd promised Saul he'd stop by.

"I can come now."

"*Schur*, that would be *gut*. *Danki*."

He hung up and drove to Saul's farm, mumbling to himself all the way. So much for his good memory.

Saul and his wife, Esther, greeted him effusively when he arrived. The family was just sitting down to supper, so he was invited to join them. He found himself seated at the table with six children who gave him big smiles and studied him with open curiosity.

Food, family, and faith. He'd never been surrounded by so much since those summers with his grandfather. Heads were bent for the blessing for the meal. Mark heard Esther whisper, "Patties down," and he cracked an eye open to watch the toddler in the high chair near him put her pudgy hands on her tray. She grinned and showed a mouth with a half dozen baby teeth. Then he saw Esther trying to suppress a smile. He shut his eye again and listened to Saul.

Mark took the bowls and platters the children passed him, impressed with how even the littlest child managed them. Silence reigned as appetites sharpened by chores were appeased.

Now that cooler weather had arrived, the women baked more, so tonight they dined on stuffed pork chops, sweet potatoes, butter beans, and homemade applesauce. Esther served blackberry cobbler made from berries the children had picked, and told a funny story about them surprising a snake under a bush.

"*Mamm* wouldn't let me keep him," one of the boys said, sounding aggrieved.

"He needed to stay with his family," Esther replied.

The meal done, the table cleared, she supervised the older children washing and drying the dishes while Saul and Mark went to the living room to study the papers about the permit.

Mark hadn't dealt with such matters at his firm, but it was a fairly simple thing. He reviewed it with Saul, who had a better understanding of it than he'd thought.

"I guess I didn't really need to bother you with it," Saul said a bit sheepishly.

"It's no problem. They have to make it sound official, I think, so people will do as they say. But sometimes they go overboard with their language. Makes it so that we have a whole profession like mine possible," he quipped.

He'd brought a legal pad with him, so he drafted a reply letter and read it to Saul. "I'll type this up and bring it by tomorrow for your signature."

"*Gut*. How much do I owe you?" Saul asked, looking visibly relieved.

He told Saul it was *pro bono*, explaining the term as he had to Miriam. "But I wouldn't turn down some cookies, if you have any on hand. I got some from Lovina the other day."

"Done." Saul grinned. "Or there might be some blackberry cobbler left."

"I doubt it. I had two helpings."

But Esther produced a plastic container with some cobbler for him and his grandfather, and looked pleased he wanted it.

As Mark headed home, he winced as he passed Miriam's house. Should he stop? He kept on driving, making excuses. He needed to get the letter typed and printed. Lay out his clothes for tomorrow. Polish his good shoes. Pack extra copies of his resume in his briefcase. He had to set the alarm, get to bed, make sure he got some rest. No telling what traffic would be like, so he had to get an early start.

It was no surprise to him that he wrestled with his conscience for a long time before he could sleep. And when he got up in the morning, his sheets were as tangled as if he'd wrestled with them all night.

Twenty-Five

Miriam smiled. She knew she was dreaming, but she just didn't want to wake up.

Mark was kissing her. And patting her cheek. Hard. Rather too hard to be romantic.

She woke and blinked as she stared into her youngest *schweschder's* face. "Katie! What are you doing here?"

Giggling, she climbed up into her bed.

"Katie!" her *mudder's* voice called from down the hall. "Where did you go?"

"She's in here, *Mamm!*" Miriam called back.

Their *mudder* walked into the room and put her hands on her hips. "She climbed out of her crib again."

Katie bounced on the bed and giggled.

Sarah sighed. "It's hard to be upset at such a good-natured *kind.*" She held out her arms. "*Kumm,* let's get you dressed and we'll get some breakfast."

"Fast!" Katie agreed. She let her *mudder* pick her up and carry her from the room. "Bye-bye, Meer!"

"Bye!" Miriam tossed aside her quilt, swung her legs over the side of the bed, and set her feet on the floor. Almost immediately she pulled them up and winced at the chill. She pulled on stockings, shoes, then dressed and did her hair quickly.

It was a mad rush getting breakfast on the table, helping the little ones with their oatmeal and toast, and doing last-minute grooming before they headed out the door for *schul.*

There wasn't a spare moment to think of Mark. Well, she did glance at John's house as they walked past it. Mark's car was gone. He'd certainly gotten on the road early for his interviews, she couldn't help thinking.

She wished him well. She really did. At least, she wanted to. It was selfish to want him to stay when he wanted to be back in his world.

Well, she'd never claimed to be perfect. She strived to be, but it would be so very immodest to think she was, after all. Hadn't she been told *"der hochmut kummt vor dem fall"*—pride goeth before the fall?—all her life?

Her *bruders* and *schweschders* rushed past her after she unlocked the front door of the *schul*. They set their lunchboxes in the cubbies built for their things, then ran outside to play until it was time to start lessons.

Miriam fetched a broom and swept gold and red leaves from the porch and steps. The trees were shedding them so fast. Soon their limbs would be bare. Winter wasn't so far away now. Spring and fall always seemed too short in Lancaster County.

She felt a pang of loneliness as she stood there in her domain. *Schur,* her *bruders* and *schweschders* were playing only a few feet away. But she was already lonely for Mark.

Shaking her head as if she could drive the thought away, she went back to sweeping the steps.

Kinner began arriving, looking eager. They climbed the steps, put their lunchboxes in their cubbies, then ran back outside to play until she called them inside.

She gave them all a few extra minutes. It was such a lovely day and she knew they would buckle down and work hard when they were asked. She put the broom away, glanced at the clock, then walked back outside.

"*Kinner, kumm!* Time to start *schul!*" she called and clapped her hands.

She stood clear of the door and greeted them as they clambered up the stairs and chorused their greetings. Only Naiman dragged his feet as he walked toward her and climbed the stairs.

"Why can't we play longer?" he grumbled as he reached the top step.

"Because it's time to learn now. And the sooner everyone learns their lessons, the sooner they can go outside for recess."

He grinned at that and hurried inside. *Recess* was his favorite word.

She closed the door. As she walked to the front of the room, she spied Jacob tugging on the pigtail of little Rachel who sat in front of him. She gave him her best stern frown. He let go immediately and raised the lid of his desk to get out paper and pencil.

The morning passed quickly with lessons and recess, and before she knew it, it was time for lunch.

She roamed the room, helping the younger children open the wrapping on their sandwiches and unscrew the cap on their thermoses. The scents of peanut butter and jelly sandwiches and homemade soups filled the air.

She'd packed her favorite egg salad and brought a thermos of hot chocolate. It was the same lunch she'd enjoyed in the same room of her childhood. The only difference now was the position of her desk. She found such continuity comforting and couldn't imagine anything better.

After the *kinner* consumed cookies and whoopie pies and cleaned their desks, they returned their lunchboxes to the cubbies and got to play outside for a brief time. Sometimes she joined in the play, but today she sat on a bench and watched, keeping a close eye on social interactions. Sometimes she learned as much about the *kinner* from the way they got along as she did in conversations about lessons.

That reminded her that she needed to respond to the circle letter she'd received a few days ago from another teacher. This time the topic was about what each teacher was planning for the Christmas play.

"Hello!" Lovina called as she came up the path to the *schul*. "It's such a beautiful day, *ya?*"

"*Ya. Danki* for coming to help this afternoon."

"I enjoy it." She sat beside Miriam.

"How are you feeling?"

"I still have sad times," Lovina admitted in a low tone. "But God has blessed me with three *kinner* and I must trust that He knows best. The doctor says there's no reason we won't have another *boppli.*"

"*Gut.*" Miriam patted her hand.

"And how are you feeling? I heard Mark went into Philadelphia today for an interview."

"The Amish grapevine is working well as always, I see."

Lovina laughed. "*Ya.*"

Something hovered at the edge of Miriam's vision, then darted toward Lovina. "A dragonfly," she murmured.

"I've seen so many since … since I lost the *boppli*," Lovina whispered as she held out her hand.

The winged creature landed on it and sat there, flexing its transparent wings, seeming to study her with its gemlike eyes.

Then, as a *kind* approached Miriam, it fluttered off and the moment was gone.

"I have to go potty," Rachel confided, jumping from one foot to the other. "Can I go to the bathroom?"

"You *may*," Miriam said, gently correcting her grammar. Then she turned to Lovina. "Well, I guess we should get started on our arithmetic." She stood and clapped her hands to get the attention of her scholars.

SSS

As Mark drove into Philadelphia, he thought about how little both places he loved ever changed.

The city was old and beautiful and valued its history. His grandfather's farm had been in the family for many generations and had its own history. Both were so different. Yet both were very much a part of him.

He drove to the stately building that housed the law firm where he'd be interviewing and found a parking spot. Like many buildings in this city, it had a sense of history, and its expensive wood paneling, brass railings, and thick carpets were all intended to impress. He'd dressed to impress, too, in his most subdued, navy pin-striped suit and burgundy silk tie. Impressions were everything.

William Renfrow IV, just a decade older than Mark, headed the family firm now that his father had retired. Mark had faced him many times in the courtroom, socialized with him at the country club, and partnered with him in doubles matches on the tennis courts.

A portrait of William Renfrow III hung on one wall. It portrayed him when he was perhaps twenty years older than his son, but there was no mistaking the aura of confidence, wealth, and success both men wore as visibly as their custom-made clothing.

Mark's origins had been less privileged, but he'd quickly learned how to fit in with fellow students at college in order to pursue his dream.

His heritage was a simple farm in an Amish community, and he'd never been ashamed of it. He hadn't wanted to shut that part of himself off the way his father had, but he'd had to adapt to a totally different mentality and lifestyle, even within the *Englisch* world. In some ways, this legal world made you become someone who sought for legal knowledge, were paid well, and yet were so often disrespected.

Well, he'd never needed approval so any disrespect didn't bother him. And he knew he'd helped enough clients that he felt comfortable about what he did. Even though Abraham had been resistant, he'd done good there and with Saul.

He waited while Renfrow scanned his resume. The ball was in the other man's court. In many ways, this was all a game.

"You've tried some interesting cases," Renfrow said when he took off his reading glasses and set them on his massive mahogany desk. "Of course, I have some concerns about the murder case in the news."

Mark had been prepared for that question. He just hadn't expected it to come up so quickly in the interview.

"I feel confident my former client will be found innocent of the last charges," he said calmly.

"You can understand why we here at Renfrow and Renfrow have to protect our reputation. Our reputation must remain spotless."

"Absolutely." Mark felt a sinking sensation in his stomach. "My reputation is extremely important to me as well. I feel so strongly that my former client is innocent, I am paying a private investigator out of my own pocket to look into the matter."

"I hadn't heard anything about that."

"Investigations are best conducted privately whether they're by a private investigator or the police."

"Indeed."

The rest of the interview followed a predictable path. Renfrow asked about the all-important billable hours—the way a firm made income—and what Mark's goals were for the future.

They exchanged handshakes when the interview was over. It was perhaps telling that he hadn't been offered a tour of the firm.

He walked out of the building and into the sunshine outside. Well, he'd given it his best shot. Time would tell if he'd be asked back for a second interview with the partners of the firm.

But he didn't see a future with Renfrow and Renfrow.

He checked his watch. It was early for lunch, but he'd eaten little before hitting the road. Pulling out his cell phone, he texted Lani and asked if she had time to meet him for lunch. She'd told him to let her know the next time he was in town, so he'd texted her last night.

"I can meet you in half an hour," she texted back and named the restaurant where they'd often eaten, not far from his old firm.

The restaurant's location near the courthouse and many law firms made it a favorite spot for lunch and dinner. Mark and Lani had often combined work and a quick meal here, or ordered it for delivery when they couldn't find the time away from the office. Since it was such a pretty day, he chose the patio and was waiting at a table when she rushed up a few minutes late.

"Sorry, got stopped on the way out of the office." She hugged him hard. "It's so good to see you! And you look so much better than you did last time I saw you."

"You always liked this suit."

She laughed. "It's not that. You're tanned and you don't look stressed. Even after an interview. How did it go?"

He was saved from responding when a server approached their table. "Mr. Byler, it's good to see you!" she said, smiling. "We haven't seen you in ages."

"Been out of town," he replied. "I'll have an iced tea, please."

Lani gave her order and when the server walked away, she turned to him. "Okay, spill. How did it go?"

"I don't see them hiring me. William brought up the murder case. It's obvious he's concerned about negative publicity that might attach to the Renfrow and Renfrow name."

"Well, I never did like him." She sighed. "You know what they say, when one door closes, another opens. You just wait, you're going to get a much better job than that."

"You can't get a better firm than Renfrow and Renfrow."

Their food was served and he closed his eyes and bent his head. He opened his eyes to find Lani staring at him, her fork halfway to her mouth.

"Sorry," she mumbled. "You didn't use to do that."

"My grandfather's influence."

"I think it's lovely. I forget to do it. Thank God, I mean."

They ate and he told her about the other interview he had lined up for the afternoon.

"Mark? Is that really you?"

He looked up. "Tiffany." Somehow he hadn't thought the day could get worse. He'd been wrong.

"You're looking good."

"That's what I was just telling him," Lani said.

Tiffany didn't take her eyes off him to acknowledge Lani. "So what are you doing back in town?" She gave him an appraising look.

"Taking care of a little business."

"I see."

Their server set drinks down on the table. "Miss? Will you be joining the table?"

"No, I'm meeting a friend." Tiffany didn't even look at the server. "I'm meeting Reece. Oh, here he is now."

Reece was a partner in Mark's old firm. "Hey, Mark, didn't know you were back in town." He turned to Tiffany. "Did you get us a table? I have a two o'clock appointment with a client." He turned back to Mark. "Give me a call, we'll have lunch and catch up."

"Will do." He watched the man walk away. "Won't do," he said to Lani.

She looked miserable. "I'm sorry, I didn't know they were seeing each other."

"Doesn't matter," he said, and discovered he really meant it. "Finish eating. I know you have to get back to the office."

"So tell me how the job search is going. What other firms have you applied to?"

"You mean which ones haven't I applied to?"

Lani ignored her favorite chicken Caesar salad and touched his hand. "I'm so sorry. I'm sure something will turn up soon."

"Eat," he urged. "So how's the kid? Still enjoying school?"

The time passed too quickly as they talked and ate. All too soon, he was signaling the server for the bill.

"Time for you to get back to work. I'll give you a call next time I'm coming into town."

"I'm sure it'll be real soon and we'll be celebrating a job offer." She gave him another hard hug and left.

He pretended he didn't see the sparkle of tears in her eyes.

The server brought the leather folder with the bill. He tucked his credit card inside and handed it back to her.

Reece hurried past just moments after Lani left.

"It seems we've been abandoned." Tiffany stood before the table.

"Yes, well, I'm afraid I have to run, too."

"So, are you back to work?"

"I've been keeping busy handling some interesting cases lately," he said.

"I didn't realize you were back at the firm. Reece didn't say anything."

"I'm not working there." The server brought the folder. He pocketed his card, signed the bill, careful to add a tip, and stood. "Listen, Tiffany, it's been good to see you, but I really have to go."

"No hard feelings?"

"No, no, of course not."

"Good." She walked away.

"No feelings whatsoever," he murmured when she was out of earshot.

He walked to his car and sat there for a few minutes, tapping his fingers on the steering wheel. Then, after a glance at his watch, he headed for the other interview.

It went much the same way as the interview at Renfrow and Renfrow. The head of the firm even used nearly the same dialogue—the firm's reputation had to remain aboveboard.

Mark sighed. Wasn't someone considered innocent until proven guilty? Maurice certainly wasn't being regarded that way by Mark's peers and he, as his former attorney, was being slandered by association.

It was so disillusioning.

His plan had been to drive back to Paradise today, but he needed to think and be alone.

He started the car and headed to his condo. Lani had a key and had been picking up his mail and forwarding it, keeping an eye on things. He let himself in and found nothing had changed since the last time he'd been here. Walking over to the glass doors leading out to a terrace, he walked outside and sat in one of the wrought iron chairs. He had an amazing view of the skyline from here, a far cry from the fields of his grandfather's farm.

His gaze fell on the big pots where he grew flowers and ornamental bushes. Last summer he'd had a few tomato plants, some lettuce and peppers. He was good at growing things, and he'd enjoyed spending a little time with his hands in the rich earth and watering them and nurturing them. He'd had Lani and her daughter over for dinner twice, and they'd enjoyed carrying home a basket of ripe tomatoes and some peppers.

The pots were empty now. He hadn't been here to plant anything.

His thoughts went to the place where he'd been spending his time harvesting the crops his grandfather and some of his friends had planted.

And they went, inevitably, to Miriam. He wondered if she thought about their kiss. If she was upset with him about it.

And he wondered what she was doing right now. He checked his watch. It was about time for school to be over. He pictured her standing in the doorway of the little school house she loved, watching her scholars, as she called them, chattering as they gathered their sweaters and lunch boxes and headed home.

She'd enjoy some quiet time and wouldn't be able to leave until everything was in order. He'd visited that school house once after she got the job, seeing it as a milestone as much as his own college graduation which she'd attended with his grandfather. All the desks had been lined up with such precision, the blackboard was washed clean, nothing was out of place. She'd been so thrilled to be given the job, so eager to teach. It was the place she'd seemed to be born to be.

He remembered what his grandfather said about God having a plan for everyone. He could clearly see that plan for Miriam, had thought he'd seen one for himself even if he didn't give Him credit for it enough.

He was trained to always be thinking, planning, even plotting his course and that of the clients he served. Maybe that was why he didn't give God enough credit.

Now he sat here in this place and tried to calm his thoughts, open his mind to guidance from above. Shadows lengthened and he felt a little chilly as a cool breeze swept through the terrace, ruffling the leaves on the ornamental bushes and carrying the scent of some fall blooms from another terrace.

Still he sat, waiting.

Twenty-Six

Miriam couldn't help noticing Mark's car wasn't parked in front of John's farmhouse the next morning as she and her *bruders* and *schweschders* walked to *schul*.

He'd told her he had interviews in Philadelphia. She'd thought he'd drive home afterward. But he hadn't. Had he gotten a job? He was so qualified, maybe they'd asked him to start right away. She wished she knew how such things worked. All she had to go by was her own experience. The men in charge of hiring for the *schul* had approached her for the position of teacher and she had started two weeks later. But that was because the last teacher had died and they needed another teacher for the fall.

She continued walking on to the *schul* and went about her day trying not to think about him. But every time she got a spare moment, she wondered what he was doing. Was he sitting at a new desk? Seeing old friends?

Seeing his former fiancée?

She couldn't think of that.

Whatever God planned for Mark, it didn't look like it included her. It was time to deal with that truth once and for all.

She had to make sure that they didn't ever put themselves in a situation where they were alone like the other day. It had secretly thrilled her to know he was attracted to her. She couldn't deny that. But it couldn't go further.

Lovina came by after lunch again to help some of the slower readers. After the scholars left for home, the two of them shared some hot tea Lovina had brought in a thermos.

"Have you heard how Mark's interview went?" Lovina asked as they settled down at Miriam's desk.

"*Nee.*"

Lovina opened a plastic container of cookies and offered them to her. Miriam wasn't really hungry, but she took one out of kindness.

"So how can I help you plan the Christmas play?" Lovina asked as she chose a cookie for herself.

Miriam got out a pad of paper and a pencil. "I made out a list of roles for the *kinner*. Several of the *kinner* are shy so I want to give them roles that help them build confidence. These *kinner* I've circled are good at memorization, so some of the longer parts would be *gut* for them. And this is the list of hymns they'll sing."

"You've done a lot of planning."

"I know it seems early, but time passes so quickly."

Except for today, she thought. The day had seemed to drag so. She wanted to know what had happened at Mark's interview.

"Are you *allrecht?*"

"Hmm? Oh, *ya*, sorry."

"Abraham can build anything you need for the play. The doctor may be taking his cast off next week."

"That's *gut* news."

"I'll make the punch and cookies. And you know Fannie Mae will want to be asked to bring her spice cake. I'll ask the other *mudders* and give you a list of what they can bring for refreshments."

Miriam wrote the details down in her careful, precise script.

Mark would probably be long gone by the time Christmas came. Oh, he might come back to spend the holiday with his grandfather as he sometimes did, but with a new job he wouldn't get much time off.

"—the rest of it."

She jerked back to attention. "Rest of it?"

"I think we should put this off until tomorrow," Lovina said. "You're looking tired."

"I'm sorry. I didn't sleep well last night."

Lovina patted her hand. "Try to get to bed early tonight." She looked closer at her. "I hope you're not coming down with something."

Miriam didn't tell her friend that she had gone to bed early last night, only to lay awake most of the night thinking about Mark. She wasn't coming down with something. She was lovesick.

A few minutes later they were rolling down the road. Lovina chattered about hosting church services that weekend and Miriam was trying hard not to look to see if Mark's car was parked at John's.

"Oh look!" Lovina exclaimed. "Mark's back!"

And so he was. He was just pulling into the driveway.

"Let's see how things went!" Lovina exclaimed. Without waiting for Miriam to reply, she turned into the drive.

So much for her plans to avoid him. Miriam smiled weakly as Mark walked over to the buggy.

"Well, it seems we were passing at just the right moment," Lovina said brightly. "We were just wondering how your interviews went."

"Fine. Now I wait to be called for a second interview."

Was it her imagination, or did he seem less confident than he had the other day? Why didn't he meet her eyes?

"I'm sure you'll hear from them soon," Lovina said. "Maybe you'll get more than one job offer."

"That would be nice."

"We'll pray for you, won't we, Miriam?"

"Of course." She tried for an encouraging smile.

"Thank you."

"Well, I'd better get home and see about supper." Lovina said. "*Gut-n-owed.*"

"You, too," he said as he stepped away from the buggy.

Miriam watched him walk back to his car to retrieve his briefcase, and her heart ached at the sight of his slumped shoulders and slow steps.

They got back on the road and Lovina resumed chattering about how she needed to *redd* up the house and get together the supplies for the light meal that would be served on Sunday.

Miriam thanked her for the ride when Lovina stopped in front of her house.

"I'll see you Sunday."

"*Ya*, see you then."

She went inside. Her *mudder* was singing as she stood at the stove. Katie sat in her high chair chewing on a *zwieback*.

"Hi, *Mamm*, I'm home." She set her lunch box down on a kitchen counter, hung her sweater on a hook by the back door, and leaned down to kiss Katie.

Sarah turned and smiled at her. "Did you have a *gut* day?"

"*Ya*, Lovina and I did some planning for the Christmas play, which is why I'm a little late. I'll be right down to help you."

"Take your time."

She heard her *mudder* singing as she climbed the stairs to her room carrying her book bag. It was tempting to sink down on the bed. She was tired, but not from work. *Nee*, she knew it was from feeling a little blue.

Well, feeling blue was just being self-indulgent. She freshened up then went downstairs. "How can I help?"

"Peel the potatoes?"

"*Schur*." Miriam sat at the table and began peeling.

"So, you and Lovina are planning the Christmas play? That should cheer you up. You love putting it on."

Miriam glanced up and caught her *mudder's* knowing look. "Lovina saw Mark coming home and stopped. She asked him how his interviews went, and he didn't sound very confident."

"Hmm. Would they tell him the same day if they didn't want to hire him?"

"I just don't know. I didn't want to ask."

"Well, time will tell. You know our time is not God's time."

Miriam nodded. She knew that well.

✒✒✒

Mark found his grandfather sleeping in his recliner.

He was so still, the rise and fall of his chest so faint, that for a long terrible moment Mark wondered if he was truly sleeping. His heart skipped a beat and his briefcase slipped from his fingers. It landed with a thump at his feet.

John jerked and his eyes flew open. "Oh, you're back."

"Yeah, sorry, I didn't mean to drop this and wake you." His heart resumed beating.

"Just resting my eyes a bit." He sat up and used his feet to push the footrest back. "Are you hungry? Got a pot of chili sitting on the stove. I was hoping you'd get home soon and we could eat together."

"Sorry I ran a little later than I thought. Traffic was bad in Philly."

They walked into the kitchen and Mark frowned when he saw the chili. It looked ... cooked down in the pot. He turned the gas flame off under it. Would it have continued to cook down until it burned and caused a fire?

"Sit, I'll get the bowls." Mark washed his hands, got the bowls, and ladled chili into them. There was a box of oyster crackers on the counter. His grandfather always loved to sprinkle the round, thumb-sized salty crackers atop his chili.

Mark bent his head for the meal blessing and remembered how surprised Lani had been when he'd done it at lunch yesterday. It was part of his daily routine now.

"So, tell me, how did it go?"

Mark gave a brief rundown and his grandfather listened as he ate.

"I guess I'll be losing you soon," he said as he scraped the bottom of his bowl.

Mark shrugged. "I don't know about that. The publicity still hasn't died down about my client being arrested a second time for murder." He rose and took his grandfather's bowl to the stove to ladle him a second helping.

When he sat again, he didn't pick up his spoon, but studied his grandfather as he ate. Was it his time away—brief as it had been—or had his grandfather aged even more than when he'd come here after being banished from his firm?

"You're not eating much."

Same eagle eye, even if he was older.

"Had a big lunch."

They cleaned the kitchen, then went out to do the evening chores. Whitey, his favorite, greeted him by rubbing his nose on Mark's sleeve. Mark portioned out feed and hauled fresh water. Then, with another Whitey nudge on his arm, he laughed and pulled out the quartered apples he always brought for the horses.

Chores done, Mark closed the barn door and walked with his grandfather to sit on the back porch.

"Won't be able to do this much longer. We're going to have an early winter."

"Really?"

John nodded. "Feeling it in my bones."

Dusk fell. Mark set his chair moving with a push of his foot. He looked out on the fields and thought about the very different view he'd enjoyed the night before.

And how this one felt more like home.

He set his foot down abruptly.

"Something wrong?"

"No," he said slowly. *Something's right*, he realized. *Something is very right.*

"I'm going in. Want some coffee?"

"Not right now. I think I'll sit out here for a while."

His grandfather stood, patted his shoulder just as he had so often. Mark's throat tightened. He reached up and put his hand over his grandfather's hard, worn one, and squeezed.

"*Gut nacht*," he said.

His grandfather's hand trembled under his and then he withdrew it. "*Gut nacht.*"

Mark listened to his slow, steady steps back into the house. There was the clatter of crockery as his grandfather fixed his coffee. Then the night fell silent. Even the crickets were quiet, probably tucked up for the coming colder weather.

He sat there for a long time, listening for His voice.

On Sunday, he attended services at Abraham and Lovina's house. He listened hard to Samuel's message, sang the hymns, and was greeted by his friends and fellow church members as though he'd been gone for longer than two days.

The Amish grapevine had traveled with its usual speed and it seemed everyone knew where he'd gone and why.

"*Gut* to see you here today," Samuel said as he settled down in a seat next to Mark.

"It's *gut* to be here." He blinked when he realized he'd slipped again into Pennsylvania *Dietsch*.

Samuel inclined his head and studied him seriously. "How are you doing?"

"You mean the interviews?"

He shook his head. "*Nee*. I know this is a time when you must be questioning God."

"Trying not to question. Well, I have questioned," he admitted. "But now I'm trying to listen."

Samuel laughed. "Listening is *gut*. I'm working on it myself."

"Seems like you have that down."

His eyebrows shot up. "Really? *Nee*. It would be wrong for anyone to think they do, don't you think?"

"I hadn't thought of it that way." Mark pushed aside his plate. "I thought I had my life all laid out. This has been a detour I hadn't expected."

"Detour?" Samuel stroked his beard. "You always seemed so certain what you wanted and went after it. Could it be that it wasn't what *you* wanted after all? Could it be what *He* had for you?"

Mark worked through that. "If that's true, why would I suddenly not have my job?"

"Only God knows that. And a detour isn't always a bad thing, right? It's a different path we have to take for some reason. Maybe the road washed out. Maybe a new one that'll be better is being built."

"Maybe it's to take us on a road less traveled?" Mark mused, remembering the poem.

"*Ya*. I remember that." Samuel sipped his coffee, then set down the empty cup. "Maybe it isn't just a straight road. Maybe we should be thinking it has detours and alternate paths."

"Maybe I should start my own practice," Mark said. "Maybe even do it here, so I could help my grandfather with the farm."

"Samuel, Mark, more coffee?" Lovina asked as she stopped by their table with a pot.

"*Danki*, Lovina."

As she poured coffee into their cups, Mark happened to glance up to see Miriam talking with a man he didn't recognize.

"Mark? Cream?"

He dragged his gaze back. "Yes, thanks."

"That's Luke, a cousin of Abraham's from Ohio," she told him. "He's come to help us for a few weeks."

"That's nice," Mark said.

Lovina moved on to another table.

"So, to return to our conversation," Samuel prompted. "It reminded me of something that happened to me some time back. I had an out of town trip and had an *Englisch* driver who was very impatient with traffic. He had perhaps five cars in front of him on a two-lane road and he couldn't pass. They were all apparently going too slow for him. Soon I noticed the cars start signaling and turning off one by one. But it still wasn't fast enough for him. He kept getting closer—being a 'bumper sticker,' I believe you call it."

He took a sip of coffee. "It got down to the last car and he couldn't wait. He pulled out to pass the car and the driver suddenly turned without signaling. My driver nearly hit him."

Samuel looked up when his wife appeared with a tray of cookies. He smiled and took one. "*Danki.*"

Mark accepted a cookie and thanked her. "So what I'm hearing is that, if the driver had been more patient, all of the cars would have turned off and he wouldn't have had a near-accident." He bit into the cookie, chewed thoughtfully. "If I follow your analogy, I should be more patient."

Samuel grinned. "Always knew you were a *gut* talker. Never knew you were so *gut* at listening to a simple man's story."

"You might be Plain, but you're not simple."

"*Danki*, Mark." Samuel stood. "You know, sometimes there are reasons why God's answer is 'Wait.' Now, I think I'll get my *fraa* and head on home."

Mark glanced around. He didn't see Miriam or Abraham's cousin. He frowned. Then his gaze fell on his grandfather sitting at a nearby table talking with one of his friends. Apparently he wasn't ready to leave yet. Mark took another bite of his cookie and decided he was in no hurry to get on the road home.

Twenty-Seven

It wasn't often Miriam met someone new at church.

Those attending were almost always family and friends in the community she'd known since she was born. But on occasion, members had a relative from another community, another state, or invited an *Englisch* friend to attend.

Lovina had introduced Luke, one of Abraham's cousins from Ohio, to Miriam before the service, and Miriam had become aware of his gaze ever since.

It disconcerted her a little. While she'd gone to singings and other church sponsored youth events, she'd never felt the same intense attention from a young male—especially not by one so attractive. Luke had caught the eye of other *maedels* today as well. He was tall, blond, and had the deepest blue eyes. The fact that he'd come to help his cousin with his farm showed a lot about his character.

Miriam was flattered that he showed interest in her and asked if they could go for a ride so she could show him around Lancaster County.

She didn't have the slightest interest in him. But she knew she should think about him. She hadn't been interested in other men in the community.

And she had to get over this crush she had on Mark. Her *mudder* had tried to make her see that she couldn't look in his direction.

But she found herself seeking out a glimpse of Mark. She saw him sitting with Samuel, talking earnestly. What were they talking about? Mark looked so thoughtful as he listened to Samuel. Was he telling Mark one of his favorite parables from the Bible? He so loved the way Jesus taught with parables …

She sighed.

"Something wrong?"

She jerked her attention back to Luke. "Sorry, I was just thinking about something."

"That's the guy who helped Abraham and Lovina, isn't it?" Luke asked. She nodded.

"Abraham says he's a lawyer from Philadelphia."

"He is." Maybe not this minute, but he would be soon, she told herself. Maybe it was time to be realistic and stop thinking she could ever be anything more than friends with Mark.

"I'd like to show you around," she told Luke.

"You would?"

"*Schur.* I have to finish helping Lovina, but I should be ready to go in about ten minutes."

"I'll go hitch up the buggy."

She managed a smile. "*Gut.* I'll be out as soon as I can."

Lovina slipped an arm around her waist. "I couldn't help overhearing. He's such a nice man, isn't he?"

Miriam tore her glance away from Mark and turned to look at her friend. "What?"

"I didn't mean to eavesdrop, but I heard what you told Luke about showing him around," Lovina said. "You go on. The other women can help me clean up."

"*Allrecht*, I will." Miriam walked past Mark, who sat alone staring into his coffee cup, and went into the front bedroom to retrieve her jacket.

The scent of snow was in the air when she stepped out onto the porch. Sometimes fall felt as short as spring here in Lancaster County.

She stood, shivering a little, and was relieved when Luke pulled up in front of the house. After she got inside, she looked around. The buggy had been repaired so expertly it looked new.

"So which way should we go?"

"Take a left. I don't remember ever seeing you here before."

"It's my first time. I just got in last night." Luke glanced around. "The trees are nearly bare back in Ohio. It's nice to see the colors of the leaves here."

"They'll be gone soon. We're supposed to have an early winter."

He nodded. "I can smell snow in the air."

"What do you do back home?"

"My family has a farm."

She'd guessed that. Those who grew up on farms were good at predicting the weather.

"Abraham was telling me about the price of the land here." Luke shook his head.

"Farmers have been squeezed out for *schur*. Tourism has gotten bigger here."

They enjoyed a ride through the countryside and compared stories of growing up in families with many *kinner*. Luke had six *bruders* and two *schweschders*. As the youngest, he hadn't helped with raising them as she had.

"I guess being the eldest helps you with your teacher work."

"My *bruders* and *schweschders* would tell you it helps me torture them during the summer. I worry that they'll backslide when they're not in *schul*, so we do different lessons using arithmetic and English."

He laughed. "That *would* be torture."

"They're always well ahead of their grade level when we return in the fall," she said a little defensively. "Anyway, I'm busy planning the Christmas play. Will you be here then?"

"Depends on how long Abraham needs me." Luke glanced at her and their gazes met. "I think I'll enjoy my time here."

Miriam looked away, feeling her cheeks heat. "We can go into town, if you'd like to see it. Traffic will be busier this time of year. With so many tourists on the road, you'll need to keep an eye out. Pull over if they get impatient behind you."

"I will. We're getting more tourists in our area as well, although from what Abraham says, you have more here."

As she predicted, traffic got heavier. She pointed out the shops and restaurants that were popular. Shops owned by the Amish were closed on Sundays, but there were still tourists clogging the sidewalks and window shopping.

Miriam debated asking Luke if he wanted to stop for something to eat after they'd been out for several hours, but decided not to. Abraham might be expecting him, and besides, it wouldn't do to appear too forward.

She listened to the rhythmic sound of the clip clop of the horse's hooves on the road and her thoughts drifted back to the first time she'd driven Mark around the area the first summer he'd visited.

"The horse is so slow," he'd said. "I thought the Amish bought retired race horses for their buggies." Then Mark must have realized he'd sounded critical because he admitted that it might be slow going because he was used to riding in a car.

"*Schur*, cars get you where you're going faster, but it's nice to relax and enjoy the ride, don't you think?" she'd asked. "Don't you *Englisch* have a saying about stopping to smell the roses?"

"I smell something that doesn't smell like roses," he said and she laughed. "We sure don't get that smell when we ride in a car."

She'd stopped and showed him her favorite place—a little pond where they'd taken a picnic lunch a lot that summer. Did he remember those picnics and the dreams they'd shared there by the pond?

"I'm getting a little hungry," Luke said, breaking into her thoughts. "You?"

"A bit. There's an ice cream shop not far from here. They have really good hot dogs and their soft ice cream is the best."

"Show me the way," he said, giving her a big grin.

Red, Abraham's horse, seemed to move a little faster when they approached the ice cream shop. If he was anything like her family's buggy horse, it was probably because he knew he'd get a drink of water and some shade while they were parked there under a big oak tree.

It took two hot dogs and the whopper-sized ice cream cone for Luke's "little" hunger to be satisfied. Miriam had one hot dog and the kid-sized cone.

Soon he drove her home. She was glad she'd agreed to go for a ride with him. It had been a pleasant enough afternoon and she'd enjoyed him acting as if he enjoyed her company.

But as he drove off, she stood there wishing it had been Mark she could have spent the afternoon with. She sighed and went inside the house.

SSS

Mark opened the latest bill from his private investigator and winced.

"Bad news?" John asked.

"Just a bill." He folded it and slid it back inside the envelope.

"Need some cash?"

His offer made a lump rise in Mark's throat. "Thanks, but I'm good." He sorted through the rest of the mail Lani had forwarded to him and didn't see anything pressing. "Did you get some good mail?"

John had brought in quite a stack of mail for the two of them. "Got some seed catalogs." He stood and walked to the stove. "Coffee?"

Mark nodded and gestured at a catalog. "May I?"

"*Schur.*" He set a mug before Mark. "It's time to order for spring planting."

"Really?" He scanned the pages. "So are you planning to plant the same crops, or doing some crop rotation?"

That led to an hour's discussion about his grandfather's plans, explanations of methods, questions from Mark about the positives and negatives of crop rotation. It was a pleasant way to pass the time on a rainy afternoon, and he could tell his grandfather appreciated his interest.

"Maybe you'll be around for planting season."

Mark felt such mixed emotions at the hope he saw in his grandfather's face, heard in his voice. "Well, I'm hoping I'll have a job by then, but maybe I can come back and help. We'll see."

He hesitated. It was on the tip of his tongue to mention the idea he had about opening his own practice here instead of in Philly, but he changed his mind. It wouldn't be good to get his grandfather's hopes up about him staying if it didn't work out.

"I talked quite a while to Samuel at church on Sunday. He said some of the same things you have about God having a plan for my life. He seems to think I need to be patient, not try to plot my course. And listen."

"That so?" His grandfather's mouth quirked in a grin.

"I always liked Samuel. Never thought he'd end up being a lay minister."

John rose and poked in the bread box on the kitchen counter. "Cinnamon roll?"

"Sure. These Miriam's?"

His grandfather took a huge bite of one, chewed, and swallowed. "*Ya*. She dropped them off earlier."

She was avoiding him. So far she'd stopped by three times and he'd missed her.

John pulled a catalog over and thumbed through it, occasionally taking a paper napkin and wiping frosting off a page.

Mark got up for more coffee and filled his grandfather's mug. "So, you want to make out the seed order?"

"You don't need to go do something on that fancy laptop of yours?"

"It can wait."

He was learning to slow down a little, not constantly try to figure out his life. And who knew how many more moments he'd have with his grandfather if he got a job in Philly soon?

John reached behind him to open a kitchen drawer and pulled out a pad of paper and a pencil. He jotted down his order for the past year, and as he talked and wrote, Mark wondered if he had inherited his sharp memory from his grandfather.

The prices in one catalog were cheaper than the other, and Mark asked why he was ordering from the more expensive company. That led to a discussion of the merits of each company. In his grandfather's opinion, the more expensive company treated Amish farmers much better than the company that tried to lure them with cheaper prices. Like most of the Amish farmers locally he also used organic methods of growing crops that saved on fertilizers and other chemicals that weren't good for people or the land.

Before he knew it, the afternoon had passed and it was time for supper. John pulled a plastic container from the freezer, opened it, and dumped it into a pot on the stove. "Vegetable beef soup. Waneta brought it over last week while you were out of town. I put it in the freezer for a night when we didn't want to cook."

"That's most of the time for me."

He chuckled. "I really appreciate how Miriam makes sure I have good meals. And Waneta likes to drop off a pie occasionally."

"Rain's stopped," Mark said, glancing out the window as he carried the mugs to the sink. He watched his grandfather stir the soup as it thawed in the pot. Back home he'd have nuked it in the microwave. Well, he wouldn't have had something homemade to nuke. Warming it here took considerably longer than a microwave, but the scent of the soup was mouth-watering and worth waiting for.

Mark pulled out his cell phone and checked his email. Like his snail mail, it contained nothing important.

He got out bowls, sliced bread, and set the table while his grandfather puttered at the stove stirring the soup.

The meal was simple but filling and just right on a cool, damp night. Mark had eaten at some four star restaurants back in Philly, but none compared to meals like this.

They were just finishing when he felt his cell phone vibrate in his pocket. He excused himself to take the call in the other room.

"Mark? Lou. Got some news for you."

He could hear the note of suppressed excitement in the private investigator's voice. "What's up?"

"I got proof it was a set-up in your client's case. Found a witness willing to talk."

Mark listened as Lou supplied the details. A witness claimed the real murderer was a member of a gang Maurice had been a part of years before who had a grudge. The police had obviously been happy to be able to arrest Maurice and close the case.

"The witness is nervous," Lou said. "I set him up in a motel outside town, advanced him some money for expenses. How fast can you get here to talk to him?"

Mark glanced at the kitchen clock. "I can leave now. Go sit on him, make sure he doesn't bolt."

"I'm parked outside the motel right now."

"Good. Be careful. I'll call you on the road." Mark disconnected the call and turned to see his grandfather watching him with a worried expression. "The private investigator found a witness related to that murder case. I have to drive to Philly tonight."

"It can't wait until morning?"

Mark shook his head and grabbed his jacket from its peg by the back door. "Guy's scared. I have to talk to him, take him to see the police as soon as possible for his own safety." He grabbed his car keys, paused to think if he needed anything from his room.

"Give me one minute," John said, heading back into the kitchen. He returned with a thermos and a paper bag. "Coffee and a couple of those cinnamon rolls for the road."

Mark took them and gave his grandfather a hug. "I don't know how long I'll be gone."

"Drive careful. The roads will be wet and it may sleet."

"I'll be careful." He shook his head. "Do you know what this means? If someone else murdered the man my former client's accused of, he'll be cleared. Again."

John nodded. "And your boss will have to give you your job back."

"He doesn't have to do anything. But yeah, it clears my name of the cloud that's hung over it since the arrest. But I'm not going to think that far ahead yet. I have to get to Philly before the witness has a chance to change his mind."

"I'll pray for you."

"Thanks. I'll be in touch."

He rushed to his car and took off in a flurry of gravel.

Twenty-Eight

Miriam stared at John. "Gone? Mark's gone?"

He nodded. "Went rushing back to Philadelphia last night. The private investigator called him, said he needed to come right away. Seems he found someone who can help clear his client."

She set her tote bag on the kitchen table. "That sounds like very *gut* news." She forced herself to pull the plastic containers from the bag. Mark had waited so long for his client to be vindicated. He must have been ecstatic that he'd been proven right. "I guess this means he'll be given his old job back."

John paused in the act of pouring a cup of coffee. "*Ya*." He set the percolator back on the stove. He sat down at the table and stared at the mug in his hands without drinking the coffee.

"I'm sorry," Miriam rushed to say. "I shouldn't have said that. I didn't mean to make you sad."

He lifted his gaze, and Miriam's heart ached at the sadness in his faded blue eyes. "It's *allrecht*. I'm being selfish, thinking of myself."

"If that's being selfish, I've been selfish, too," she confessed.

"You?"

She nodded. "I've loved Mark being here. He's been my friend for so many years."

"I had hopes ..."

"Of him taking over the farm," she finished.

"More."

"More?" She sank down into a seat at the table opposite him.

"I'd hoped the two of you would be more than friends."

Miriam avoided his eyes, afraid that if she looked at him, he'd see too much. "John, Mark loves his work and his life in Philadelphia. As much as he's seemed to enjoy being here, I think he really wants to be there again."

He sighed heavily. "He took off in such a hurry, he left ruts in the gravel in the drive. I had to go out and rake the drive this morning."

She could just imagine the sight of Mark driving off in such a rush. "Well, it's time Mark gets to show his boss he was wrong to treat him the way he did."

John grinned. "He has quite the champion in you. There's a fire in your eyes, *kind*."

"I don't like it when people are treated badly. It's not right."

"*Nee*, it's not. Sometimes we are treated badly, and sometimes it moves us to make change whether we want to or not. But it's part of what God planned, after all."

"I know. And we're supposed to forgive, turn the other cheek."

"Well, all will be *allrecht*." He patted her hand. "It always is no matter what we think at the time. God's in every situation, not outside of it. Now, what have you brought us today?"

Miriam felt mixed emotions when she left John's farm a little later. She hadn't had to avoid Mark, but now she might not get to see him for who knew how long.

Life could *schur* take some disturbing turns.

"Luke stopped by while you were gone," her *mudder* told her when she walked into the kitchen. "I invited him for supper."

"That's nice," she said without much enthusiasm.

Sarah turned from washing green peppers in the sink. "Should I not have done that?"

"*Nee*, it's *allrecht*."

"Is something wrong?"

"Mark's gone off to Philadelphia again. John said he got *gut* news."

She brought the colander of vegetables to the table, sat, and began to chop them. "A job?"

"Not yet." Miriam filled the tea kettle, and while the water heated, she told her *mudder* what John had said. "So I expect it won't be long before Mark gets his job back."

"So that is *gut* news."

"*Ya.*" For Mark, not her. Or John. "John's already thinking that means Mark won't be staying on at the farm."

She sat there, chin in hand, elbow propped on the table, watching her *mudder* core a pepper.

Sarah tilted her head. "Sounds like someone just woke from her nap.

"I can finish those."

"*Danki.*" She went upstairs.

Miriam finished coring the peppers, then began chopping an onion. A tear plopped on her hand, then another. Before she knew it, tears were rolling down her cheeks as she indulged in a good cry.

"Why Miriam, what's wrong?"

She glanced up to see her *mudder* staring at her as she bounced Katie on her hip.

Mortified, Miriam reached for a paper napkin from the holder on the table. "Onion."

Sarah settled Katie in her high chair and gave her a cookie, then came to stand beside Miriam's chair. She touched her shoulder "Are you feeling sad about Mark?"

"It's wrong of me, I know. Mark loves his job. And he deserves to have his boss apologize for sending him away." She tried t smile. "John said I was a champion for Mark."

"I was hoping ..."

"That I'd become interested in Luke?"

"*Ya.*"

"He's well read and we have interesting conversations. But ..."

"But?"

"He isn't Mark."

"*Nee*, no one is. Or ever will be."

"So I should look elsewhere. I know."

The back door opened and her *dat* walked in, bringing with him a gust of cold wind. He shut the door quickly. "Thought I'd see if there was any coffee on."

Katie squealed.

"Hi, little one." He shed his jacket and black felt hat and hung them on a peg.

Sarah rose and poured him a cup of coffee. He sat at the table, sipped his coffee, and smiled when she set a plate of cookies before him.

"Something wrong?" he asked Miriam.

"Onion," she said at the same time as her *mudder*.

"I see." He bit into a cookie, chewed it, and looked thoughtful. "I guess I interrupted girl talk."

"Now you're being silly."

Katie babbled in apparent agreement.

"Luke's coming to supper," Miriam said. "He's Abraham's cousin from Ohio, here to help him with the farm while Abraham's arm is healing."

"That's *gut*."

Miriam glanced at him, trying to read his expression. "It is?"

He nodded and finished his cookie. "Family should help family."

"*Ya*."

"So what are we having for supper?"

She couldn't help laughing. "Always the same question. What's for supper?"

"All men are the same," Sarah said. "Or so I hear from my friends."

Miriam got two baking pans and set the peppers in them. "Here's a hint," she said, tucking her tongue in her cheek. She turned on the oven then got hamburger from the refrigerator to brown it for the stuffing in the peppers.

He finished his coffee and set the mug in the sink. "Well, I'm back to work." He donned his jacket and hat and left, leaving a gust of cold air as he closed the door.

The stuffed peppers and the scalloped potatoes her *mudder* had already prepared and set on the counter would warm the kitchen as they baked. Miriam got a basket of apples to peel for a crisp that could go in when the peppers and potatoes came out. It would be done by the time supper was eaten and be *gut* with some ice cream.

"I'm going upstairs to see why it's so quiet," her *mudder* said. "It's not always a gut thing when *kinner* are quiet."

"True."

Katie munched happily on a piece of apple while Miriam worked. Her spirits lifted as she peeled the apples and talked to Katie. It was hard to stay moody around such a happy *boppli*.

She tried not to think about how another marriage season had passed. God *schur* was taking his time to show her the man He'd set aside for her.

Mark met Lou in the parking lot of the motel where the private investigator had stashed the witness.

"Glad you could drive right in," Lou said as he extended his hand in welcome.

"I'm glad you found a witness. Now if we can just get him to agree to go to the cops with us."

Lou knocked on the door, gave his name, and the door opened.

The witness greeted Mark warily but let them in. Jerome Smith was in his late twenties and exuded the kind of tough guy image a short man wore like clothing. The room was dim, but Mark could see his pupils were dilated from fear. Or drugs.

Jerome had grown up in the same neighborhood as Mark's client, and they knew each other well. They'd gone to school together—often played hooky together—and been gang brothers for a brief time.

Mark's client had left the gang behind and Jerome was trying to. "Some of the gang members set Maurice up."

Mark pulled a yellow legal pad out of his briefcase. "How do you know this?"

"Dude, I was having a beer with him and two other guys when they decided to frame Maurice," he said. His Adam's apple bobbed as he swallowed hard. He broke out in a sweat and a nervous tic flickered at the corner of his mouth as he gave Mark the name of the gang member and his possible whereabouts.

"Why didn't you come forward sooner?"

"Because I happen to want to keep breathing." Jerome pulled out a pack of cigarettes and lit one. "Besides, it's my word against theirs. What if I go to the cops with you like Lou here wants me to, and I get arrested, too? They can charge me with being an accessory."

"I told him you'd go in with him, make sure that doesn't happen," Lou spoke up.

"Lou's right."

"No charge?"

"None. And we'll arrange for protection if the police don't until after the trial." His savings was going to take a hit if the district attorney didn't step up for it, but it would be worth it. His professional reputation had suffered from his former client being wrongfully charged.

Jerome finished one cigarette and lit another from the end of the first one. "These are scary dudes, man. You have no idea coming from where you do."

He'd really have a laugh if he knew where Mark had been a few hours ago. "I'm a criminal defense attorney," Mark said. "Most of my clients are not choir members." Fortunately, however, they had been innocent.

"Let me call someone I know on the force." Mark got out his cell phone and started dialing.

Jerome turned to Lou. "How about some food before we go see the cops? It's been a long time since dinner. And this place doesn't have room service."

"We'll get you something on the way to the police station," Mark promised as he waited for the captain to pick up. "As soon as my client's sprung, I'll buy you the biggest steak you ever had at the best place in town."

Jerome lit another cigarette. "Deal."

Mark talked with the captain who sounded dubious but agreed to meet. He disconnected the call and turned to Lou. "Do you mind riding along? I'll bring you back for your car."

"Sure." He turned to Jerome. "Hand over anything you shouldn't have on you when we go to the police station. And anything stronger than cigarettes."

"What about you? I know you have a gun on you. I saw it when your jacket fell open."

"I have a concealed weapon permit."

Jerome pulled out a switchblade and handed it to Lou, who took it without blinking and tucked it into his pocket.

Mark started for the door, a little unnerved at how casual both men acted about the knife. He hadn't thought about Jerome having anything like that on him as he talked.

He'd been naïve.

"Wait a sec," Lou said. "Let me take a look around before the two of you go out."

They waited while he checked the parking lot then gave the go-ahead. Mark drove them to the police station, stopping at a fast food drive-through as promised, and giving Maurice's new attorney a call to let him know about developments.

His old friend sounded like he'd woken up, but he came quickly to attention when Mark told him what had happened.

"That's incredible news. I'll meet you at the police station. It'll take me about twenty minutes."

"See you there." Mark disconnected the call.

Captain Thornwell was waiting for them when they arrived. "Well, well, Jerome Smith, you've decided to chat with us again."

Jerome slid a nervous glance at Mark.

"Mr. Smith is here to volunteer information on the Maurice Johnson case, as I told you," Mark inserted calmly.

Thornwell gave him a cool glance. "Seems he didn't want to volunteer any information when our detectives talked to him some time back." He shrugged. "Follow me. We'll have us a little talk."

Two long hours later, Jerome was signing a statement and it was done.

"I've talked to the D.A. about arranging protection until we round up the two suspects," Thornwell said as he took the signed statement.

Jerome let out a shaky sigh. "Never thought I'd be trusting cops with my safety."

"Never thought I'd be offering you protection," Thornwell replied curtly.

Mark handed Jerome a business card. "Call me or Lou if you need anything. Otherwise I'll be seeing you when you testify."

"Thanks, man."

"Thank you for doing the right thing."

"Tell Maurice I'm sorry I didn't come forward before."

"I will."

Mark turned to Lou. "Let's go get your car." He waited until they got inside and were on their way. "Great work."

"Thanks."

"Got your last bill. I'll give you a check and you let me know the additional charges."

"Will do."

"Want some coffee?" he asked as they came up along a coffee shop.

Lou winced. "Had enough of the cop shop stuff to ruin my stomach lining, thanks. Think I'll just head home and get some sleep. What about you?"

"I'm exhausted. I think I'll stay overnight at my place. Besides, there are some things I want to do before I head home."

"Good idea."

He pulled into the motel parking lot and stopped next to Lou's car. "Don't forget to add the charges for Jerome's stay and food, whatever you spent out of pocket."

"I know the owner of the motel. He gave me a special price for his stay." He held out his hand. "Good working for you. Looking forward to more when you get back to work."

"Yeah," Mark said slowly. "Me, too."

He drove to his condo, tired but exhilarated at the turn of events. Tomorrow—he glanced at the time—no, later today, he'd be talking to Maurice and letting him know about the impending arrests. Then he'd be staying in touch with Maurice's new attorney to make sure the system released Maurice as soon as possible.

Mark programmed his coffee maker—no percolator on the stove

here—then walked into the bedroom, undressed, and fell into bed. His last thought as his head hit the pillow was how Miriam would react to his news.

He woke several hours later. He'd always been an early riser, but these days he woke even earlier on the farm. Tossing aside the duvet, he headed for the shower. He had a lot to do today.

"Oh mercy, have you got more bad news for me?" Maurice's mother asked as he climbed the steps to her porch a little later. Her mouth trembled.

She'd aged twenty years since he'd seen her last. Maybe that would change when he told her the good news. "I'm not Maurice's lawyer right now, but I have something to tell you."

She cried. Mark knew about happy tears. These were thrilled tears. She hugged him so tight he thought she'd crack a rib.

"I wanted you to be first to know," he said. "I'm on my way to see your son now."

"Praise God, praise God," she kept saying as she took the handkerchief he offered.

"Your son's lawyer will see that he's released as soon as possible, but it won't be today so you need to be patient. Now, I'm going to go see Maurice and give him the good news."

"Tell him I'll fix him his favorite supper."

"I will."

Maurice had aged as he sat in jail awaiting trial. His face looked puffy, his skin pale, and the orange jumpsuit hung on his thin frame.

He tried to grin when he saw Mark. "I know, I look awful. And you look great. You been lying on a beach somewhere?"

Mark laughed and shook his head. "Been working in the fields on my grandfather's farm. Not sitting around like you." He held out his hands. "And I have the calluses to show for it." They were a farmer's hands. He sobered. "I didn't forget you. Neither did a friend of yours. Jerome Smith."

"Jerome?" He gave Mark a wary look. "Cops told me he didn't know anything when they talked to him."

"He had a lot to say to them last night. He gave them a statement and they're rounding up the leader of the gang and some of his buddies. The charges against you are going to be dropped."

Maurice jumped to his feet to hug him, but the guard standing nearby ordered him to sit.

"Your mom gave me a bear hug," Mark said. "And she said she'll be cooking your favorite supper as soon as you're home."

He climbed into his car and headed home.

To Lancaster County, not his condo.

Twenty-Nine

Miriam took a big pot of ham, navy bean soup, and a pan of cornbread to John's house for his supper.

She wanted to ask if Mark had returned, but had the answer when she pulled into the drive in her family's buggy and his car wasn't there.

So she delivered the basket of food, talked briefly with John, and returned home. Luke stopped by her house and asked if she wanted to go for a drive, and she agreed. Might as well, she told herself, and excused herself to run upstairs for her jacket and bonnet. It was an awful reason to be with someone—because she had nothing better to do and the man she loved wasn't around ... or likely to be.

Well, too late now. She had to make the best of it.

She slipped into her jacket and tied on her bonnet, and found herself avoiding her own gaze in the mirror over her dresser. When she went back downstairs, she smiled at Luke and they went out to the buggy.

"I'm going home next week," he said as they rode along one of the country roads. "Abraham got his cast off today and he won't need my help anymore."

"Oh. I didn't realize you were leaving so soon."

"It's been nice getting to know you."

"You, too."

He pulled the buggy into a fast food restaurant drive-through. "I thought we could get some hot chocolate."

"I could have made some to bring if I'd thought of it. Saved the money. Let me pay for it." She reached for her purse.

"It's my treat," he said firmly.

After he took the cups from the young woman at the window, he handed one to Miriam, then drove the buggy back onto the road. "The thing is," he began, then trailed off.

"The thing is?" she prompted.

"I'd like to get to know you better. I was thinking maybe you could come visit my family. Ohio's pretty this time of year."

She knew where this was going. "Luke, I'm sorry, but I can't do that. I have my job here at the *schul*."

"Oh, right." He sipped at his drink. "Maybe I could stay here a little longer."

"You're not needed back on your family's farm?"

"It's a slow time of year."

"True." Now what? She couldn't let him spend time here thinking they would get to know each other better when she wasn't interested in him.

Why couldn't she be? He was handsome, caring, a hard worker.

But she couldn't make herself care about someone romantically when her heart yearned for someone else. And there was no question that she did. She sighed.

"So maybe I'll ask Abraham and Lovina if they'd mind if I stayed here a little longer." Luke kept his eyes on the road.

Miriam heard the hope in his voice and hated hurting him. "Luke, I'm sorry. I like you as a friend, but I'm not interested in having a relationship with anyone."

He pulled the buggy over onto the shoulder of the road. "Anyone? Or just me?"

She bit her lip and hesitated.

"Never mind. I think I know the answer to that. I've seen the way you look at the *Englisch* guy."

"You have?" Her hand flew to her throat. If a newcomer had noticed, who else had? Other than two close friends and her *mudder*. "We've been friends for years," she said carefully.

"Just friends?" Luke stared ahead, not looking at her.

"There can't be anything more. He's got his own life in Philadelphia."

"But you care for him."

It was a statement, not a question. She sighed. "*Ya*, I do."

"It's so ironic," he said. "There's someone back home I used to think about. But I realized I just didn't love her."

"I'm sorry."

Luke gave a half-laugh. "We're a pair, aren't we?"

"*Ya.*"

He checked traffic and pulled back onto the road. They rode in silence for a time, sipping their hot drinks. Miriam searched for something to say.

"I guess your family will be happy to have you back for Christmas."

"How are the plans coming for the Christmas program at your *schul?*"

Ach, now they had a safe topic for conversation. Bless him for his kindness. He really was a nice man.

Miriam chatted freely about the rehearsals, told a funny story about Jacob forgetting his lines, and described the decorations the *kinner* had been making.

Her gaze wandered as they passed John's farm and she faltered for a second, then recovered.

"Is it snowing back home?" she asked quickly to cover her lapse.

"Has been for the past two weeks."

"I love when it snows." Well, that was inane. She was grateful when he pulled into her driveway. She turned to him. "*Danki* for the drive and the hot chocolate. And Luke, it's been nice knowing you these past weeks. I'm glad you came to help Abraham. I hope I'll see you again at church before you leave."

He smiled at her. "It's been nice knowing you, too. I hope you find a *mann* worthy of you."

"And I wish you well finding the woman God's set aside for you." She slipped from the buggy, walked up the steps to the porch, and waved to him as he drove away.

Her *mudder* was fixing a cup of tea when she walked into the kitchen. "You're back early. Want some tea?"

Miriam shook her head. "We got some hot chocolate." She took off her bonnet and jacket and hung them on the pegs by the back door.

"So how is Luke?"

She sat at the table. "He may be going back to Ohio soon. He said Abraham got his cast off today." She pushed the bowl of tea bags closer to her *mudder*. "I'm kind of relieved. I liked being friends, but he was looking for more." She watched her *mudder* dunk her tea bag in the hot water in her mug. "I tried to like him, *Mamm*. I really did."

"He's a likable man."

"*Ya*. But there has to be more."

"Perhaps with more time?"

"He asked me to visit him. I said *nee*. I can't leave *schul* and if I look into the distance I don't want to leave here, leave my scholars, leave my family."

"Even for love?"

She shook her head. "I don't want to make that choice. I'm hoping I don't have to for any man."

"'For I know the thoughts that I think toward you, saith the LORD, thoughts of peace, and not of evil, to give you an expected end.'"

"Well, for now I feel like His plans for me are to teach at the *schul*," Miriam said, rubbing at her forehead. A headache was beginning to make itself felt. "I think I'll go lie down for a few minutes, if you don't mind. I have a headache."

"*Ya*, that sounds like a *gut* idea."

Miriam took an aspirin and washed it down with a glass of water. She went upstairs and lay down on top of her bed. She listened to the wind stirring the bare branches of the big oak tree near her bedroom window. It was a *gut* time to be inside, warm and secure.

As she lay there waiting for the headache to go away, she wondered where Mark was tonight. If he was not just warm and secure, but happy. If he'd gotten such *gut* news about his former client being cleared of the murder charge, then perhaps Mark had already gotten a call from his firm. Perhaps he was even out celebrating with his *Englisch* friends.

She wanted him to be happy. Even if his happiness made her miserable.

SSS

Mark's cell phone rang as he was driving to Lancaster County. He used the hands free feature to answer.

"Mark! Saw the news about the charges against your client being dropped. Congratulations."

It was his boss at the law firm. "Thank you, sir."

"Surprising turn of events."

"Yes."

"Give my assistant a call tomorrow and set up an appointment for us to meet."

"I'll do that. Thank you, sir." Before he could say anything else, he heard the click of disconnection.

Well. He'd gotten the call he'd wanted for so long. How many times had he dreamed about it, imagined how he'd feel about receiving it?

Now it just felt anti-climactic.

Mark remembered what a passionate champion Miriam had been, how she'd expressed outrage that his boss hadn't stood by him.

He couldn't wait to tell her about the call.

He couldn't wait to see her.

If he were honest, he couldn't wait to get to the farm.

He tapped his fingers on the steering wheel. Tanned, callused fingers. Farmer's hands, he'd said to Maurice. He had earned every callus with hard manual labor that he loved.

He suddenly realized he hadn't missed his legal work in weeks. That gave him pause. He'd always loved spending his summers on the farm. He'd felt so at home here and loved the work.

He had work in the city.

He had love and family and a growing faith on the farm.

The realization struck him with the force of a physical blow. His heart pounded so loud he swore he could hear it. He rubbed at the ache in the center of his chest. What if he'd never been forced to take a leave of absence?

Instead of punishing him, God had opened him to a deeper understanding of what he'd been missing. So busy making a living that he hadn't made a life? It wasn't a cliché. It was his truth.

The flashing red light in his rearview mirror made him glance at the speedometer. Great. He'd been going more than ten miles over the speed limit.

He pulled over, produced his license and registration when the police officer asked for them, and apologized profusely. He didn't assist clients with traffic offenses, but it went against all he'd been taught about offering up self-blame.

It was his good fortune that the officer gave him a warning and handed back his identification.

He got back on the road and watched his speed the rest of the way home. The sight of the exit for Paradise had never made him so happy.

His grandfather looked up with a huge smile when he walked into the house. "Well, well, look who's here. How did it go?"

"It couldn't have been better!"

John got up a bit creakily from his recliner. "I waited supper for you. Have you eaten?"

"I had a bagel for breakfast."

"A man can't get by on a roll for breakfast and nothing for lunch."

Mark followed him into the kitchen and watched as he pulled a big soup pot from the refrigerator.

"Miriam brought ham and navy bean soup and cornbread over the day you left. There's plenty left."

They fell into their easy routine of moving around the kitchen, warming food, setting the table, pouring glasses of cold water.

His grandfather's gray head bent over the blessing of the meal reminded Mark of Lani's surprise when he'd said a quiet prayer the day he'd met her for lunch.

As he spooned up the hearty soup, Mark told his grandfather all about Lou finding the witness, about taking him to the police station, and how Jerome had expressed a desire to break away from the gang life.

"I have a friend who can help him do that," Mark said as he buttered a piece of cornbread.

"So in saving the life of an old friend, he might be saving his own."

Mark paused, struck by the simple wisdom of his grandfather's words. He nodded.

"So now what happens?"

"The wheels of justice start turning. Maurice's new attorney will make sure he's released and the record of his arrest expunged. And who knows, Maurice could well have a case for a false arrest suit, but I have the feeling he's going to be so grateful to have his life back, he won't pursue that."

"And what about you?"

"Me?" Mark stared.

"Now will you get your old life back?"

Mark felt the tension his grandfather was trying to hide.

"My old boss called me as I was driving home."

"To your condo?"

"No. Here. Home."

"Oh?"

"Funny thing. I didn't feel anything when he said to call his assistant tomorrow and set up a time for us to talk later this week." He laid his spoon beside the soup bowl and held out his hands. "When I went to see Maurice to give him the good news, he was embarrassed at how bad he looked. Being in jail, wondering if you're going to lose your life ... well, he'd lost weight, his skin was sallow. Anyway, I guess he could tell from my expression how surprised I looked at his appearance. But he told me I looked good. Asked if I'd been spending time at the beach. I showed him these hands."

John looked confused. "And?"

"They're farmer's hands now, and I'm proud of them."

"What are you saying?"

Mark saw the hope in his eyes. "I'm a farmer. And I'm here to stay. I'm home, *Grossdaadi*. If you still want me here."

Tears sprang into John's eyes. "Welcome home, *grosssohn*. Welcome home."

Mark reached for his handkerchief and remembered that he'd given it to Maurice's mother earlier that day. He pulled a paper napkin from the wooden holder on the table and handed it to his grandfather.

"Do you suppose I could get out of helping to clean up the kitchen this once?"

"Of course. I imagine you're tired from all the excitement."

"Not tired. Just want to go see Miriam."

"*Schur.* She'll be so happy to hear your *gut* news."

"That's not the only reason I want to see her."

"*Nee?*"

Mark shook his head. As much as he wanted to tell his grandfather he hoped for more good news that day, he needed to see Miriam. For all he knew, she'd become serious about that Luke guy. Butterflies fluttered in his stomach at the thought. He didn't want to get his grandfather's hopes up.

"Be back soon."

"Take your time."

Mark wanted to say, "Wish me luck," but it wasn't luck he hoped for. He'd done his best to wait for God's plan for him. And now he hoped Miriam was part of His plan.

He rushed out the door to hitch the buggy up to go see her.

Thirty

"Miriam?"

"Mhh hmm?" She blinked. The room was dim. She must have fallen asleep.

"Mark's here to see you," her *mudder* said from the doorway.

She sat up and rubbed her eyes. Was she dreaming?

"*Kumm* downstairs."

"*Allrecht.*" She swung her legs over the side of the bed and wondered if she was still asleep.

She hurried over to the mirror, redid her hair, and pinned on a fresh *kapp*. It took just a few minutes to change her dress, but there was nothing she could do about the sleep crease in her cheek. Sighing, she went downstairs.

Mark sat with a cup of coffee while the family finished supper. He smiled at her when she walked into the room.

"You're back."

He nodded. "I thought I'd see if we could go for a drive."

"I – *schur.*"

"I didn't call you for supper," her *mudder* explained. "I thought you needed the rest more. Do you want to fix me a plate for you? Mark says he's already had supper."

"I'll eat later," Miriam said as she slipped into her jacket and tied on her bonnet.

They walked outside.

"Where's your car?"

"Back at the farm."

"Something wrong with it?"

"No."

She frowned as he climbed into John's buggy and picked up the reins. He'd taken her for a drive in John's buggy before, but seemed to prefer his *Englisch* car. There was an air of suppressed excitement about him.

"Actually, it's probably better if I don't drive the car for a day or two," he said with a grin. "I almost got a speeding ticket on the way home."

"You?" She stared at him.

"Well, it's easy to do if you're distracted and driving a car like mine."

"I suppose. It's just that I thought ..."

"You thought?"

"I guess I think you're perfect."

He laughed. "Hardly." He sobered. "You're the only perfect person I know."

Now it was her turn to laugh and shake her head. "I had this dream the other day. I was standing on some stairs and my *bruders* and *schweschders* were below me. When I woke up, I realized that I've always tried hard to teach and inspire them. But lately they've been letting me know they get tired of lessons at home. I've had trouble leaving the teacher at *schul*." She stared at her hands. "And we inspire by doing and being, not by teaching and telling."

"True." He reached into the back for a blanket and handed it to her. "Are you warm enough? These things aren't the warmest this time of year."

Miriam spread the blanket over her lap and legs. "I'm fine. *Danki.*"

"I put some hot chocolate in a thermos."

"That sounds *gut*. Do you want some?"

"No. Just had a cup of your mom's coffee. You have some since you haven't eaten."

She picked up the thermos, unscrewed the top, and poured some hot chocolate into it.

"How's the headache? Your mom said you came home with one and you were lying down."

"Better."

"Maybe we should stop and get you something to eat."

"This is enough. I'm not really hungry." She took a careful sip of the chocolate, making sure it wasn't too hot. "You put little marshmallows in it."

"That's the way you like it."

He remembered!

"So how did it go?" she asked as he looked both directions before easing onto the road.

"Couldn't have gone better. The witness Lou found made his statement to police, they've picked up two gang members who murdered the man Maurice was accused of killing, and Maurice should be getting out of jail very soon."

"That's *wunderbaar*."

He nodded.

"I thought maybe, when you didn't come back yesterday, that your boss had asked you back to work."

"He called when the news broke on TV today. Said to call his assistant and arrange for a meeting with him later this week."

She twisted her hands in her lap. "That's *gut* news."

He nodded. "Guess so."

"You *guess* so? Why, what he did was so unfair to you, he—" she broke off when he chuckled, and froze when he picked up one of her hands and kissed it.

"It's a lucky man who has such a champion."

"Are you laughing at me?"

He turned to her and studied her with a serious expression. "Never. I'm not sure if I could have gotten through these past months without your support."

"Yes, well, John believed in you, too."

"He did. But not in the same way. You understood better. Just as you always have."

"That's what friends are for."

"Friends, Miriam? Or more?"

Her heart leaped into her throat. "I … if you go back to your world, there can't be more. You know that."

"Do you want more, Miriam?"

"You're not being fair."

Mark looked down at her hand. "No, I'm not. What if I said that *I* want more?"

"More?"

"So many Amish couples start off as good friends. Then they get married."

"What are you saying?" Her throat was suddenly dry. She took a sip of the hot chocolate and tasted the sticky sweetness of marshmallow.

"I wonder if we'd have gotten married."

SSS

Miriam choked.

Mark hadn't realized he'd shock her that much. Or that she'd have such a violent reaction. He thumped her on her back until she held up her hand.

"Stop!" she gasped. "I'm *allrecht!*"

"Shocking thought, huh?"

Miriam wiped the tears from her eyes. "Let's say unexpected." She took another sip of the hot chocolate and felt better.

Maybe it was too soon. Maybe he should wait, let her get adjusted to the idea.

No, he'd never been one to take the easy way, the slow and patient way.

"I love you," he said. "It's taken this time here to realize it, Miriam."

"You love me as a friend." She said it slowly, cautiously.

"As a friend. And more. Did I wait too long, Miriam? I know you've been seeing Luke." He reached for her hand, wanting the connection.

She shook her head. "I only saw him when I thought you and I could never be more than friends. Mark, I've loved you for years."

"Years? Why didn't you ever tell me?"

"I was so afraid you'd think I was just a foolish Amish *maedel.*"

"You could never be foolish. Marry me, Miriam."

Tears rolled down her cheeks and her lips trembled. "I can't do that, Mark. I wish I could be the biblical Ruth, but I can't leave my family, my church. This life. I'd be shunned if I married *Englisch.*"

"I guess I'm not explaining myself very well." He squeezed her hand. "I know we haven't touched much. It's not something a single man does with a young Amish woman. But feel my hand, Miriam. Do you notice anything different?"

She took it in both of her hands and stroked it, feeling the calluses. When she looked up at him he saw that she felt them.

"I realized today that I have farmer's hands now. I've always loved working here on the farm, but it was a part-time love, something that was a small part of my life. It's more now, Miriam, because of you and my grandfather." He gave a half-laugh. "And in some ways, because of the whole detour in the life I thought I wanted." He took a deep breath. "I'm staying, Miriam. Here. On the farm. And I hope you'll be my wife and help me with it."

"But you said your boss wants you back."

"He can't have me. I'm staying, with or without you. But I hope with you." He looked down at her hands. "I won't offer you an engagement ring. That's not done here. But you'll have my heart and my promise that I'll do everything I can to make you happy."

She started to speak, but he raised his hand and touched a finger to her lips. "I have to talk to Samuel, find out what I need to do to join the church. Maybe I should have found out what's necessary before I asked you, but I needed to know if I had any chance with you."

"It's not a life that's easy for an *Englischer*."

"Well, half *Englischer*."

"Very *Englisch* sometimes. What about your condo? Your car with the fancy initials?"

"Things. " He shrugged. "Miriam, do you really think I don't know this isn't an easy life? I'm not looking for easy. I'm looking to have a life with love. Family. Friends. Community."

"Are you *schur*?"

"Very *schur*."

She laughed and it was a sound of pure joy. "Oh, I couldn't dream something this *wunderbaar*."

"Then you'll marry me."

"*Ya*, I'll marry you and be your *fraa*."

They kissed and sealed the promise. When they drew apart, her eyes were shining with love.

"Let's go tell John," she said

Mark nodded, picked up the reins with one hand, and drew her close. "I told him I was staying on the farm, but I didn't tell him about you. I didn't want to get his hopes up."

"He's hinted to me that he hoped we'd get together, but I told him that could never happen." She looked up at him. "I wonder how much of his asking you to come here was wanting to pass the farm to you, and how much might have been some matchmaking."

"You might be right. Planting seeds?"

She nodded.

It was early still, but Mark wondered if his grandfather would still be up. They found him sitting in his recliner reading the *Budget*. Not only did he look wide awake, but his gaze instantly latched onto Miriam holding his hand.

"Granddad. We have something to tell you."

John shot out of his chair with the agility of a much younger man. "*Ya?*"

"We're getting married. I need to talk to Samuel, find out what I need to do. But we're getting married in the church. Miriam will be my wife. My *fraa*," he said, testing the Pennsylvania *Dietsch* word he'd be using more when he lived here.

John beamed and embraced Miriam first, then him. "I can't believe it. God is *gut*," he said and he pulled out a handkerchief and wiped his eyes. "It's more than I hoped for." He looked at Mark. "She's always been like a *grossdochder* to me."

"And you like a *grossdaadi* to me," Miriam said, wiping away her own tears.

"Have you told your parents?"

Miriam shook her head. "We wanted you to know. But I don't think my *mudder* will be surprised. She knows how I feel about Mark."

"You should go tell them now."

"Later," Miriam said. "Mark and I have a lot to talk about."

"Then I'll let you young people talk. *Gut nacht.*" He hugged them both and made his way to the stairs that led to his bedroom.

"We'll start with some practical things," Mark said, taking her hand and leading her into the kitchen.

"Practical things?"

"Food first. You haven't eaten. Can't have you passing out from hunger."

She laughed. "That's not likely."

He released her hand and opened the refrigerator. "Looks like there's some ham and navy bean soup left. It's really good."

"Is it?" She gave him an impish grin.

"I had two helpings at supper. Or would you like me to make you some eggs? I make good scrambled eggs."

She sat at the table. "I had no idea you cooked."

"A single man learns to or he ends up eating too much takeout. Well, I've been known to do that because I used to work too much, but yes, I can cook a little."

He warmed the soup, got what was left of the cornbread from the bread box, and set it before her with the dish of butter. When the soup was warm, he ladled it into a bowl and served her.

"Miriam, what do you really think your parents will say when we tell them?"

"They'll be happy if they know I'm happy," she said firmly. "They've known you for years."

"Still …" he trailed off. "I got the distinct impression they were concerned when we would go for rides in my car."

"That was when you were an *Englisch* attorney and could take me away from them, from the church and the community."

"True."

She picked up her spoon, then hesitated. "Mark, aren't you worried about what *your* parents will say?"

He reached for her hand. "Like you said, they'll be happy if they know I'm happy," he told her, using her words and the firm tone she'd used as well.

She smiled. "I hope you're right."

"Eat."

Mark sat with her while she ate, in the room where she'd so often prepared meals for his grandfather and him. They would share many evenings like this in the years to come. John would move into the *dawdi haus*—the living quarters the *Englisch* called a mother-in-law apartment—and be a daily part of their lives. If they were lucky, children would one day sit around this old wooden table like he had from the time he'd come here to spend summers with his grandfather, like his own father had until he'd left the community. Miriam would be such a good mother and teach them as she did her own brothers and sisters and the children at the school she loved.

"You're being quiet," she prompted.

So he told her his thoughts, and as she listened, her tears flowed once again.

Mark pulled a fresh handkerchief from his briefcase. She stared at it in surprise. He shrugged. "Kind of an old-fashioned thing, I guess. But I like having one on hand."

"It's not old-fashioned here."

He glanced at the clock. "I wonder if Maurice is home yet. His mother told me to tell him she'd cook him his favorite supper as soon as he got there."

"You're *schur* you won't miss your work? Your life?"

"That work was part of my life. I can still use it to help people in a different way, like I did with Abraham and Lovina, and with Saul. But I want a different life here, on the farm, with you."

He took her hands in his. "There's a saying in my old world. You can work so hard you make a living but you don't make a life. I started making a life when I came home this time."

He spotted the seed catalogs lying on the kitchen counter. "The other day, my grandfather and I made out the order for the seeds for the spring planting. Just think. I'll get to plant crops this time, and see them all the way through to the harvest. I've never had the chance to do that before. I imagine it'll be like worrying and watching over your own children." He smiled at her. "I think I'm going to like doing that a lot. As long as I have you by my side."

Glossary

ab im kop—off in the head. Crazy.

ach—oh

allrecht—all right

boppli—baby

bruder—brother

daed—dad

danki—thank you

dat—father

dawdi haus—a small home added to or near the main house into which the farmer moves after passing the farm to one of his children.

Der hochmut kummt vor dem fall.—Pride goeth before the fall.

Deitsch—Pennsylvania German

dippy eggs—over-easy eggs

dochder—daughter

eck—the corner of the wedding table where the newly married couple sits

Englisch—what the Amish call a non-Amish person

fraa—wife

grossdaadi—grandfather

grossdochder—granddaughter

grosseldres—grandparents

grosskinner—grandchildren

grossmudder—grandmother

grosssohn—grandson

guder mariye—good morning

gut—good

gut-n-owed—good evening

hochmut—pride

hungerich—hungry

kapp—prayer covering or cap worn by girls and women

kind, kinner—child, children

kumm—come

lieb—love. Term of endearment

liebschen—dearest or dear one

maedel—young single Amish woman

mamm—mom

mann—husband

mudder—mother

nacht—night

nee—no

newehocker—wedding attendant

onkel—uncle

Ordnung—The rules of the Amish, both written and unwritten. Certain behavior has been expected within the Amish community for many, many years. These rules vary from community to community, but the most common are to have no electricity in the home, to not own or drive an automobile, and to dress a certain way.

redd up—clean up

roasht—roast. A stuffing or dressing side dish.

rumschpringe—time period when teenagers are allowed to experience the *Englisch* world while deciding if they should join the church.

scholars—Amish students

schul—school

schur—sure

schweschder—sister

sohn—son

verboten—forbidden, not done

wilkumm—welcome

wunderbaar—wonderful

ya—yes

zwillingbopplin—twins

Discussion Questions

Spoiler alert! Please don't read before completing the book, as the questions contain spoilers!

1. John Byler owns a farm that has been in his family for generations. He'd hoped to pass it on to his son, but then his son left the Amish community. His only hope of keeping the farm in the family is for his grandson to take it over. Is there anything you own that you hope to pass on to someone in your family?

2. The Amish believe God sets aside a marriage partner for them. Do you believe this? Do you believe in love at first sight?

3. Miriam has had a crush on Mark, an *Englischer*, for years. She longs for him to take over John's farm, but she's torn because Mark loves his work in Philadelphia. Do you think she should have told Mark about her feelings for him sooner?

4. Mark thought he had his life all planned out, then he ran into a detour. Some say when one door closes another opens. What would your advice be to Mark?

5. Mark waits and waits for his firm to call him back to work. Have you ever become upset with God when His timing isn't yours? What did you do?

6. John tells Miriam he hoped she and his grandson might become more than the good friends they've been for years. Do you think John was playing matchmaker by offering the farm to Mark?

7. Mark feels part of two worlds—both the Amish and the

Englisch. Have you ever thought about joining a church or way of life different than the one you were raised in?

8. Miriam is the eldest child in her family. What is your birth order? How has it influenced your life?

9. Miriam loves her job as a teacher. Did you have a favorite teacher? Why was that teacher your favorite?

10. Mark discovers working on the farm—something he did as a teenager in the summers—is something he loves. Have you ever changed not just jobs but careers? Why? What happened?

11. The Amish don't believe in pressing charges or suing. When someone in the community is hurt by an *Englischer,* Mark finds himself frustrated that he can't use his legal skills to help them. Do you think the teen driver learned anything from what Mark did to help the Amish family?

12. What do you think will be the hardest adjustment Mark will face living the Amish life? What will be the easiest?

Pumpkin Whoopie Pies

For the Pumpkin Cookies:

    3 cups all-purpose flour

    1 teaspoon salt

    1 teaspoon baking powder

    1 teaspoon baking soda

    2 tablespoons ground cinnamon

    1 tablespoon ground ginger

    1 tablespoon ground cloves

    2 cups firmly packed dark-brown sugar

    1 cup vegetable oil

    3 cups pumpkin purée, chilled

    2 large eggs

    1 teaspoon pure vanilla extract

For the Cream-Cheese Filling:

    3 cups confectioners' sugar

    ½ cup (1 stick) unsalted butter, softened

    8 ounces cream cheese, softened

    1 teaspoon pure vanilla extract

Directions:

Preheat oven to 350 degrees. Line two baking sheets with parchment paper or a nonstick baking mat; set aside. In a large bowl, whisk together flour, salt, baking powder, baking soda, cinnamon, ginger, and cloves; set aside. In another large bowl, whisk together brown sugar and oil until well combined. Add pumpkin purée and whisk until combined. Add eggs and vanilla and whisk until well combined. Stir flour mixture into pumpkin mixture and whisk until fully incorporated. Using a small ice cream scoop, drop heaping tablespoons of dough onto prepared baking sheets, about 1 inch apart. Bake until cookies are just starting to crack on top and a toothpick inserted into the center of each cookie comes out clean, about 15 minutes. Let cool completely on pan.

For the filling:

Sift confectioner's sugar into a medium bowl; set aside. Beat butter until smooth. Add cream cheese and beat until well combined. Add confectioners' sugar and vanilla, beat just until smooth. (Filling can be made up to a day in advance. Cover and refrigerate; let stand at room temperature to soften before using.)

Assemble the Whoopie Pies:

Line a baking sheet with parchment paper and set aside. Transfer filling to a disposable pastry bag and snip the end. When cookies have cooled completely, spread filling on the flat side of half of the cookies. Sandwich with remaining cookies, pressing down slightly so that the filling spreads to the edge of the cookies. Transfer to prepared baking sheet and cover with plastic wrap. Refrigerate cookies at least 30 minutes before serving and up to 3 days.

About the Author

Barbara Cameron is a gifted storyteller and the author of many bestselling Amish novels. Harvest of Hope is her new three-book Amish series from Gilead Publishing.

Twice Blessed, Barbara's two-novella collection, won the 2016 Christian Retailing's Best award in the Amish Fiction category. Two of her other novellas were finalists for the American Christian Fiction Writers (ACFW) awards. She is the first winner of the Romance Writers of America (RWA) Golden Heart Award. Three of her fiction stories were made into HBO/Cinemax movies.

Although Barbara is best known for her romantic and Amish fiction titles, she is also a prolific nonfiction author of titles including *101 Ways to Save Money on Your Wedding* and two editions of *The Everything Wedding Budget Book*.

Barbara is a former high school teacher and has also taught workshops and creative writing classes at national writing conferences, as well as locally. She currently teaches English and business communication classes as an adjunct instructor for the online campus of a major university.

Barbara enjoys spending time with her family and her three "nutty" Chihuahuas. She lives in Jacksonville, Florida. Visit her website at barbaracameron.com.